DEADLY RUSE

For my daughters, Melissa Ellis and Melanie McMillan.
Thank you both for your unconditional love and support.

A MAC McCLELLAN MYSTERY

DEADLY RUSE

E. MICHAEL HELMS

SEVENTH STREET BOOKS®
AN IMPRINT OF PROMETHEUS BOOKS
59 JOHN GLENN DRIVE • AMHERST, NY 14228
www.seventhstreetbooks.com

Published 2014 by Seventh Street Books®, an imprint of Prometheus Books

Cover design by Grace M. Conti-Zilsberger
Cover image © Media Bakery

Inquiries should be addressed to
Seventh Street Books
59 John Glenn Drive
Amherst, New York 14228
VOICE: 716–691–0133
FAX: 716–691–0137
WWW.SEVENTHSTREETBOOKS.COM

18 17 16 15 14   5 4 3 2 1

Library of Congress Cataloging-in-Publication Data

Helms, E. Michael.
    Deadly ruse : a Mac McClellan mystery / by E. Michael Helms.
        pages cm
    ISBN 978-1-61614-009-0 (paperback) — ISBN 978-1-61614-077-9 (ebook)
    1. Retired military personnel—Fiction. 2. Marines—Fiction. 3. Florida Panhandle (Fla.)—Fiction. I. Title.

PS3608.E4653D434 2014
813'.6—dc23

                                                                                    2014023931

Printed in the United States of America

CHAPTER 1

I'd never been a big believer in coincidence until the night Kate Bell and I strolled out of O'Malley's Theater after watching *Dead Man Walking*.

O'Malley's shows classics from yesteryear and other oldies, and instead of row after row of conventional seating, tables and chairs occupy most of the auditorium, where couples or small groups can enjoy dinner while viewing the night's offering of cinematic magic.

Not that I considered 1995's *Dead Man Walking* a true oldie, but to the teens and twenty-somethings in the audience I suppose the flick qualified. After all, I'd served with several old salt Vietnam vets during my career with the Marines, and to me the Vietnam War was ancient history, much like World War II and Korea had been to the younger set. It's all relative.

I'm not much of a Sean Penn fan, although I think he's a fine actor. I guess it's his politics that rub me the wrong way. But Kate's a big fan, and any excuse to spend time with her is good enough for me. We enjoyed grilled grouper sandwiches with the trimmings and a pitcher of beer while I suffered through the movie.

When R. Lee Ermey (a career Marine himself), who played the rape/murder victim's father, tossed do-gooder Sister Helen out of his house I almost cheered, while the scene brought Kate to tears. Ugh. And when they finally strapped Matthew Poncelet's no-good lying ass into Gruesome Gertie and fried the bastard, I did let slip a rather loud "Ooraah!" From the look she gave me, I thought Kate was going to slap the taste out of my mouth.

"You just don't get it, Mac," she said, still dabbing at her eyes with a napkin as we left the theater and stepped into the cool, early-spring night air.

"Sure I get it," I countered as we strolled down the sidewalk toward my Silverado. "He raped that girl and murdered her and her boyfriend. Then they fried his butt. What's not to get?"

Kate reached over and pinched my arm. "You're about as sentimental as Godzilla. I don't know why you even—

"Dang," she said, interrupting herself, "I forgot my purse."

Kate turned and rushed back into O'Malley's, leaving me several steps behind. Just as I stopped under the marquee I sidestepped a tall, dark-haired man and bumped head-on into an attractive redhead clutching his arm. She was wearing a tight black pantsuit that did nothing to hide a knockout figure.

"Sorry," I muttered, standing aside as they hurried down the sidewalk. I forced my eyes back into their sockets and rushed through the door after Kate. She had stopped dead in her tracks between the concession stand and the doorway leading into the auditorium and was shaking like she'd been poleaxed. I double-timed to her side, hoping she wasn't having a heretofore-unmentioned epileptic fit or some similar medical malfunction.

"What's the matter?" I said, quickly wrapping an arm around Kate to steady her. She'd turned as pale as the mound of popcorn in the theater's popper.

"That man," she said, just as her legs buckled. I caught her with my other arm and pulled her close. She trembled against my chest, her ragged breath coming in rushes. "That was . . ." and just like that she fainted.

～～～

With an usher's help I managed to get Kate to a chair inside the theater. I sent the young man after Kate's purse as another usher arrived with a cool, damp cloth. I wiped Kate's face with the cloth and declined the young lady's offer to call 911 since Kate's breathing had calmed and she was beginning to show signs of coming around. Her eyes fluttered several times and then opened. In a few seconds she sat upright and glanced around.

"What in the world?" she said, looking confused.

"You fainted. How're you feeling?"

"Okay." She still looked woozy.

"You sure? I can call a doctor."

"No, I'm fine." Then her eyes grew wide and she looked around the theater, turning her head this way and that. "That man I passed in the lobby . . . it was Wes!"

Okay, I don't claim to be the brightest star in the celestials, but in our months together I was pretty damn sure I'd never heard Kate mention any Wes before. Who the hell was this guy Wes? I felt like a contestant on *Jeopardy*. Then the lightbulb flashed on—her late boyfriend, Wes Harrison, who had drowned over a decade ago in a boating accident.

"Kate, listen to me. That couldn't have been Wes. Wes is dead." A reasonable enough conclusion, I thought.

"No, no . . . you don't understand," Kate said, making about as much sense to me as her feelings of compassion for the killer in the movie we'd just seen. "That really was Wes!"

Kate had a wild look in her eyes, an expression I'd never seen on her face before. For a minute I thought she was going to keel over again. I grabbed her by both shoulders and gave her a gentle shake. She was still milky pale. "Kate, please listen. Wes drowned in a boating accident, remember?"

Kate nodded. "But it was Wes." She stared at me like I'd just stepped onto Earth from an alien spaceship. "You don't get it, Mac," she said, her voice breaking up.

Now where had I heard *that* before? Oh yeah, out on the sidewalk a few minutes earlier heading for my pickup while Kate was informing me what a lousy movie critic I was. "Okay. What don't I get?"

Kate turned and stared toward the lobby for a long moment and shook her head. "Dang, Mac, Wes is still alive!"

CHAPTER 2

By the time I dropped Kate off at her house I'd almost convinced her that seeing Wes Harrison was most likely a simple case of mistaken identity, "almost" being the operative word. I knew she wasn't fully convinced that her eyes or mind had played a cruel trick on her, but she'd calmed down enough to promise to chew on my explanation for a while.

Tomorrow being Saturday, Kate had to be at her job at Gillman's Marina by six-thirty, so we called it a night. After making plans to meet for dinner and drinks after work, and a less-than-romantic good-night kiss, I drove to Gulf Pines Campground and my twenty-two-foot Grey Wolf camper trailer that I called home.

It was a quarter to eleven when I unlocked the door and stepped inside, but I wasn't the least bit sleepy. Kate believing she'd actually seen a dead man walking had me wound tight. Undressing to my socks and skivvies, I put on a sweat suit and my house slippers. I opened a cabinet door next to the sink, grabbed a tumbler, and poured myself a hefty three fingers of single-malt Scotch from a bottle of The Dalmore I kept on hand for special occasions. I figured Kate seeing a ghost from her past qualified. I stepped outside into the chilly night and took a seat atop the picnic table that serves as the centerpiece of my front yard, such as it is.

Spring had officially arrived five days ago, but a late cold front made the past few nights feel more like winter along the Gulf Coast of the Florida Panhandle. I took a sip of the smooth twelve-year-old whiskey and stared through the pines at the stars dazzling the black sky like a million fine-cut diamonds. Another month would mark the first anniversary of my retirement from the Marine Corps after twenty-four years of service, and I still hadn't figured out what to do with the rest of my life. The Marines had been my home since the day after I turned eighteen, and at times I still felt like a homeless waif.

Last spring, shortly after departing Camp Lejeune and the Corps, I'd come to St. George, a small coastal town that wealthy retirees were bent on transforming from a sleepy fishing village into a mecca for artsier tastes. I'd planned to spend a couple of weeks fishing and lazing on the beach while mapping out my future. I'll spare the details, but finding a body one morning while fishing for speckled trout near Five-Mile Island, and the consequences that followed, had prompted me to stay. Okay, meeting Kate Bell had a little something to do with my decision, too.

Kate. I sipped more Scotch and thought about her fainting spell earlier tonight and how upset she'd been. Kate is no wimp, anything but, so she must've really been convinced she'd seen this Harrison guy. That was impossible, of course; the man had been dead for twelve years, and I don't believe in ghosts. But what if it *was* him? Did that mean the others were alive, too? There had been three guys aboard the boat that day, if I remembered her brief account of the incident correctly. Had they planned and managed to pull off some elaborate scam for whatever reason? That idea was loony. No man in his right mind would've given up a life with Kate to work some scheme with a couple of other schmucks and then disappear into thin air. No, Davy Jones had claimed those three unfortunates.

I drained the last of the fine whiskey and headed for the warmth of the trailer. I felt a shiver run down my spine as the wind moaned through the swaying pine tops. Damned if it didn't sound like a ghost.

⁓〇

Because she'd opened the store that morning and the busy season hadn't yet arrived for the marina, Kate got off work at four that afternoon. We'd agreed to meet at four-thirty at St. George's most popular hangout, The Green Parrot Bar and Grill, for happy hour and an early dinner. Saturday night was also karaoke night on the back deck, so there wouldn't be a dull moment, not that there was ever a dull moment when I spent time with Kate. Hell, I might even decide to sing myself if the mood struck and I got buzzed enough.

I'd been helping Jerry Meadows move a new food cooler into the campground office/store that afternoon and was running a few minutes late. Jerry and his wife, Donna, own and operate Gulf Pines. I'd rented site 44 from them for almost a year, and we'd become fast friends. They were like the favorite aunt and uncle I'd never had.

It was pushing five by the time I parked, and I hurried across the Parrot's lot. I saw J.D. Owens coming down the wooden crossover that spans the dunes to protect them and the sea oats from foot traffic. He was leading a bedraggled but attractive young lady by the arm. As they crossed the sidewalk and stepped onto the pavement, I could see that his hand, firmly gripping her bicep, covered a tattoo. In my quick head-to-toe survey I also noticed her belly button and left eyebrow were pierced. She looked eighteen, twenty at the most, and like a lot of young beach-goers trying to get a head start on a tan, she wasn't exactly dressed for the weather. She was decked out in flip-flops, ragged hip-hugging denim short-shorts that were way beyond tight, and a print midriff-baring tank top at least two sizes too small. The top barely covered what it was designed to cover, and there was enough cleavage showing to cause a blind man to wander into rush-hour traffic. A pair of hummingbirds hovered over flowery vines at the tank top's strategic points. Lucky hummers.

"Hey, Mr. McClellan," J.D. greeted me with a grin. I still couldn't convince the lanky young police officer to call me Mac, even though he'd saved my bacon last summer.

"*Sergeant* Owens," I said, giving him tit for tat. J.D. had been awarded a medal of valor and a meritorious promotion to sergeant when he helped me bust up a drug operation last summer that was indirectly related to the body I'd found.

J.D. flushed. He hadn't taken well to being hailed a hero by the community or being addressed by his lofty new rank, for that matter.

"Who's your friend?" I was trying hard not to stare at the girl, who was tall but still a head shorter than J.D.

He gave the girl a quick glance. "Oh. This is Dakota, my cousin. Boyfriend trouble. Her and some girl got into a little altercation down on the beach, so I'm taking her home." He turned a couple of shades deeper. "*Her* house, I mean, not mine."

Dakota made a throaty noise that might've been a growl and blew a strand of tangled, bleached-blonde hair out of her big brown eyes. It was only then I noticed the purplish mouse below her right eye and a small split on her full upper lip still seeping blood. "Hey, I know you," she said. She flicked out her tongue—also pierced—and licked at the blood. "You're the guy that found Maddie Harper's body. I saw you and J.D. on TV the night y'all played hero busting them drug dudes."

A well-known local family had made a fortune smuggling drugs into the area for years via their commercial fishing fleet. Their son, Maddie's boyfriend, had gotten greedy. His solo venture into the marijuana trade had ended tragically.

"Nice to meet you, Dakota," I said, trying my best to keep my eyes above her chin, which was no easy task. She flashed a curled-lip Elvis snarl.

I turned my attention to J.D. "I need to talk to you about something. Give me a call when you get some time."

"Yes, sir," J.D. said, giving Cousin Dakota a "let's go" tug.

"Ouch, you bastard!" she spat as they passed by me, heading for J.D.'s blue and white cruiser. "Friggin' pig!"

"One foot in front of the other," I muttered, heading for the stairs leading down to the back deck and fighting the urge to turn around, "just one foot in front of the other."

⌇⌇

Kate was waiting at our favorite table next to the rail overlooking the beach, sipping on a glass of white wine. I half-expected her to be pissed because I was thirty minutes late, but when she spotted me coming her way she greeted me with that special smile of hers. I was glad to see she seemed to be in a good mood, especially after last night's drama.

"Dang, Mac, you missed the show," Kate said as I sat down oppo-site her, the cute, tiny gap between her front teeth highlighting the smile still spread across her face. The glow from the orange ball of sun just starting to touch the gulf's horizon highlighted her shoulder-length auburn hair.

"Yeah? What show?"

Kate waved a hand toward the beach. "A catfight on the beach, just past the volleyball net about fifteen minutes ago. This pretty brunette was catching rays with a guy when some scruffy-looking blonde walked up cussing like a sailor and started kicking sand all over them. The girl on the blanket jumped up and the two of them went at it. They were throwing punches and pulling hair like a couple of pro wrestlers."

I grinned. "Yeah? How come The Fabulous Moolah didn't step in and break it up?" Kate's brothers had dubbed their tomboy sister "The Fabulous Moolah" when they were kids, in honor of Lillian Ellison, one of the greatest lady wrestlers of all time. I'd learned this valuable tidbit from Kate's younger brother, Mark, when he'd done a big favor for us during the case I'd stumbled into last summer.

Kate half-rolled her eyes. "Very funny, Mac, ha ha. Anyway, the girl in the bikini almost lost her top. If J.D. Owens hadn't shown up when he did, somebody might've really gotten hurt."

My grin stayed intact as the image of bouncing female anatomy flashed through my mind. "Who won?"

Kate hesitated and arched her brow. "Nobody, thanks to J.D. I would've put my money on the blonde, though. What's with the guilty look?"

I couldn't help myself. "You mean the girl wearing short-shorts and a tank top with hummingbirds hovering on her chest?"

Kate's brow rose higher. "Let me guess. You ran into J.D. and the half-dressed perpetrator out front."

I grinned again and nodded. "That 'scruffy blonde' J.D. busted is his cousin, Dakota. Talk about kissing cousins."

Kate reached across the table and gave my arm a playful slap. "You're incorrigible."

I ordered some jalapeño poppers and a pitcher of Michelob with two frosted mugs, and we sat there enjoying the sunset while a solo guitarist played soft rock and beach tunes. I'd been waiting for Kate to mention last night's ruckus, but she was acting as if it had never happened. Patience has never been one of my greatest virtues, so I figured I'd take a chance. Big mistake.

"So, how're you doing with the Wes Harrison thing?"

Kate frowned. "I've been trying not to think about it." She stared into her mug for a minute before looking up. "I know what I saw, Mac, and I saw Wes."

I washed down a bite of popper with a swallow of beer and let out a breath. "Look, I believe *you* believe what you saw, but—"

Kate slapped the table. "I am *not* crazy! I saw Wes last night as sure as I'm seeing you right now!"

"But it's—"

"Fine, don't believe me then." She grabbed her purse and stood up.

This short fuse wasn't like Kate at all. I reached out and gripped her wrist. "Where're you going?"

"Home."

"What about dinner?"

"I'm not hungry."

"But tonight's karaoke. I was even thinking about getting up there myself."

She shook loose of my grasp. "Have a good time."

CHAPTER 3

I tried calling Kate several times the next day, but she didn't answer her home or cell phone. Finally I gave up and drove to her house. Her Honda CR-V wasn't in the driveway. I knew she wasn't scheduled to work that Sunday, but by midafternoon and more unanswered calls, I drove to Gillman's anyway just to make sure.

"She came in early this morning and asked for a few days off," Linda Gillman, who was working the store register, told me. As newlyweds, Linda and Gary Gillman had found their way down to the Gulf Coast from Minnesota and in two decades had built a small, struggling business practically from scratch into one of the finest marinas on the Panhandle coast. A tall, striking woman in her midforties, Linda had the same pale-blue eyes and whitish-blonde hair as their teenaged daughter, Sara, though Linda's was cut almost mannishly short.

On my way out I walked over to Sara, who was busy placing packages of hooks and other fishing tackle on metal rods extending from the shelves. "No, Mr. Mac," she said in her Southern drawl that had somehow managed to override her parents' heavy Minnesotan accent. "I didn't get a chance to talk to her this morning. She did seem pretty upset about something, though."

"Any idea about what?"

Sara shook her head, causing her long ponytail to swish like a horse's flicking away flies. "No, sir, but yesterday she said something about needing to find an old friend or something like that."

~⁀⁀◡

That night I was watching the local ten o'clock news when headlights flashed through the trailer's windows. Tires crunched over the gravel drive, and a vehicle pulled to a stop behind my Silverado. Thinking it might be Kate, I hurried to the door and opened it. The driver-side door of a white, older-model Toyota Corolla swung open, and a pair of long legs emerged, followed by the rest of a tall, shapely figure. It took a minute for my eyes to adjust enough to recognize Cousin Dakota striding toward me.

"Hey, McClellan," she said, climbing the steps and slipping past me through the doorway without waiting for an invitation. Before I could speak she'd made herself comfortable on the small sofa along the opposite wall, legs crossed, arms outstretched along the back.

At least she was decently dressed this time, although the modest white shorts and sky-blue blouse were more suited to summer than this chilly early-spring night. Makeup covered the mouse under her eye, and lip gloss hid any signs of the split. Her hair had even met up with a comb or brush.

"Dakota," I finally managed to force out with a nod. "What brings you here?" *And how the hell do you know where I live, anyway?* I added to myself.

Ignoring my question, she moved her arms from the sofa's back and dug through a small purse in her lap I'd somehow failed to notice when she'd invited herself in. The sleeve slipped up her bicep, exposing the tattoo J.D.'s hand had covered when I'd seen the two at The Green Parrot yesterday afternoon: a ring of barbed wire with alternating butterflies and honeybees. *Float like a butterfly, sting like a bee* flashed through my mind. After a moment she blew out an exasperated breath and glanced up. "You got a cigarette?"

I shook my head. "Don't smoke."

Dakota forced another breath through pursed lips. "Figures." She uncrossed her legs and pointed to the bottle of Michelob I held in my hand. "How about one of those?"

I chuckled and shook my head again. "I don't think so. You know, contributing to the delinquency of a minor? I doubt Cousin J.D. would approve."

"I'm twenty-one."

I snickered. "Yeah, so am I."

"Oh, give me a friggin' break." She did the Elvis thing with her upper lip and fished through the purse again. Her appearance may have climbed up the ladder a couple of rungs, but her language was still in the gutter. "Here," she said, handing me a laminated card that looked about the size of a driver's license.

It was, and on the surface it appeared to be the real deal. Up-to-date Florida license, local address; Dakota Blaire Owens, date of birth February 22. According to this, she was legal. "You and George Washington, huh?" I handed the license back. "Sorry, I'm not buying."

Dakota snatched the card and made that throaty growl I'd heard her give J.D. as she rummaged through the purse some more. "Will this do?"

I took the other card she held out. It was a student photo ID for Chipola College, which was about forty miles north of St. George near the town of Marianna. Everything checked out with the info on her driver's license. I stared hard into those big brown eyes for a long moment. She didn't blink or flinch. I handed the card back. "Okay, but just one," I said, opening the fridge and grabbing a bottle of Michelob. "You're not driving away from here buzzed." I twisted off the cap and handed it to her.

"Thanks," Dakota said. She tilted the bottle and knocked back a healthy swig as I sat in the recliner across from her.

"Now, what brings you here?" I repeated.

She crossed her legs again, wagging an Adidas-covered foot slowly back and forth. "I've been wanting to meet you for a while, is all."

"Yeah? Why?"

One eyebrow arched, and her lips crept into a coy smile. "It's not every day you get to meet a real hero."

"Hero?" I took a quick swig of beer and snorted. "You got it wrong, young lady. Your cousin's the one who bailed my butt out of trouble. If anybody's a hero, it's J.D."

Dakota sat there smiling and wagging her foot. I was beginning to feel uncomfortable, even a little intimidated by this barely legal siren who was only a few months older than my own daughter. Just what the hell was she really doing at my place at ten-thirty on a Sunday night? My gut told me hero worship had nothing to do with it. "So, what're you studying at Chipola?" I said, more to alleviate my own uneasiness than to make small talk.

Dakota's foot stopped wagging. She took a sip of beer and ran a finger in circles around the rim of the bottle. "What the crap do you care?"

"I asked, didn't I?"

Dakota took a final swallow, got to her feet, and placed the half-empty bottle on the lamp table beside the sofa. "Thanks for the beer, McClellan," she said, grabbing her purse and heading for the door.

I stood up. "You're welcome."

She stopped as she swung the door open. "Maddie Harper was a friend of mine," she said, her back to me. "I appreciate what you did for her, finding her killer and all."

I just stood there. What the hell do you say to that?

Dakota started down the steps. She stopped and turned. "Hey, McClellan, do me a favor, okay?"

"Depends. What is it?"

The gusting wind caught Dakota's hair, blowing it across her face. She brushed it out of her eyes with her free hand. "Keep an eye on J.D. for me. He can use your help."

CHAPTER 4

Monday the weather turned warmer, and I spent most of the day in my rental boat cruising the bay and wetting a few lures. While I didn't catch anything worth keeping, it was nice getting out on the water again after a colder-than-normal winter and blustery first week of spring. It also helped distract me some from fretting about Kate.

By noon Tuesday I still hadn't heard a word from Kate. My concern was turning into worry. It just wasn't like her to disappear and treat me like I didn't exist. We'd worked together to find out who'd been responsible for Maddie Harper's death and had grown close in the time we'd known each other. After Labor Day Kate took ten days off from work, and we'd hitched up the Grey Wolf and made a beeline for North Carolina. First stop was UNC-Wilmington, where my son Mike is on a baseball scholarship, then on to Raleigh and NC State where daughter Megan is studying to become a veterinarian. Kate and the twins hit it off better than I'd expected, and both kids seemed happy I'd found someone to fill the void caused by their mother's and my divorce.

On our way back to St. George, Kate and I spent an enjoyable few days cruising the Blue Ridge Parkway and exploring the Great Smoky Mountains National Park. We'd grown even closer on our little trip, and the "M" word slipped into my thoughts for a quick visit a time or two.

Like most couples, we'd had our little disagreements, but never before had Kate shut me out over anything. It was obvious I'd underestimated just how deeply this Wes Harrison matter was affecting her.

I fished through my wallet and found Mark Bell's business card. Mark worked in graphics at a print shop in Destin, Kate's hometown, located on the coast some seventy miles west of St. George. He'd given

me the card last summer when Kate and I called on him with an envelope full of less-than-sharp black-and-white Polaroids we hoped he could
improve. Mark worked his magic, and the results were beyond what
I could've hoped for. The enhanced photos proved to be a big help in
busting up the drug op and bringing Maddie Harper's killer to justice.

I turned the card over and punched in Mark's personal cell number
he'd jotted down on the back. He answered on the second ring.

"Mark, it's Mac McClellan."

"Hi, Mac. I had a hunch I might be hearing from you." His voice
sounded unenthused at best, which I figured couldn't be a good sign.

"Have you heard from Kate? She took off a few days ago but didn't
let anyone know where she was going."

There was a brief silence, broken by the sound of something clanking
and Mark's muffled voice talking to someone. "Sorry, Mac, it's kind of
busy around here right now. Kate's staying at our parents' house."

A wave of relief flowed through me just knowing she was safe.
"Could I have their number? Kate won't answer her cell phone."

Another hesitation. "I don't know. She seemed pretty upset at you
over something."

"Did she tell you what about?"

"No, just that she needed her space for a while."

"What about your parents? Did she mention anything to them?"

"Not that I'm aware of. They're still in Arizona. They've been
spending winters at an RV park on Lake Havasu the last few years. I
doubt Kate would want to dump anything on them."

Other than Mark, I'd yet to meet Kate's family. As close as we'd
become, she'd never offered to introduce me to her parents or two older
brothers. I hadn't pushed the matter. If she wasn't ready to commit
to anything other than an unspoken exclusive relationship, so be it.
"Going steady" seemed a bit juvenile, but I guess that best describes
what we'd had going the past several months.

I took a few seconds to get my thoughts together. "Listen, Mark,
do you remember a guy named Wes Harrison?"

"Wes? Sure. He was Kate's boyfriend," Mark said. Then his tone changed, like he'd possibly let a secret slip out without thinking. "You do know about Kate and Wes, don't you?"

"Yeah. He died in a boating accident in the gulf, right?"

"Right. Along with Eric Kohler and Robert Ramey. They drowned when a squall capsized their boat. There was also evidence of a fire in the engine room that might've been a contributing factor. That was a bad time. It damn near killed Kate."

I'd known the incident had claimed three victims, but it was the first time Kohler and Ramey's names had been mentioned. The fire was also news. I heard what sounded like a pen or pencil drumming on a desktop for a few seconds before Mark said, "What does Wes Harrison have to do with this?"

I took a deep breath and let it slide out. "Kate and I were at the movies in Parkersville Friday night. Kate forgot her purse on the way out. She went back to get it and . . . she claims she saw Wes in the lobby."

The drumming stopped and a brief silence passed. "That's crazy. I mean, they never found any of the bodies, but . . ."

"Yeah, that's what I thought. But now I'm not so sure. Kate's pretty damn convinced she saw the guy, and I'm starting to believe her."

Another quick silence, then, "You got a pen handy, Mac?"

I'd just finished jotting down the Bells' home phone number and ended my conversation with Mark when J.D. Owens pulled into my driveway. I stepped out to greet him as his car door opened. "Sorry for not giving you that call yet," he said, climbing out of his blue and white Ford cruiser. "We been shorthanded with Chief Tolliver down in Clearwater attending that Police Chiefs Association meeting."

I grinned. "You got the new chief trained yet?"

J.D. flushed at my little joke and returned the grin. "Yes, sir, just about. Beth's been keeping him on his toes."

I'd met Chief Brian Tolliver shortly after the St. George City Council hired him in October. Tolliver was around my age, maybe a couple of years younger, and of average height and build. Picture a fortyish Huck Finn, and you've described the new chief to a T. He'd spent fifteen years with the Tallahassee police and knew his stuff. In the short time Tolliver had been on the job he'd managed to expand the department by two full-time officers and was hounding the council to hire one more. Counting Chief Tolliver and Sergeant Owens, the St. George Police Department now boasted a force of four full-time officers plus Beth, the dispatcher, who had undergone an almost overnight makeover in appearance with the new chief's hiring.

"What'd you want to talk to me about?" J.D. said, getting down to business.

I decided not to mention Dakota's little visit Sunday night or her request that I keep an eye on J.D. No sense complicating matters. I motioned to the picnic table, and we both took a seat on top with our feet resting on the bench. A couple of blue jays began scolding a squirrel in a nearby pine. "I need some information on a man. I thought you might check police records and see if you can come up with anything."

"What's the name?" J.D. said, pulling a small notepad and pen from his shirt pocket.

"Wes Harrison."

J.D. looked up. "Wes? That his full first name?"

I shrugged. "It's all I've got. Maybe it's Wesley, something like that." I hadn't told Kate that I planned on looking into Wes's background. She was upset enough as it was, already.

The young sergeant jotted down the name. "What'd this guy do, Mr. McClellan? I mean, I can't go looking into somebody's background without just cause."

I took a breath and gave J.D. the whole spiel about what had happened at O'Malley's Friday night, plus a description of the guy Kate had sworn was Wes Harrison.

"What about his eye color?" J.D. said.

I thought for a minute. "Kate didn't say."

J.D. frowned but didn't say anything. Professional courtesy, I guess. When we were finished, J.D. knew as much as I did about the three amigos and their alleged descent into Davy Jones' Locker. "I know it sounds far-fetched, but Kate swears it's this Harrison guy she saw. If the man *is* alive, something mighty fishy must've been going on back then."

J.D. nodded. "And you say this accident happened over in Destin about twelve years ago?" he said, checking his notes again.

"According to Kate." I was impressed with how confidently J.D. went about his business, how much he'd matured in the months since the drug bust.

J.D. stared across the crushed shell-and-gravel road and tapped pen against pad. "Seems like I remember hearing about that accident way back then. Funny, who would've thought Miss Bell would've known them guys?"

I watched as the blue jays gave up their game with the squirrel and flew across the campground toward the office where Jerry and Donna kept several feeders filled with seed. "Yeah, sometimes it really is a small world."

Kate returned my call around nine-thirty that night after I'd left a second message on her parents' answering machine. It took some doing, but I finally convinced her that I now believed she'd seen Wes Harrison at O'Malley's. Kate had never lied to me before, and I felt like a louse for ever doubting her. If she saw Wes Harrison that night in the lobby, she saw Wes Harrison. I apologized and promised I'd do everything in my power to help her get to the bottom of Wes's sudden resurrection from the dead.

Kate was due back to work at Gillman's on Saturday, but she asked if I could drive to Destin in the morning. There were a couple of things she wanted to check out, and she'd feel more comfortable if I was there to help. What the hell was I going to say, no? She gave me the address and directions to the house, and I promised to meet her there at ten sharp Wednesday.

We exchanged good-nights, and I was about to click off when

Kate shouted, "Wait!" into my ear. For the entire conversation something had been troubling me about the sound of Kate's voice. I couldn't pinpoint what it was, but something told me all wasn't right with our world. What I heard next didn't do a whole lot to ease my concern.

"Mac, please don't think I'm going crazy, but I believe Wes might be searching for me."

CHAPTER 5

Following the directions Kate had given me the night before, I drove through the newer, more touristy part of Destin to the western end, where Highway 98 becomes Harbor Boulevard. I turned right onto Benning Drive. At the end of Benning I made a left on Calhoun that brought me to the Bells' home, an older but well-kept two-story wooden structure overlooking Choctawhatchee Bay near the mouth of Marler Bayou. The large front lawn was shaded by several tall pines and two sprawling live oaks, one on either side of a concrete driveway. I pulled into the drive and stopped behind Kate's CR-V, which was parked outside a detached two-car garage.

As I climbed out of my Silverado the screen door of the house flew open. Kate, dressed in faded jeans and a green sweatshirt, bounded across the big porch and down the brick stairs and was in my arms before I'd made it halfway along the sidewalk leading from the garage to the house. The bear hug and warm kiss made the trip well worth the trouble already.

"I missed you, Mac," she said, pressing her cheek against my chest. "Sorry I took off the way I did."

I hugged her tight and kissed the top of her head. "Glad you're safe."

I followed Kate into the house, accepting her offer of fresh-brewed coffee. We stepped from the foyer into the great room with its high ceiling and wood-burning fireplace. The spacious room was comfortably fitted with overstuffed sofas and chairs and matching tables. Beach scenes in rustic driftwood frames hung on the walls, and family photos through the years crowded the mantel above the fireplace. It was easy to see the Bells were a tight-knit bunch. If rooms could talk, this one would've shouted, "Family!"

The kitchen was located at the back right corner of the house. While Kate poured the coffee I took a seat at the dining table in an alcove along the outside wall. Tall windows provided a view across the greening lawn with the bay in the distance. In the middle of the oak table sat a cardboard box roughly twice the size of a shoebox. Next to the box was a small stack of what appeared to be photos of various sizes. I kept my curiosity in check, figuring they were turned face-down for good reason.

Kate handed me a mug of steaming coffee and sat in the chair to my right. She took a sip from her cup, reached across the table, and scooped up the photos. "These are all the pictures I could find of Wes," she said, placing them in front of me. The top photo showed two smiling young men holding fishing rods and standing side by side on a dock with open water in the background. They were about the same height with lean athletic builds. One had dark, wind-tousled hair with bangs that fell across his forehead. The other was a sandy blond and wore his longish hair swept back; I guess the term "ruggedly handsome" might fit, but "surfer dude" came to mind instead.

"This is a picture of Eric and Wes," Kate said. She tapped a finger-nail on the blond. "That's Wes."

A red flag waved inside my head. Was Kate hallucinating? I didn't get a real good look at the man I'd sidestepped at O'Malley's, but he'd had dark hair, neatly styled and parted on one side, if my memory served me. Okay, so maybe he'd cut and dyed his hair. I could buy that. But the nose was all wrong. The Wes in this photo had a definite honker with a noticeable hump midway up; the theater Wes's nose was straight and not nearly as prominent. The chin didn't look right either, for that matter. It was too square.

I hesitated and took another sip of coffee. Here I'd gone and blabbed to Kate that I believed she'd seen Wes Harrison at O'Malley's, and now I was about to make a liar out of myself. What the hell; it was time to bite the bullet. "Kate, the guy I saw had dark hair," I said, trying to be as diplomatic as possible. "I realize he could've dyed his hair easy enough, but the nose and the chin don't fit at all."

To my surprise and relief Kate placed a hand on my forearm and gave a little squeeze. "I know. But did you see his eyes?"

His eyes? The truth is, after a quick glance at the man I'd been too distracted by the redhead I'd bumped into to notice his eyes. I took a closer look at the photo. Nothing I saw jogged my memory. "No, what about his eyes?"

Kate grabbed the photos and flipped through a few. She pulled one from the stack and placed it before me. "Here. This is a close-up of Wes."

I picked it up. It was a mug shot. Same grin, swept-back blond hair, hooked beak, and square chin. But the eyes jumped out at me like a pair of throbbing thumbs. The left eye was blue, the right brown. I glanced up at Kate.

"It's called heterochromia," she said. "Don't be too impressed. I had to look it up. It's fairly rare in humans. You see it a lot more in animals."

I took a breath and let it out slowly. "Why didn't you mention the eyes before?"

"I don't know. Maybe it was the shock of seeing Wes again after believing he was dead all these years. I was starting to think you were right, that it couldn't have been him. That's why I had to come here and look at the photos again. I had to prove to myself that I wasn't imagining what I saw."

"Okay, but what about the nose? I got a good enough look at the guy to tell the nose is all wrong. The chin, too."

"Plastic surgery," Kate said. "That's the only thing it could be. When I passed him in the lobby that night we made eye contact. There's no mistaking those eyes. And I *know* he recognized me. His mouth dropped open before he turned away."

"You *are* talking about the guy who was with the redhead, right?"

Kate's brow arched. "Dang, Mac, nothing sneaks by you, does it? Yes, the guy with the redhead."

I still wasn't convinced the man I'd seen at O'Malley's was the man in the photo I was holding. I wracked my brain trying to remember more details of the theater Wes's face, but I came up blank. I hadn't noticed his eyes, but Kate had. What were the chances of running into two men with eyes like that in a lifetime? Miniscule at best.

"Okay. You saw Wes Harrison at O'Malley's the other night," I said, playing along. "But what makes you think he's searching for you?"

Kate finished a sip of coffee and held the mug at chin level in both hands. "Maybe during the accident he was badly hurt and lost his memory besides having to have his face reconstructed. What if he's slowly regaining his memory and somehow is starting to remember our relationship together?"

"That's it?" I'd been expecting Kate to come up with more than a flimsy house of cards to support her belief that Harrison was still among the living.

"Well, yeah."

"You're really reaching. No Hollywood B-movie would buy into that scenario."

She looked close to tears. "Maybe not."

"You believe Eric Kohler and Robert Ramey might still be alive, too?"

Kate's eyes widened. "How do you know their names? I never mentioned them."

"Mark told me. So, you think they're still kicking around somewhere too?"

Kate set the mug on the table and stared into it a few seconds before looking up. "I guess. I mean, if Wes—"

"Why, Kate?"

Kate frowned, her forehead wrinkled. "Why what?"

I let out a deep breath. "If the three of them are still alive, what were they up to? Did they stage their own deaths? And why the hell would Wes Harrison do that to you, the woman he loved?"

Kate's chin quivered, and she wiped away a tear tracing down her cheek. "I don't know, Mac. It doesn't make any sense. I just know in my heart that I saw Wes the other night."

I got up and wrapped my arms around her. She pressed her face into my shoulder. After a moment she turned away and blew her nose into a paper napkin she'd grabbed from a holder on the table.

"I'm sorry. I know all this sounds crazy," she said, dabbing her eyes with the folded napkin. "But I know it was Wes I saw at O'Malley's. And I don't know why they would've staged anything, *if* they did. That's not like Wes at all."

I knelt beside Kate's chair and took a minute to get the words straight in my mind. "Have you considered the possibility that Wes is the one who pulled this thing off, whatever it was? What if he had some reason to get rid of Kohler and Ramey and disappear, making it look like the three of them had died in the storm?"

Kate pushed her mug away. "I can't believe that. I *won't* believe that! Wes and Eric were too close, Mac. They were more like brothers than friends."

I sighed and squeezed Kate's hand. "Okay then, looks like we've got our work cut out for us."

Hightower Investigations was located on Harbor Boulevard in a two-story brick building atop a New Age tea and aromatherapy shop. Frank Hightower and Jim Bell, Kate's father, had been best friends since high school. The two had joined the Navy together after graduation and were shipmates aboard a carrier during the middle years of the Vietnam War. They had remained close friends after their hitch ended. Mr. Bell had owned and operated a successful tackle and marine supply business for many years, while Frank Hightower pursued a career with the Okaloosa County Sheriff's Department. Upon retiring, Hightower opened his own private eye operation.

I trailed Kate up the outside stairway to a landing overlooking a side street that dead-ended near the waterfront. Gulls wheeled high in the cloudless blue sky above Destin Harbor. Masts of sailboats and charter boats' flying bridges were visible along the docks.

Not bothering to knock, Kate turned the brass doorknob and stepped inside. I followed close on her heels. A wiry man with a shock of gray hair stood up from behind a black metal desk with a pair of matching file cabinets centered along the back wall. He wore gray slacks and a blue dress shirt but no tie. A two-inch scar above his right eye paralleled his furrowed brow. He looked to be in good shape for someone in his sixties. He took off the wire-rimmed glasses he'd been wearing, and as he recognized Kate his ruddy face broke into a big grin.

"Katie, how's my best girl?" he said, hurrying around the desk to give her a warm hug.

Kate returned the hug and patted him on the back. "Uncle Frank, it's good to see you."

"And you must be Mac," Frank said, glancing over Kate's shoulder at me. "I've heard good things about you, young man."

We shook hands, and I pointed a thumb at Kate. "My PR department must've preceded me," I said, hoping he'd take it for the joke I intended. His hearty laugh told me he did.

"Now, Katie girl," Frank said as he motioned for us to sit in twin chairs fronting the desk, "what's this about you wanting me to look into a missing person case?" He sat on a corner of the desktop and crossed his arms. "Just who is it that's gone missing?"

For the next few minutes Kate laid out the whole spiel about running into Wes Harrison at O'Malley's, including mentioning Harrison's unusual eyes. The more emphatically Kate stated her case, the deeper the frown on Frank's face grew. Finally, he held up a hand like a cop stopping traffic.

"You know I worked on that case, Katie. We searched the coast and the inland waterways for days, just in case the tide—"

"But it was *him*, Uncle Frank. There's no mistaking his eyes. And I know he recognized me."

Hightower tilted his head and glanced at me. "Mac?"

My jaw tightened. I sure as hell had hoped to avoid being put on the spot like this. "Like Kate said, I didn't get a good look at the guy, but if she says it was Wes Harrison, I believe her."

Frank stared at me a couple of seconds and then grinned. "Good answer." He turned to Kate. "Let's have a look at the photos."

Kate handed Hightower the manila envelope she'd brought containing a few of the better shots of both Harrison and Eric Kohler. There was also a photo of Rachel Todd, Eric's sister, posing on the beach with Kate, Wes, and Eric. Frank moved to his chair, sat down, and spread the photos out on the desk. After eyeballing them a moment he said, "You two bring your chairs back here."

Kate and I stood and moved our chairs to Frank's right as he double-clicked an icon on the monitor that sat just left of center on the desk. "This is a face-identification program," he said, as Kate and I settled in. He winked at Kate. "Fringe benefit, courtesy of the Okaloosa Sheriff's Department."

We spent the next half hour poring over dozens of face shapes, chins, noses, eyes, hair, skin tone, and every other feature you could think of until Kate was sure the face on the monitor was a near spitting image of the Wes Harrison she'd seen at O'Malley's last Friday. From what little I could remember, I had to agree. This could be the man with the redhead I'd bumped into. Neatly styled dark hair, chiseled jaw line, straight nose.

For the next five minutes Frank followed Kate's suggestions until the eye colors on the monitor matched those of the younger Wes's odd eyes. "That's him!" Kate said, coming out of her chair and hugging Frank from behind. "That's the man I saw in the theater!"

After Kate settled down, Frank scanned a close-up of Eric Kohler onto his hard drive. He worked his magic, and in a few minutes Wes's best friend had aged over a decade and put on a few pounds. He then cropped Rachel from the beach photo and progressed her age. Frank printed several color copies of the newly resurrected Destin gang and saved the files to a flash drive. He handed the printouts and drive to Kate. "It's a start."

~⌒

It was late afternoon when we finished our business at Hightower Investigations, so Kate and I invited Frank for happy hour and dinner at AJ's Seafood and Oyster Bar. The invitation was Kate's idea. Frank had been widowed a couple of years back, and Kate thought he could use the company. Besides, being an old friend of the family, he had a lot of catching up to do with Kate.

Frank followed us in his silver Jeep Cherokee as I drove the few blocks west to AJ's, located on the harbor a short distance from Destin Bridge. The afternoon was mild, so we followed our hostess to a table on the downstairs deck with a nice view of the harbor. There was a decent crowd even though spring was still struggling to gain a firm foothold in the Panhandle. Several seafaring patrons had tied their boats to AJ's visitors' dock for happy hour or an early dinner.

After the waitress brought our drinks and took our dinner orders, I decided it was time to get down to the matter of money. I had no idea what PIs in this area charged. Old family friend or not, I thought Hightower's fee might be a little steep for Kate's budget, so I bit the bullet and spilled the question.

Frank and Kate glanced at each other and exchanged slight smiles. "I've got a proposition for you, Mac," Frank said. He took a sip from his bourbon and water. "How would you like to go to work for me?"

I eyeballed Kate, who quickly averted her eyes and sipped her wine while staring out at the harbor. I shook the ice in my tumbler of Dewar's and tried to decipher just what the hell Frank Hightower was getting at. He took another drink, set his glass on the table, and turned in his chair to face me.

"I know about your little adventure last summer, Mac. You handled yourself like a pro according to what I heard."

I took a hefty swallow of Scotch and stared Frank in the eye. "Yeah? Heard from who?" I frowned and shot Kate a glance. I've never cared much for people talking about me behind my back, good or bad. Evidently Kate and "Uncle Frank" had done more catching up than I was aware of.

Frank must've caught my expression. "Listen, Mac, Katie did clue me in about what the two of you were up to, but I've got other sources in your neighborhood."

"Bo Pickron, for example?"

Frank's eyes narrowed. "I knew his old man pretty well when he was sheriff of Palmetto County. We even worked together on a few cases when county lines got crossed. Fine man. And yeah, I know his son a little. He's got the makings of a good lawman *if* he ever learns to keep his personality out of the job. But there's a couple of old hands still with Palmetto County who I keep in touch with now and then. You've got the cojones for the job, Mac."

I wondered just who, besides Kate, Frank had been in touch with. Other than Sheriff Bocephus Pickron, I'd had little contact with members of the sheriff's department. I swirled a sip of Dewar's around my mouth and let it trickle down my throat. What the hell. The old man was obviously fond of Kate and was probably trying to help her by helping me. "So, what's your proposition?"

Frank picked up his glass and stared at the contents for a moment. "I've been thinking about branching out to the east. Panama City's not far from your neck of the woods. I've done some work around PC, but there's more than I can handle here. I know you're retired military and probably don't need the money, but you're still a young man, Mac. So, here's the deal. You agree to work for me. I'll be your sponsor and show you the ropes while you take the proper courses and all the other BS required to earn your legal PI license. Meanwhile, you'll be helping me find out what's going on with Katie's old friends. I pay for the courses, you work the case, and we call it even. Katie won't owe a dime."

I knocked back a healthy swig of Scotch and stared at the horizon where the top edge of the sun was about to dip into the Gulf of Mexico. Maybe I'd see the elusive "green flash" and take it as a sign I should accept Frank's offer. A few seconds later the gulf swallowed the sun; no green flash, no omen. I'd spent almost a year since my discharge trying to decide what to do with the rest of my life. Hell, maybe Frank's proposition was my omen.

I signaled to our waitress, pointed to my empty glass, and held up three fingers indicating drinks all around. "What if I try it for a while and decide being a PI's not for me? I'm no quitter, but I don't want to waste time spinning my wheels doing something I don't like."

Frank drained his glass and set it back on the folded paper napkin he'd been using as a coaster. "All I'm asking is that you give it an honest shot. If it doesn't work out, you walk away. No questions, no obligations. Fair enough?"

I had retired from the Marines as a First Sergeant. That rank commanded respect and pulled a lot of weight with both enlisted personnel and officers. Starting over at the bottom of the heap didn't exactly thrill me. And I'd be taking orders from Frank, a former swabbie.

Kate was still pretending to be fascinated with the sights of the harbor. I reached over and touched her arm. She turned to me, her auburn hair reflecting the golden glow of sunlight still lingering on the horizon. I searched her eyes. "Kate?"

She sighed and said, "It's your decision," just as the waitress arrived with our fresh round of drinks.

When we'd been served I grabbed my tumbler of Dewar's and held it up in a toast. "To Mac McClellan, boot private eye."

CHAPTER 6

Later that evening Kate and I were watching a movie on her parents' big-screen TV when my cell phone rang. Kate grabbed the remote and put the movie on pause as I answered.

"Mr. McClellan, this is J.D."

"Good evening, Sergeant Owens."

"I mean, Mac."

"Much better, J.D. What's up?"

"I ran that name you asked me about, that Wes Harrison? I checked with the FBI National Crime Information Center and came up with a bunch of guys, but I ruled out all but a couple. They're both around the right age and match the description you gave me."

I got up and made a scribbling motion at Kate. "Hold on a second J.D., I'm getting something to write with." Kate hurried across the room and was back with a pad and pen in a few seconds. I told her to go ahead with the movie, a chick flick that had me struggling to stay awake. I moved to the kitchen so I'd be out of earshot.

Because of the new info on Harrison's eyes, anything J.D. had dug up was a long shot at best. But what the hell. He'd gone to the trouble; the least I could do was hear him out. "Okay, go."

I heard paper shuffling. "The first guy's name is Wesley Jerome Harrison. Thirty-nine years old; born in Indiana but moved to Tallahassee with his family in 1985. He's got a rap sheet as long as your arm; breaking and entering, auto theft, possession of stolen property, stuff like that."

I jotted it down. "Jail time?"

"Yes, sir, mostly county slammers across the Panhandle, but he spent two years in Raiford for assault and battery. He roughed up an old lady during a home invasion."

"A real sweetheart. When was he in the state pen?"

J.D. cleared his throat. "That's a problem. It was after the boating accident."

The chances that our Wes Harrison faked his own death and then beat up some elderly woman a couple of years later were almost nil. Unless. . . . "What about his eye color?"

"Hold on . . . brown."

Wesley Jerome wasn't our man. "What about the other guy?"

Turns out the other Harrison was a generic Wes, no middle name, with hazel eyes. He was a Mississippi native with a similar small-time record. This Wes's only saving grace was that he'd managed to stay out of real trouble to date.

I thanked J.D. and was about to end the conversation when an idea popped up. "Did you happen to run across any surfer dudes with blond hair and weird-colored eyes in that database?"

There was silence for a moment. "Any whats?"

"I'll catch you later, J.D."

Thursday morning I drove back to St. George armed with some books and manuals Frank had loaned me about the PI business. Kate was staying in Destin a couple more days to visit with friends and family but promised to be home in time for work Saturday morning.

When I got back to the campground I called J.D. on his personal cell phone. He was on duty but agreed to meet me at my trailer as soon as his shift ended at four. When J.D. arrived I filled him in on the new info I'd learned in Destin and showed him the photo of the younger Wes Harrison.

J.D. let out a whistle. "So, this is what you meant by 'surfer dude' last night, huh."

"Yeah. That's the Wes Harrison Kate knew back in Destin."

J.D. glanced up from the photo. "But he doesn't look—"

"Here's the Harrison Kate saw at O'Malley's." I handed him the computer-generated likeness of the new Wes. "She thinks he's had plastic surgery. Compare the eyes."

Another whistle.

"Kate swears the man she saw at O'Malley's last Friday had eyes just like this. Does that FBI database have photos?"

J.D. was studying the printouts again. "Some," he said without looking up.

"I hate to be a pain in the butt, but would you check through it again? He might've had a juvenile record or some kind of run-in with the law before Kate ever met him."

J.D. nodded. "They got a juvenile offender file if I remember right. And a missing and unidentified persons file, too. I think that one's got victims of storms and accidents where they didn't recover a body."

We talked a few more minutes until J.D. had to leave to get ready for a date with Hailey, the girl he'd been seeing the past year. I handed him copies of the old and new Wes as he was leaving. "I owe you, J.D."

"No, sir, you don't owe me. What you did for Maddie and all, I mean." Halfway to his cruiser he stopped and turned. "I'll get on this soon as I can . . . Mac."

The young man was learning.

⁓

It took several days of filling out paperwork, submitting various documents, and a couple of phone interviews, but by the second Friday in April I was dutifully enrolled in an online certified PI training institute headquartered downstate. Forty hours of training were required. By busting my butt and taking advantage of Frank's help, I hoped to complete the course work inside a month, six weeks tops.

That would still leave me enough free time to do some actual footwork on Kate's case during my studies—strictly off the record, of course, until I had my license. No way could I risk landing Frank or his business in hot water with state authorities. But if Wes Harrison was really alive and kicking somewhere, I aimed to find out. Kate was doing her best to be patient, but I could tell she was chomping at the bit.

So, in the week before my enrollment paperwork was finalized I went to work. First I browsed through the books Frank had loaned me. A couple were mostly "how to" material on the private eye trade for the novice; another, more technical in scope, contained info on numerous available resources valuable to the profession, both online and elsewhere.

For starters I accessed the archives of the *Northwest Florida Sun*, Okaloosa County's leading newspaper, searching for coverage of the accident. Pay dirt. I turned up seven articles, beginning with the boat being reported overdue from a fishing trip. The Coast Guard discovered the capsized and fire-damaged vessel the next day. The official search for survivors was suspended a few days later. Speculation was that the men had been at anchor fishing when the storm came up. While attempting to restart the gas engines an explosion occurred, possibly from inadequate ventilation in the engine room. That might have led to a loss of steering. Foundering in the growing sea and taking on water, the vessel capsized.

There were also obituaries for Ramey, Kohler, and Harrison. Ramey's obit was lengthy and flattering, damn near a bio. Harrison's and Kohler's were barebones.

Robert Alton Ramey was thirty-nine years old at the time of the accident. A respected jeweler and gemologist, he owned both Ramey's Gems and Jewelry of Atlanta and Ramey's Fine Jewelry in Destin. Coming from old money, Ramey succeeded his father and grandfather in one of Atlanta's oldest and most respected jewelry establishments. He'd grown up in a ritzy neighborhood of North Atlanta's upscale Buckhead district, not far from where the family business was located.

Never married, Ramey spent the majority of his time at his Atlanta location but made numerous visits to the Gulf Coast to keep tabs on the Destin business. He was well-known in social circles for throwing lavish parties at his Atlanta home, his extravagant waterfront home in Sandestin, and aboard the vintage yacht he'd inherited from his father, a forty-foot Chris Craft Conqueror.

From all accounts, the silver spoon had never left Robert Ramey's mouth, from his privileged birth till his untimely death, and he'd taken full advantage of it. He was survived by his mother, Mrs. Edmond Randolph (née Darla June Spence) Ramey, and a couple of aunts, uncles, and cousins.

Eric James Kohler, twenty-eight, hailed from Waxahachie, Texas. Manager of Ramey's Fine Jewelry, he'd been a resident of Destin for the past four years. He was survived by a sister, Rachel Todd of Pensacola. Short and sweet.

The info on twenty-seven-year-old Wes Harrison was scant. He was single, a native of California, where his surviving family resided, and had also been employed with Ramey's Fine Jewelry. He'd been a resident of Destin for two years.

Kate hadn't exactly been a geyser of information, but she had spilled a few interesting tidbits. Eric Kohler was already employed by Robert Ramey as manager of the Destin store when he and Kate were introduced at a mutual friend's party. No sparks flew, but their shared interests in fishing and diving led to a close but platonic friendship.

Rachel Todd was Eric's half-sister and only living relative. A licensed pilot, Rachel worked for a Christian missionary organization headquartered in Pensacola and made frequent trips to South America. Kate had spent time with her on a few occasions, and, although not close friends, they'd gotten along well enough.

Wes Harrison hailed from the San Diego, California, area. Before moving east he'd received training as a gemologist. He met Kate and Kohler while SCUBA diving shortly after his arrival in Destin. The three buddied-up on the dive trip and became fast friends. Upon learning Harrison was a trained gemologist, Kohler introduced him to Ramey, who hired him as a buyer working mainly out of the Destin store. Eventually, Kate found herself drawn to Harrison, and the two began dating.

I was on my way to Kate's house Monday around six p.m. for dinner when my phone rang. I hadn't heard from J.D. in over a week and hoped he might be calling with info on Wes Harrison. It was Frank Hightower.

"I've got some new dope on Eric Kohler for you," Frank said.

Hearing that, I pulled onto the shoulder of the road and grabbed the small notebook and pen I kept in the center console. "Shoot."

"I talked to a few jewelers around the area. Both of Robert Ramey's businesses held membership in the Diamond Council of America. The DCA is a not-for-profit headquartered in Nashville. They've been in business since 1944. They've got a top-notch reputation in the jewelry trade and their training carries a lot of prestige. Having the DCA membership plaque hanging on your wall is evidently good for business.

"Our boy Kohler had a couple of certificates for training courses offered by the DCA to its members' employees. My guess is Ramey insisted Kohler take the training when he hired him to run his store."

I jotted down the info, intending to do my own research on the DCA. "What else?"

"One thing bothers me, Mac. Kohler had to have earned his DCA certificates *after* he went to work for Ramey. So why would Ramey hire Kohler and put him in a managerial position right off the bat when he had no prior training or experience in the jewelry business? At least none that I've been able to dig up. For a smart businessman like Ramey, that doesn't make much sense."

"Good question. Maybe Eric had a business degree or something related. I'll mention it to Kate. She might know something."

"Okay, but go easy, Mac. Katie was friends with Kohler. I don't want to see her hurt."

"Will do."

"Anything on your end?" Frank asked.

"I've got a cop friend checking FBI databases to see if there's anything on Wes Harrison. Kate doesn't know about it yet."

"The Owens kid who saved your hide last summer?"

"Yeah."

"Good move. You can't have too many reliable contacts in this game, especially a cop. Anything else?"

I gave Frank a quick rundown on what I'd found in the newspaper archives.

"How old did you say Ramey was when the accident happened?" Frank asked.

"Thirty-nine, according to the articles and obit."

"Okay, keep digging. Things tend to snowball once they get rolling. Find out if Ramey's mother is still alive. If she is, you're headed for Atlanta."

I was about to ask Frank what the hell good it would do to interview an eighty-something-year-old woman who might be half-senile when a blue light cut the darkness. I glanced in the rearview mirror as a city cruiser pulled up behind me. "Gotta go, Frank, the cops just showed up."

~⌐)

"You're not going to like this," I said when Kate answered the door. I handed her the printouts J.D. had given me a few minutes earlier. It had taken the young sergeant a week's worth of spare time searching the FBI's crime info site, but he'd struck real pay dirt.

"Kate, meet Weston Russell Harrison."

Kate stood in the doorway, staring at the photo of a teenage Wes Harrison and scanning the criminal report J.D. included with it. Her mouth dropped open. "What in the world!"

I stepped inside, pulling Kate with me, and closed the door. "Yeah, seems ol' Wes wasn't the all-American golden boy he led you to believe."

Kate finally looked up. "Gang activity?"

Long story short: Weston Russell Harrison grew up in a well-to-do family living in La Jolla Shores, a popular beach and vacation community of greater San Diego. His father owned half interest in a real estate company while his mother taught economics at nearby University of California-San Diego.

For whatever harebrained reason, while a sophomore in high school Wes and a bunch of his friends formed a gang composed of mostly upper-middle-class whites. Calling themselves the Red Vikes after their school mascot, the Vikings, their specialty soon became auto theft, made all the more convenient by transporting and selling their goods south of the border. Returning with cash and drugs, they marketed their ill-gotten gains primarily to classmates and other friends.

There were a few run-ins with the law, but high-profile lawyers plus the perps' tender age got most of the charges dropped or reduced to misdemeanors and probation. Then the Vikes decided to branch out into prostitution. They brought attractive señoritas across the border and began pimping them to their friends and others in the community. They paid the Mexican girls a pittance of the fee, but it was a hell of a lot more money than they could make on *their* side of the border. The Vikes even recruited a few willing local girls from their school, giving them half of the take for their trouble.

Then came the bust. Wes and about a dozen of his cohorts wound up in the San Diego County Jail. Expelled from school, the Harrison family's slick lawyers worked their magic to get the charges reduced to misdemeanors and time served, along with a few years of probation.

The now-repentant Weston Harrison went to work for his uncle, who owned a jewelry store in the exclusive business district of La Jolla Shores. Keeping his nose clean, young Wes dutifully earned his GED and learned the ins and outs of the jewelry trade from the extensive on-the-job training his uncle provided. After a couple of years, and with money being no object for the Harrisons, Wes enrolled at the nearby Carlsbad campus of the Gemological Institute of America, where he earned a Graduate Gemologist diploma. Sheepskin in hand and his probation obligations fulfilled, Wes Harrison packed up and headed east.

"That's not the Wes Harrison I knew," Kate said, looking stunned and shaking her head as she finished reading the report.

"The man at O'Malley's wasn't the Wes you knew either," I said, following her into the kitchen. She set the printouts on the table, grabbed a spoon on the stovetop, and stirred the pan of shrimp scampi as I opened the fridge for beer. My stomach growled when I smelled sautéing shrimp. I'd been trying to lose a little weight and had skipped lunch.

"Dang, the sauce is drying out," Kate said, rapping the spoon against the rim of the pan. "Hand me the butter, would you?"

I found the butter dish, grabbed a couple of beers, and elbowed the door shut. Kate looked a little pale but composed. She added a generous dash of olive oil to the scampi and reached for the butter. "Maybe I'm wrong, Mac," she said, her back to me as she cut a chunk of butter and dropped it into the pan. "Maybe it wasn't Wes I saw that night. My mind could've been playing tricks on me, like you said."

I twisted the tops off the beers and set one on the counter next to the stove. "You really believe that?"

Kate added a splash of white wine, stirred the pan a final time, and turned the gas burner off. She turned, picked up the beer, and took a sip. Her eyes locked with mine. "No."

Wes Harrison had been up to no good as a kid, and it was a sound bet he'd been up to no good when Kate knew him. The question was, up to what? But there was something else bugging me. "You've got Wednesday off, right?"

Kate nodded as she swallowed. "Yes, why?"

"We're going to Pensacola."

CHAPTER 7

We crossed the Pensacola Bay Bridge around noon that Wednesday and followed Bayfront Parkway to East Main in downtown Pensacola. I hung a right on South Jefferson and drove north a few blocks to the headquarters of Sacred Word Missions located in an old two-story brick building. From my Internet research the day before, I'd learned that Sacred Word Missions, Rachel Todd's employer during the time Kate knew her, had occupied this same location since before World War II. The nondenominational organization sponsored dozens of missionaries in South America, most located in Venezuela. I parked the Silverado in the mission's small lot, and Kate and I headed for the entrance.

Inside the reception room a slender woman with silver-streaked hair and glasses perched on the end of her nose smiled from behind a desk. "Welcome to Sacred Word," she said. She stood and straightened her modest dress. Removing the glasses, she let them dangle from a strap around her neck. "I'm Mildred Comer. How may I help you two this morning?" She glanced at her wristwatch. "Oh my, this afternoon, I should say."

I introduced Kate and myself. "I believe I spoke with you yesterday. We have a one-thirty appointment with Dr. Garrett."

Mildred's eyes lit up. "Why yes, from St. George, wasn't it?"

"Yes, ma'am."

Mildred picked up the phone and punched a button. "A Mr. McClellan and Miss Bell are here to see you." She paused a moment. "Yes, sir, I'll send them right on back.

"Dr. Garrett will see you now," Mildred said and gave us directions.

Our footsteps echoed on the worn hardwood floor as Kate and I followed a hallway to its end and then turned left down another to the fourth door on the right. *Lawrence C. Garrett, Th.D.* was painted in block letters on the door's opaque glass window.

I glanced at Kate. "Ready?"

She nodded. I took a deep breath and knocked on the door.

"Come in, come in," a deep, friendly voice called.

Opening the door, I stood aside for Kate and followed her in. A tall, large-framed man in his midsixties with a ruddy complexion strolled around a cluttered wooden desk and offered his hand. "Larry Garrett," he said as we shook, "so nice to meet you."

Kate and I introduced ourselves and sat in the two padded leather chairs Garrett offered. "Now, how may I be of service?" he said, moving back to his own chair behind the stout desk. His thick hair and matching eyebrows were cottony-white.

I pulled one of Frank Hightower's business cards from my shirt pocket and handed it to Garrett. "I represent Hightower Investigations," I said, figuring that as long as I didn't try to pass myself off as a licensed PI, I wasn't breaking any rules or laws. "We're trying to locate someone who worked for Sacred Word Missions as a pilot in the late nineties."

Kate handed me the best photo she'd been able to find of Rachel, the same waist-up shot of Kate, Wes, Eric, and Rachel standing on the beach together in swimwear. Rachel was about three inches shorter than Kate, around five-five or so, a very pretty brunette with dark eyes and a petite build. In the photo she was wearing a modest white one-piece suit. Kate's skimpy black bikini top didn't make it any more comfortable to show the photo to a man of the cloth, but like I said, it was the best shot she had.

"It's my understanding that she used to pilot an airplane for your ministry somewhere in South America." I handed the photo to Garrett. "Her name is Rachel Todd."

I swore his jaw twitched when I mentioned the name. His wrinkled brow furrowed deeper as he picked up a pair of glasses from the desk. "Rachel Todd, did you say? Hmm." He put the glasses on and studied the photo.

"Yes, sir. That's Rachel on the right, next to her brother, Eric Kohler," I said when he seemed hesitant. Maybe he didn't recognize Kate from the photo, although that seemed unlikely.

Garrett's lips tightened. He stared at me over the rims of his glasses. "Brother?"

"Actually, her half-brother," Kate offered. "Eric was friends with my boyfriend. They both died in a boating accident several years ago."

Garrett studied the photo for another moment. He removed the glasses and set them and the photo on the desktop. "My condolences, Miss Bell. When was this photograph taken?"

"In the late nineties," Kate said, "a few weeks before the accident."

"I see. And may I ask why you're trying to locate Miss Todd now, after all these years?"

I took another deep breath and let it out. "Three men supposedly lost their lives in that accident. Their boat capsized during a storm, and all three were declared lost at sea. But now we have reason to believe that at least one of them might have survived."

"I see," Garrett repeated. He glanced down at the photo and tapped a finger beside it a few times before looking up. "Yes, I do remember the young lady. But I don't recall her ever mentioning anything about a brother or half-brother. She was raised in an orphanage in Texas from infancy until she was thirteen or fourteen, at which time she was adopted by the Todds, an upstanding older Christian couple who provided her with the loving home she deserved."

Kate made a kind of choking noise. When I looked she'd turned nearly as pale as she had the night she saw Wes Harrison at O'Malley's. The Destin gang's story seemed to be coming apart at the seams. I reached over and placed a hand over hers.

"Miss Todd did work for us around that time," Garrett continued. "She flew shipments of translated Bibles and study guides and other supplies to our missionaries in the field. She was a lovely young woman and a commendable worker, but . . ."

I didn't like where this conversation seemed to be headed, and I highly doubted it was anything Kate or I wanted to hear. "But what?"

Garrett raised a hand to his brow and massaged his forehead. "I hate to be the bearer of bad news, but Miss Todd's plane apparently crashed somewhere in the jungle around that time."

Kate and I sat dumfounded while Garrett explained the bombshell he'd just dropped in our laps.

"Miss Todd was delivering a load of New Testaments and food staples to our missionaries working with the Warao Indians in Venezuela when her plane disappeared," he said. "She'd been following the Orinoco River west when for some inexplicable reason the plane veered off course heading south. It was last spotted over Canaima National Park in southeastern Venezuela, which borders Guyana and Brazil. Despite an intensive aerial search the wreckage was never located."

Garrett hesitated for a moment, looking pained. "After a few weeks, and only after we'd exhausted every means of locating her, we had to presume Miss Todd was deceased. She most likely perished somewhere in the jungles of Brazil's Amazon rainforest, either from the crash or . . . well, I don't like to dwell on such things.

"No one knows why the accident happened," he continued. "Her airplane was inspected and serviced on a rigid schedule. The missionaries had radio contact with her that morning early in the flight, and then nothing. There was no distress call or any further contact from Miss Todd. She simply vanished."

"When did this happen?" I said when my mind finally stopped spinning.

"Hmm, Miss Todd's file should still be in our inactive records. Excuse me a moment, please." Garrett picked up the phone and called Mildred. A couple of minutes later she brought a folder containing Rachel's employee info. She handed it to her boss and stood patiently beside his desk.

"That will be all, Mildred."

"Yes, sir," she said and left the room.

Garrett opened the folder and leafed through a few pages until he found what he was looking for. He ran a finger along the page and stopped about halfway down. He turned the folder to where we could read the date.

Kate and I locked eyes. June 4—about two weeks after Wes and company supposedly met their fate in the Gulf of Mexico.

"Do you have an address or phone number for Rachel's parents?" I said.

"I'm sorry, but Miss Todd's parents both passed away shortly after she came to work for us," Garrett said.

"How about the name of the orphanage where she grew up?" What the hell, it was worth a shot.

He shook his head. "I'm sorry. It's against Sacred Word's policy to release such information without a proper warrant from the authorities."

I was really fishing without bait now. "Could I have a quick look at the file?"

Garrett frowned and stared at me like I'd completely flipped my lid. "I'm afraid that's not possible."

~~~

"No wonder you never heard from Rachel after the boating accident," I said to Kate as I unlocked the Silverado. "Why didn't you try to get in touch with her here?"

Kate was still a little pale and looked stunned from what we'd learned, not only about Rachel's likely demise, I figured, but also the fact that she and Eric might not have been siblings at all. "Dang, Mac, I was a zombie for weeks after Wes's and Eric's deaths," she said. "And when I did think about Rachel I couldn't remember the name of the place where she worked. After a while, when I hadn't heard from her in so long, I guess I assumed she'd moved back to Texas. We were never very close anyway."

Kate barely said another word until we were crossing Pensacola Bay on our way back to St. George. She'd been staring aimlessly out the window at the dark, choppy water as if she'd find the answer to whatever questions were running through her mind there. Finally she turned to me. "Eric or Rachel never mentioned a thing about any orphanage. Eric said his father abandoned him and his mother when he was a baby, and his mother married a man named Todd when Eric was around three. A few months later they had Rachel." She paused for a moment. "What on earth do you think it all means, Mac?"

"I should be asking you that question."

Kate bit her lower lip, turned her head, and stared out at the bay again. "First Wes and Eric and Robert Ramey are lost at sea, and then Rachel's plane disappears in the jungle just two weeks later. It all seems a little strange, don't you think?"

I kept myself from laughing out loud. A little strange? More like a bad script from a B-grade flick. "You don't remember seeing anything about Rachel's disappearance in the newspaper or maybe on TV?"

She faced me again. "No, of course not. I wouldn't have forgotten something like that. My parents or brothers, either. We just thought she'd taken Eric's death hard and had moved back home to be with friends."

"What was the name of that town they were from again?"

"Waxahachie. It's somewhere near Dallas, I think."

I grabbed my notepad from the console and handed it and the pen to Kate. "Write down the name. Also, make a note to check the Pensacola and Destin papers for any articles they might've published about Rachel."

Kate arched her eyebrows, and I realized I was sounding bossy, something she didn't take kindly to, so I quickly added, "Please."

About halfway to Destin I called Frank Hightower at his office but got his answering machine. I tried his cell phone. He was in DeFuniak Springs gathering evidence for a cheating spouse case. I gave him a quick rundown on what Kate and I had learned at Sacred Word Missions.

"The snowball's getting bigger, Mac. Sounds to me like you need to make a trip to Texas."

"I was afraid you'd say that." I also knew Frank was right. I had to do whatever I could to find out the truth about Dr. Garrett's comment that Rachel Todd had no brother or half-brother. That statement had blown the lid off both Eric's and Rachel's credibility. Good or bad, for Kate's sake I needed to find out.

"It's a hot lead, Mac. Do your research and see if there's any orphanages in that area. If so, get out there pronto and find out if their records mesh with what Garrett has on Rachel. And while you're there, ask around town and see if you can turn up anybody else who might've known or who might remember Eric or Rachel or the Todds."

"Roger that."

"Did you find out if Ramey's mother is still living?" Frank asked.

"Not yet. Believe it or not, I've been a little busy lately."

"Well, you've got your work cut out for you. How are the lessons coming along?"

Christ, Frank must've been hyper as a kid. "At this rate I'll probably be done in a year or two."

"Get on it, Mac. You know what they say, 'Time's a-wasting.'"

CHAPTER 8

I spent most of Thursday on the Internet preparing for my trip to the Lone Star State. First, I checked the archives of every newspaper across the Florida Panhandle I could access for articles about Rachel Todd's disappearance, but I struck out. Maybe the lack of coverage was because Sacred Word Missions hadn't wanted the bad publicity that would result from one of their workers meeting with a tragic end. Or, maybe the incident was so far removed from daily life along Florida's Panhandle coast that it wasn't deemed newsworthy. After all, Rachel was a Texas native with no local next of kin to mourn her loss. It was also possible I'd just flat-out missed something during my search. I made a note to check with the Waxahachie newspaper while I was there.

I did learn there was an orphanage in Waxahachie: the Good Shepherd Christian Children's Home, which housed and cared for some sixty boys and girls ranging in age from infants to seventeen-year-olds. I jotted down the address and phone number. I found no information on the Todds, but I planned to check with the newspaper obits or pay a visit to the Ellis County Courthouse to see what I could turn up.

Kate was scheduled to work at Gillman's Marina for the weekend, so I was on my own. I called the airport in Tallahassee and booked a flight with Delta leaving Friday morning at seven. I was up well before daylight to catch the flight. After an hour-and-a-half layover in Atlanta, I arrived at Dallas/Fort Worth shortly before eleven. Grabbing my briefcase from the overhead that contained my laptop, photos, and notes, I hustled to the baggage claim to retrieve my suitcase. Twenty minutes later, I was buckled in my Ford rental and heading south on Highway 360 for Waxahachie, a forty-something-mile drive.

Several miles later I picked up Highway 287, followed it to its juncture with Highway 77 on the north side of Waxahachie, and pulled into the La Quinta Inn on nearby Stadium Drive. While checking in I grabbed a free map of the city and surrounding area from a display rack by the counter, compliments of the Ellis County Chamber of Commerce.

By two-thirty I was settled into my second-floor room with a view of the swimming pool below. I kicked back to relax a few minutes on the comfortable king-size bed. This was going to be a quick trip. I'd booked a Sunday return flight; that gave me the rest of the day and tomorrow to work through the schedule I'd laid out. There was no time to waste.

I opened the briefcase and scanned my to-do list. Good Shepherd was at the top. I wasn't even sure I had the right orphanage, but it was located in Waxahachie, the town Eric Kohler claimed to be from. And with him and Rachel passing themselves off as brother and sister, it was the best shot I had to go on. But what if Eric had lied to Kate about his hometown, or Rachel had fed Sacred Word Missions a line of bull about being raised in an orphanage? This little trip to Texas could prove to be a total wild goose chase.

I stripped down to my skivvies and made a quick trip to the bathroom to wash up and trim and shave around my beard. Kate had talked me into keeping it, even though more gray bristles seemed to be invading the reddish-blond every week. After brushing my teeth I put on clean Dockers, a blue button-up shirt, leather deck shoes, and a sports coat. Not bad, I decided, giving myself a quick once-over in the mirror. To hell with a tie.

I decided a cold call to Good Shepherd Christian Children's Home would be better than wading through a maze of telephone transfers to find the person I needed to talk to. I scanned the map as I walked to my car. The orphanage was located on the west side of town. I cranked the Ford and drove south into downtown Waxahachie. Approaching Main Street I caught sight of the Ellis County Courthouse, a huge, gothic-style structure that would look more at home in medieval Europe than modern Texas.

I took West Main to Brooksfarm Road and hung a left. Crossing under Interstate 35, I eased into the right turnoff lane and drove through a wrought iron gateway onto Good Shepherd's grounds. The winding road led to a cluster of wooden buildings, all painted the same white with forest-green trim and metal roofing. Acres of greening lawn were trimmed and weed-free. Sidewalks were neatly edged, and there wasn't a trace of litter or debris from trees or bushes to be found anywhere. The property was as well-maintained as any military base I'd seen during my twenty-four years in the Marine Corps.

A hundred yards beyond the buildings stood an athletic complex; a couple of the fields had chain link fencing and tall light poles. I parked near what appeared to be the main office building. Climbing out of the car, I heard kids' voices shouting from the direction of the athletic fields. The research I'd done on Good Shepherd emphasized how the home was dedicated to the total well-being of the children entrusted to their care, in body, mind, and spirit. My first impression was these people had their act together and practiced what they preached.

I guessed right about which building was the office. With its multi-hipped roof and wraparound porch, it looked more like a large family home from the early twentieth century than an orphanage business center. Most of the other structures on the property were elongated, reminding me of military barracks but with a more homey flair. Above the office's wide covered porch was a sign in large block lettering: *Good Shepherd Children's Christian Home, established 1934.* Below, in smaller letters, *Administrative Offices.*

I glanced at my watch. Quarter to four, no time to lose. I hustled up the stairs and across the porch to find the front door standing open behind a screen door. I figured that meant to come on in, so I did. Inside and immediately to my right was a long counter that once had probably been the bottom section of a wall. Behind the counter were a few desks, one currently occupied, and a long row of filing cabinets stacked along the back wall. An attractive young woman wearing a green skirt, white blouse, and braided blonde hair piled atop her head looked up from a desk and smiled as I approached the counter.

"May I help you, sir?" she said in a Texas drawl, standing and walking my way.

Early thirties, I guessed, with a trim and well-toned body. With her hair down she'd be a real looker. "Yes, ma'am," I said, remembering my Southern upbringing. I slipped one of Frank's business cards from my pocket, handed it to her, and gave the spiel about representing Hightower Investigations. "We're trying to find information on a missing person who might've been a resident here several years back."

When she glanced at the card, I noticed the engagement and wedding ring combo. Some lucky guy had done well for himself. "You're Mr. Hightower?"

"No, ma'am, his associate, Mac McClellan. I flew in this morning from Florida."

She handed the card back and smiled again. "Welcome to Good Shepherd, Mr. McClellan. She extended her hand. "Pardon me. I'm Melissa Banks. Who is it you wish to see?"

I shook her hand. "I'm not sure. Whoever might be familiar with the kids who were living here during the seventies and eighties."

Melissa gazed toward the ceiling and tapped her chin with an index finger. "Let's see, I believe Mrs. Brady would have been here then, and Reverend Sparks for sure," she said, thinking out loud more than talking to me. Her eyes met mine. "I believe Reverend Sparks is still in his office. Let me see if he's busy right now."

A few minutes later I was seated in the director of personnel's office facing Reverend Vernon Sparks, a stooped elderly man with thick eyeglasses whose remaining trace of hair was white as fresh snow. After the usual formalities I didn't waste any time getting down to business.

"Todd, you say?" He leaned back in his chair, his age-spotted hands pressed together like a church steeple.

"Yes, sir, Rachel Todd. I was told she arrived here as an infant and was adopted when she was around fourteen by a family named Todd."

He nodded as he slowly rocked back and forth in the chair. "Hmm, Rachel, you say? And what year would that have been, young man?"

I remembered Kate mentioning that Rachel was three or four years younger than Eric. That would make her and Rachel around the same age. "Miss Todd would be in her midthirties today, so I'd guess she would've arrived here sometime around the midseventies."

The old man stood up with the aid of a cane and hobbled from behind his desk to the open office door. He stuck his head into the hallway. "Missy, would you look in the Baby Doe files and bring me anything you can find on an infant arrival named Rachel. Also check the adoptive parents' file under last name Todd. Start with 1974 for Baby Doe, and, oh, '87 or '88 for the parents."

"Yes, sir," Melissa called from the front office, just a few doors away.

"We give our children biblical names if they arrive as Baby Doe," Reverend Sparks explained as he started back toward the desk.

"I have a photo of Rachel when she was in her twenties, if that would help," I said when Sparks was settled in his chair again. I fished through the briefcase for the photographs I'd brought and found the one of Kate, Wes, Eric, and Rachel at the beach. I handed it to Sparks. "That's her on the right. The guy next to her is Eric Kohler. He and Rachel might've been related."

Reverend Sparks sat up and adjusted his glasses. He leaned closer and squinted at the photo. His hands began to shake a little. I chalked it up to his age until the photo slipped from his fingers and fell to the floor. I hurried around the desk to retrieve the photo as the old man pulled a handkerchief from his coat pocket and mopped his brow.

He pointed to the photo I put back on the desk. "Did you say this young man's name is Eric Kohler?"

"Yes, sir. He—"

Just then Melissa Banks knocked on the door frame, hugging a couple of file folders to her breast. "Pardon me. The records you asked for, sir?"

"Yes, bring them in," Sparks said, looking a bit shaken.

She set the folders on his desk. "Baby Doe Rachel was right where you said she . . . are you all right, Reverend Sparks?"

He nodded. "I'm fine. Thank you, Missy."

She gave the old man a concerned look as she headed out the door. "Call if you need anything else, sir."

Reverend Sparks waited until the clacking of Melissa's footsteps faded and then picked up the photo and stared at it again. He laid it aside and turned his attention to the thicker of the two folders. He took his time, slowly examining page after page. "Yes, of course," he said, as if a lightbulb had suddenly switched on in his mind. "Such a lovely young child and a wonderful student, too." A faint smile crept across his face for a moment and then disappeared until his lips were drawn into a tight slit. "Until . . ."

I waited as he studied the photo another minute, which seemed to drag on for an hour. Finally he turned the photo toward me, his finger pointing to Eric. "The young man here, this is *not* Eric Kohler!" He frowned and tapped his finger so hard against the photo I thought he might punch a hole through it. "Eric was killed in the invasion of Iraq in 1991, Lord rest his soul," he said, voice quivering. "He's buried in Arlington National Cemetery." His jaw tightened and his nostrils flared. He rapped the photo again. "*This* young man is Travis Hurt!"

On my way back to the La Quinta I stopped at a McDonald's and ordered a Big Mac and fries to go. At a nearby convenience store I bought a six-pack of Budweiser. After my meeting with Reverend Sparks I didn't have much of an appetite, but I could damn sure use the beer. Maybe I could choke something down later.

Right now I had plenty enough to chew on, but it was all food for thought.

CHAPTER 9

It took three beers before I worked up the nerve to call Frank. I propped myself against the headboard with pillows and hoped he wouldn't answer. He did.

"Mac, any news?"

"Yeah, you got an hour or so?"

"It's your dime. I'm parked outside a motel in Niceville keeping tabs on some Air Force major's wife. She and lover-boy have been in there over an hour. My camera's ready, so I'm all ears until they show."

I twisted the cap off the fourth beer. "How's this for starters: Kate never met Eric Kohler. Kohler's been dead since 1991, and the guy Kate knew as Eric was really named Travis Hurt."

There was silence for a moment, then, "Damn. What else?"

"Rachel Todd and Kohler—I mean Hurt—weren't related. Rachel, the real Eric Kohler, and Travis Hurt were all wards of the Good Shepherd Orphanage here at the same time. There's a lot more, but I don't want to bore you with details."

"Bore me, Mac."

I took a big swig of Bud and grabbed my notebook. "Okay, I'm still trying to sort all this crap out myself, so I'm summarizing here. Travis Hurt's mother was a druggie from Dallas who whored around to support her habit and her son, in that order, I'd guess. When the kid was three or four she OD'd. No known surviving family, so he wound up in the orphanage here in Waxahachie. That was in the midseventies, around the same time our Rachel arrived at Good Shepherd as an unknown infant, what they call a 'Baby Doe.'"

"I know the term, Mac. Go on."

"Eric Kohler was another infant arrival, only he came with a name

61

and birth certificate. His teenage mother died giving birth; his father was only sixteen at the time and in no position to take care of a kid. The kids weren't married, and evidently none of the grandparents or other relatives wanted the responsibility of raising a baby, so Eric was brought to Good Shepherd. That was a couple of years before Kohler arrived. You with me here, Frank?"

"Yeah. Real nice of the mother's parents, huh? This world is full of assholes."

"I won't argue that, but maybe Eric was better off at the orphanage. Anyway, it turns out that all three of our kids bounced in and out of foster homes during their time at Good Shepherd. Reverend Sparks, the head honcho at the orphanage I talked to, said Eric and Rachel were model kids and he was surprised neither of them found a permanent home, not until the Todds adopted Rachel when she was almost fourteen.

"On the other hand, our boy Travis, the guy we thought was Eric Kohler, was nothing but trouble from the get-go. 'A real hellion' is how the good reverend described him. From what Sparks told me, Travis set the home-run record for the most foster homes visited by any kid since the orphanage opened in 1934. I think his longest stay in any one home was six weeks; that's saying something when you consider a few foster parents are mostly in it for the money."

"Damn. And Katie was friends with this fellow. It just goes to show you can never tell about some people."

"It gets worse, Frank."

"I can hardly wait."

"Okay, you asked for it. For whatever reason, when Rachel was around twelve she took a liking to Travis Hurt. From what Sparks said, he was the Big Man on Campus and the big bully. Also, maybe him being four years older had something to do with it, the 'older man' thing. Sparks did mention Rachel was an early bloomer. Anyway, by that time Travis had already earned a reputation for fooling around with any kid who showed him interest, male or female. He—"

"Wait, wait . . . did you say male or female?"

"Yep. Travis was a switch-hitter."

"Okay, Mac, I get the picture."

"Good. Then one night Rachel's housemother was doing a bed check and noticed Rachel's bed was empty, the old 'pull the covers over the pillow' trick. She started a search and finally found Rachel and Travis together in a dugout at one of the ball fields. They were, as Reverend Sparks so delicately put it, 'getting to know one another in the biblical sense.'"

"Let me get this straight, Mac. Travis Hurt was having sex with a twelve-year-old girl?"

"Roger that."

"That's statutory rape in a lot of states."

"Yeah, I'm no expert in Texas law, but the way Reverend Sparks explained it, Travis was several months past the age where he could've had a viable defense against the charge. Something to do with being more than three years older than the other juvenile involved, I think."

"So what happened?"

I drained my beer and opened another. "Long story short: The charge was reduced to a misdemeanor, and Travis wound up in juvenile detention for six months. But almost as soon as he returned to Good Shepherd, him and Rachel hooked up again. Travis went back to the juvie slammer, and a few months later Rachel was adopted by the Todds."

"What's the real Eric Kohler's story?"

"Eric and Travis knew each other at the orphanage but didn't get along very well. Travis was the typical older bully, and Eric was the model orphan. He joined the Army in 1990 shortly after he left Good Shepherd when he turned eighteen. A little over a year later he was killed during the invasion of Iraq."

"Sounds like this Hurt guy stole Kohler's identity. Easy enough to do, especially before 9/11. It's called ghosting, for your information."

"Yeah, I read about it in one of the books you gave me, believe it or not. It makes sense, especially since Hurt didn't have the greatest reputation when he got out of Dodge. Reverend Sparks said Hurt and

Kohler were around the same height and had the same coloration. I guess it—"

"Whoa, gotta run, Mac. The lovebirds just exited the room."

"I'll check in tomorrow," I said, but Frank's phone was already dead.

⁓

I was up bright and early Saturday morning. Got dressed, grabbed my briefcase, and drove to McDonald's for breakfast. While I was eating I opened my laptop and tried to access the Ellis County court records but struck out. Then I tried the online archives of the *Waxahachie Daily Light* and came up empty there, too. Great, this being Saturday the courthouse was closed. Maybe I should've rearranged my priorities list, but it was too late now. My best bet was a visit to the newspaper's office and finding a cooperative employee who'd be willing to help me find what I was looking for.

I finished my sausage biscuits and coffee, and headed toward downtown. One good thing about Waxahachie is that the town is easy to get around. The drive to the *Daily Light* on West Marvin took only a few minutes, almost a straight shot down Ferris Avenue that leads into the heart of town.

Inside the lobby I told the receptionist what I needed. She got on the phone, and in a couple of minutes a husky young man in his late twenties or early thirties walked into the room and greeted me with a big smile and a friendly handshake. Bill Danner was built like a linebacker, and during our chitchat heading to the room where the microfilm and other archives were stored I learned he had indeed played football at North Texas as a walk-on. A journalism major, Danner had come to work for the *Daily Light* shortly after graduating from UNT.

We entered a huge room with shelves jam-packed with thousands of yellowing newspapers from floor to ceiling along two walls. Another section of the room contained desks with computers, printers, and other electronics and equipment. I followed Danner to one of the desks and took a chair beside him. "Where do you want to start?" he said.

"I'm looking for information on a Theodore and Mary Todd of Waxahachie, both deceased. They probably died sometime in the mid-nineties. How about 1994?"

Danner turned to a desktop computer and keyed in the Todds' names. I couldn't see the screen clearly from where I sat, but a minute later he stood and motioned for me to follow him.

He stopped before another tall storage shelf, searched through several reels of film, selected a few, and then sat down at the desk. "We're hoping to go to full digital with our archives someday, but right now my best guess is we'll find what you're looking for on microfilm," he said, loading a reel into what looked like a glorified computer monitor with push buttons, dials, and other gizmos located below the screen and on a remote keyboard.

Danner grinned. "This ain't your granny's old microfiche reader that you probably used in libraries back in your day."

My day? Who the hell was I, Father Time?

"It's a Canon 800 Microfilm Scanner. This baby can handle almost any format you throw at her. Only problem is, she'll be a dinosaur herself in a couple of years."

Less than an hour later I thanked Bill Danner for his help and walked out of the *Daily Light* with several eight-and-a-half-by-eleven-inch printouts of news articles and obits added to my briefcase. Back inside the rental car I scanned the map and found Virginia Avenue, the street where the Todds had lived. It was only a few blocks away, up West Marvin.

I hung a right out of the parking lot, wracking my brain trying to remember what I'd read about conducting a neighborhood investigation from one of the books Frank had given me. I planned to knock on a few doors and find a neighbor or two who might've known the Todds, someone who might be able to provide more info on Rachel and her relationship with her parents.

Among the articles Bill Danner found was a front-page piece

reporting how Theodore and Mary Todd, ages seventy-one and sixty-nine, respectfully, met their tragic end perishing in a house fire during the early morning hours of December 26, 1997. Source of the fire was determined to be a defective or dirty chimney. A fire erupted in the flue, turning it into a giant Roman candle and setting the roof and attic on fire. A strong back draft sent sparks and embers flying out of the fire-place onto the den carpet, resulting in a toxic smoldering fire. By the time firefighters pulled the couple from the burning house, both were beyond help. Cause of death was asphyxiation due to carbon monoxide and smoke inhalation.

Daughter Rachel had been visiting her adoptive parents for the Christmas holidays. Fortunately for her, she'd caught a flight Christmas evening back to Pensacola, Florida, where she worked as a missionary pilot with Sacred Word Missions.

A red flag was waving inside my head. Rachel had missed dying with her parents in a house fire by a few hours. Rachel had disappeared from Kate's life shortly after her "brother" Eric, Wes Harrison, and Robert Ramey supposedly perished in the Gulf of Mexico, not even sticking around for the memorial service. And just two weeks later, Rachel's airplane had mysteriously wandered off course and was lost somewhere in the jungles of South America. Something smelled rotten, and it sure as hell wasn't in Denmark.

⌒

I eased along Virginia Avenue through an older but very nice middle-class neighborhood, checking addresses on mailboxes. Most of the houses sat on quarter-acre lots with plenty of shade trees and well-maintained lawns. I found the number I was looking for and pulled to the side of the road opposite the house. It was a split-level home, with tan brick and sage vinyl siding, and looked a little out of place cloistered between the decades-older wooden houses flanking it on either side. A red and white tricycle lay tipped over on the sidewalk leading from the driveway to the front steps, and a basketball hoop stood at the end of the drive. The trees were leafed out in new spring foliage, and the green yard appeared to have been recently fertilized. It was hard to imagine this being the scene of a tragic fire in the not-too-distant past.

Eeny, meeny, miny, moe. The house facing me on the left won. I opened the briefcase and slipped the manila envelope containing a few photos into my inside coat pocket. I crossed the street and followed the walkway up the steps and onto the wide covered porch. The rails were boxed in with ornate lattice. At the far right a wooden swing was anchored from the ceiling by heavy eye-hooks and chalky-white chains. A patio table and padded chairs stood at the left side of the porch, and colorful potted plants lined both sides of the front railing. With just a little imagination it could've been my grandparents' home up in North Carolina.

Using the toe of my shoe I nudged aside a battered toy dump truck and plastic fire engine parked haphazardly in front of the door. I rang the bell, and a few seconds later the front door swung open. A barefoot young woman wearing denim shorts and a loose T-shirt stood facing me behind the screen door. She shifted a curly-haired kid around a year old from one hip to the other and swept her long brown hair out of her face.

She managed a quick smile. "Hey there, can I help you?"

"Yes, ma'am." I held one of Frank's cards close to the screen where she could see it. "I'm Mac McClellan, representing Hightower Investigations. I'm trying to find out information on the people who used to live next door," I said with a quick tilt of my head to the right. "Unfortunately there was a fire and—"

"You must mean the Todds," she said, just as a youngster carrying something black and white by the neck flashed through the room behind her and disappeared down a hallway.

The young mom turned and hollered, "Jordan, I told you that puppy ain't no toy! Put him down *now!*"

She turned back to me. "Sorry, mister, but I've got to go before he kills that pup." She pointed toward my rental. "You need to talk to Mr. Chatwood across the street yonder where that car's parked. Him and his wife was good friends with the Todds.

"*Jordan!*" She hustled after the kid and was out of sight before I had a chance to thank her.

<center>~~~</center>

After ringing Mr. Chatwood's doorbell a third time the only response I'd gotten was from a yapping Chihuahua that kept leaping halfway up the screen door snapping its teeth like it was determined to rip out my throat. Damn good thing Great Danes weren't born with that disposition.

I turned and started down the steps when a hulking man in his late seventies or early eighties decked out in dusty overalls and a sweat-stained straw hat came ambling around the side of the house. He looked past me at the irritated overgrown rat.

"Hush up, Sugarbunch, this good man don't mean Daddy no harm."

Sugarbunch ceased fire and pressed her gray muzzle against the screen. The low growl told me she didn't fully take Daddy at his word just yet.

"Chester Chatwood," the man said, extending a beefy hand as he grunted up the steps into the shade of the porch. "Call me Chet. And don't mind Sugarbunch. She never bit nobody in all her sixteen years. She's just gotten a little overprotective of me since my wife passed away last year."

"I'm sorry for your loss," I said, shaking Chet's hand. "Mac McClellan, nice to meet you sir."

"Same here, Mac. What can I do you for?" he said and chuckled at his little joke.

I pointed at the house across the street. "The young lady living there said you were friends with the Todds."

Chet took off the hat and fanned himself. "Sylvie's right. Me and my Angie were real close with Ted and Mary. Say, you care for a beer? It's hot as Satan's cellar working in that garden out back."

I declined the beer but accepted Chet's offer to sit in one of the twin high-back rockers near the door. I peeled off my sport coat and made myself comfortable. A couple of minutes later Chet returned with two bottles of Miller High Life. Sugarbunch took up her vigil behind the screen door just in case I tried anything unseemly.

The other rocker groaned as Chet took a seat. He held out one of the bottles. "Sure you won't join me?"

What the hell. I grabbed the bottle and twisted off the cap. "Thanks."

Chet rocked slowly in the chair and swigged down a healthy dose of Miller. "Say, Mac, what you wanting to know about Ted and Mary?"

I slipped Frank's card from my shirt pocket and flashed it to Chet. "I'm with Hightower Investigations, out of Destin, Florida. What can you tell me about the fire?"

The pleasantness faded from the old man's weathered face. "Is that what you here for? This some kind of insurance business?"

"No, sir, this has nothing to do with insurance, not directly anyway. I'm just trying to find out all I can about what happened. It might concern their daughter Rachel."

Chet's already-wrinkled brow furrowed deeper. "Rachel? Why, she was like a granddaughter to me and Angie. Such a sad, sad thing, her passing just a few months after the fire that took Ted and Mary. It broke our hearts."

"So you knew about her plane disappearing in South America?"

"Oh, yeah. Rachel used to write us when she found the time. That missionary work kept her real busy."

I took a sip of beer while I got my thoughts together. "I checked with the *Waxahachie Daily Light* this morning. They didn't have any articles on Rachel's disappearance in their files, not even an obituary."

Chet let out a deep sigh. "Reckon that's my fault, me and Angie's. You see, we were the only family Rachel had left. Ted and Mary adopted her. Sweet thing used to call us Granny and Gramps. After a few months went by and we hadn't heard from her, we called the mission in Florida she worked for. They told us about her plane going missing."

Chet covered his face with his hands for a moment before continuing. "Me and Angie wouldn't let ourselves believe Rachel was gone. We kept holding onto the hope that she would turn up at any time. We put her on our church's prayer list and trusted that the Lord would work a miracle." He paused and sighed again. "Reckon it just wasn't God's will, is all. Anyway, time just seemed to slip away. Never did get around to having a proper memorial service for her. But who knows, maybe that miracle will happen yet, Lord willing."

The last thing I wanted to do was open up old wounds for a man who'd just lost his wife, but I needed to find out what I could while I had the chance. I hoped Sugarbunch wasn't the only family Chet had left. If I blew his image of sweet Rachel, he might need more comforting than that overgrown rat could provide.

I took my coat from the armrest, slipped out the envelope, and found the beach photo. I handed it to Chet. "Is that Rachel on the right?"

Chet took the photo and squinted at it. He moved it farther away until it was at arm's length. A smile slowly spread across his face. "That's our Rachel all right. Only, her hair is different. She must've dyed it. Rachel was the prettiest little redheaded gal you ever saw."

Bells and whistles went off in my head. *Redhead?* The woman I'd bumped into at O'Malley's was a redhead. Unfortunately, I hadn't gotten a good look at her face. But the Rachel in the photo was on the petite side, nothing like the well-stacked lady at O'Malley's. Plastic surgery? If Wes Harrison had changed his looks, why not Rachel? Chet's voice snapped me back to the present.

"Say, Mac, this fellow next to her looks familiar somehow too, but I can't place him."

"Does the name Travis Hurt mean anything to you?"

"That's it!" Chet damn near shouted. The bottle of Miller slipped from his hand and clattered to the porch deck, rolling and spewing what little brew was left. Sugarbunch resumed her imitation of a yapping four-legged pogo stick.

"That boy gave Ted and Mary nothing but trouble all through Rachel's high school years," Chet said after he'd convinced Sugarbunch he wasn't in imminent mortal danger. "They did everything they could to keep him away. But he wouldn't quit pestering the poor girl; kept coming around all hours of the day and night till they finally got a restraining order on him. He wound up getting throwed in jail, but even that didn't stop him. Rachel wouldn't give him the time of day, but he kept snooping around like a buck in rut. Never seen such a hard-headed punk in all my born days."

I resisted the urge to say I doubted the time of day had anything to do with what Rachel was giving Travis. Instead, I spent the next ten minutes giving Chet the gist of the case, including how Rachel and Hurt claimed to be siblings while living in Florida, and how the whole fatal boating incident seemed to be springing more and more leaks. I even brought up the possibility that Rachel might somehow be involved in the scam, if that's what this mess turned out to be.

Chet's face turned red and his nostrils flared. "You got no right saying that," he said. "What makes you so all-fired sure her plane didn't crash in the jungle like that missionary fellow said? Rachel was a martyr for the Lord, and you're sitting here sullying her good name. Thank God Angie's not around to hear such trash."

PI rule number one: When you're trying to get information from a subject's neighbor, especially a close friend of the subject, don't piss him off.

"I apologize if that's how it came across, Chet. I'm not trying to trash anybody. I don't have any real proof that Rachel's involved, just a gut feeling. Remember, Rachel and Travis Hurt claimed to be brother and sister, and you know that's a line of bull. That photo was taken just a few months after the fire and just before the boating accident. And then two weeks later Rachel's plane disappears. That sounds more than a little fishy, don't you think?"

He shook his head. "That's not like our Rachel, not at all. I don't know how or why she met back up with that scumbag, but there's no way she would've done anybody wrong. She was a fine Christian girl, got her education at the Assembly of God College just a few blocks yonder," he said, lifting his hand with his thumb pointing behind him like a hitchhiker. "Him and Rachel must've just run across each other somehow, is all."

It was clear that Chet had Rachel perched on a pedestal, and she wasn't about to come down by anything I had to say. "What about the fire? Do you think Travis could've had anything to do with it, maybe as some kind of payback to the Todds?"

The old man rocked and shook his head again. "Best I remember he was in jail at the time. No, wait . . . seems like he'd got out and left the state before that happened. Who knows? It's hard to keep track of things after all these years. Besides, the fire chief ruled it was an accident. Nothing fishy about that."

"What about the funeral, did you get a chance to talk to Rachel then?"

"'Course we did. Rachel stayed right here with me and Angie when she flew back home for the funeral. I told you she was like our granddaughter. She stayed long enough to settle up with the insurance company and put the property up for sale with a real estate company. Then she went back to her mission work."

Before I could come up with another question, Chet shifted in his chair and looked me in the eye. He was close to tears. "Never crossed my mind that would be the last time we'd ever see her."

CHAPTER 10

The flight back to Tallahassee on Palm Sunday was uneventful except for a little teeth-rattling turbulence somewhere over Mississippi or Alabama that prompted us to buckle up and a few passengers to mouth silent prayers. The prayers worked. The wings stayed put, and we landed safely around five p.m.

When I got home that evening I grabbed a cold beer and started to punch in Kate's number. My finger stopped in midair. How the hell was I going to tell her that Eric Kohler was really Travis Hurt and that he and his "sister" Rachel had been lovers? I called Frank instead and filled him in on the rest I'd learned from Chet Chatwood.

The Todds were well-off financially, but not showy with their money. Ted and Mary chose to live in the same house and neighborhood that Ted had grown up in, although they could've done much better for themselves. Todd owned a Ford dealership in downtown Waxahachie that he sold around the time Rachel graduated from high school in the early nineties.

According to Chet, the Todds were generous almost to a fault. They supported many charities including, among others, the Good Shepherd Children's Christian Home and the Assemblies of God University where Rachel had graduated with a degree in World Ministries and Missions.

While in high school Rachel had developed an itch to learn to fly. The Todds agreed to pay for flight lessons as an incentive for Rachel to excel in her studies, *and*—Chet Chatwood let this little contradiction slip almost as an afterthought later in our conversation—that she have nothing more to do with a certain Mr. Travis Hurt.

"Here's the kicker, Frank. Chatwood remembers that Ted Todd

had a sizeable life insurance policy to ensure Mary and Rachel would be well taken care of in case he kicked the bucket. And, he was worth a few million from his auto business. Chatwood's not sure how much, but he says he recalls Todd saying he planned to leave half to Mary and Rachel, and half to charity."

"Not a bad incentive for Rachel and Travis Hurt to hook back up and lay some plans," Frank said.

"Damn straight. Something bugs me, though."

"What's that?"

"It's hard to believe that Rachel could be so coldhearted. From everything I heard, the Todds were nothing but loving and generous to her."

"Love is a powerful emotion, Mac. Stir in a few million bills and it can become downright overpowering."

"Good point. I'd bet my next retirement check that Rachel and Travis never stopped seeing each other, except for when he was in the slammer. And once Rachel got her driver's license it would be easy for them to get together instead of Travis sneaking into the neighborhood."

"Another thing," I said. "I doubt it's a coincidence that Rachel landed a job with Sacred Word Missions in Pensacola not long after Kohler aka Hurt moved to Destin. We're talking, what . . . less than fifty miles away?"

"Yeah, but we still don't have a motive other than the insurance and inheritance, which very well *could* be a coincidence. We need more, Mac."

"Okay, why were Rachel and Hurt passing themselves off as brother and sister?"

"No clue. It still rankles me that Katie was friends with those jerks."

"Join the club."

"Let's go another route, Mac. Let's assume the guy Katie saw that night at the theater was Wes Harrison. What does that prove?"

"That Wes Harrison is still alive."

"Right. But where is Travis Hurt? Where is Robert Ramey?"

I slugged down some beer. "You said 'assume.' So now you think Kate was imagining things?"

"I didn't say that. What I *am* saying is that so far we have no crime, no motive, no nothing except our speculation that Rachel Todd and Travis Hurt knocked off her adoptive parents for the insurance and inheritance money. We've got no proof, Mac. For all we know Harrison and the others might all have drowned in the gulf and Rachel could be a skeleton inside a plane wreck somewhere in the middle of the jungle."

I drained the beer and headed to the fridge for another. "What about the redhead I bumped into at O'Malley's? We know now that Rachel was a natural redhead. That could've been her with Harrison."

"Jesus, Mac, just how many redheads do you think there are in this country? Ten, a hundred, a hundred thousand?"

"Okay, I get your point. But it's not impossible. It could've been Rachel. With a boob job and some really high heels."

"Get some sleep. And be careful how you break the news about Hurt and Rachel to Katie. She's already on thin ice over this crap."

"I thought you might tell her, Uncle Frank, being the old friend of the family that you are."

Frank snorted. "It's your case, Mac. Good luck and good night."

Thirty minutes later I'd polished off a third beer and was pouring Dewar's over a tumbler of ice when my phone rang. I checked the caller's number. It was Kate.

"I missed you," she said. "When did you get back?"

"A few minutes ago. Missed you, too. Want some company?"

"Only if you don't mind driving to Destin tonight. What did you find out in Texas?"

"Not much," I said, hoping Kate wouldn't press the subject. "We'll go over it later. What're you doing in Destin? I thought you had to work tomorrow."

"I asked Linda for some time off. I found something that might be important, Mac."

"Yeah? Like what?"

Kate let out a deep sigh. "I decided to drive to my parents' house this morning and go through some of Wes's things."

I felt my hackles rise and took a hefty swallow of Scotch. The guy had supposedly been dead for a dozen years, yet somehow the mention of his name still goaded me. "Wes's things? What are you doing with Wes's things?"

Another sigh. "How do I put this? Okay. At the time of the accident I had a key to Wes's apartment. After the accident I kept a watch on the apartment for a couple of months until the lease ran out."

"You paid the rent?"

"Yes. Actually, my name was on the lease, too. "

I took another big swig of Scotch. "So, you two were living together?" There was a long pause. "Earth to Kate."

"No, not really. I'd stay over sometimes."

"Sometimes?"

"That's what I said."

"You never mentioned that little fact."

"Dang, Mac, don't be jealous, I didn't even know you existed then."

"I'm not jealous," I said, lying through my teeth as I poured a refill.

"Yes, you are. I was twenty-three, get over it. If you're looking for a virgin I suggest you start hanging around a middle school."

"Ha ha. So, what's this important thing you found?"

"When the lease ran out I boxed up a few of Wes's things and stored them in my bedroom closet. I never got around to looking through the boxes—his personal items, I mean. But seeing him at O'Malley's that night, I got to thinking there might be something he had that could help us with the case."

Visions of Kate sitting on the closet floor swooning over photos and other crap she and Wes had shared together grated through my mind. "Can we get to the point? I'm bushed from the trip."

"See! You *are* jealous."

"Christ on a crutch, I'm tired. What did you find that's so all-fired important?"

"Never mind."

Kate said it quietly, but I knew her well enough to know she was really pissed. "Look, I'm sorry," I offered in the most appeasing voice I could muster. "I've been on the go all weekend, and the flight back home was a little hairy. What did you find?"

"A Crown Royal bag."

"A Crown Royal bag?" Christ, what could be so damn important about a Crown Royal bag? "With an unopened bottle inside, I hope?"

"No, it was full of diamonds."

⁓

I brewed a thermos of coffee and was out the door and on my way to Destin by seven-thirty the next morning. I waited until eight and gave Frank a call. I scooped him on the bombshell Kate dropped in my lap last night. We made plans to meet at his office at eleven.

Kate greeted me with a less-than-enthusiastic hug and kiss when I arrived at her parents' house around ten. I followed her into her bedroom where several cardboard boxes of various sizes were spread around the floor and on her bed. There was also a metal filing cabinet standing just outside the closet.

"I found the diamonds in the bottom drawer of the filing cabinet," Kate said, handing me the small purple Crown Royal bag. "They were at the back of the drawer behind a stack of files."

The bag was damn near full of diamonds like Kate had said, and they dazzled the eye when I poured the contents onto the bedspread. I started counting, but Kate cut me short.

"Two hundred and seventy-eight," she said. "I counted them three times."

I didn't know much about diamonds or other gems, but the ring I'd given my ex when we got engaged was a quarter carat, all I could afford at the time as a Marine corporal. Most of these were larger than that, several quite a bit larger. About a third looked like the normal diamond you'd see set in a ring, but most were irregular-shaped and not as clear or shiny as what you'd expect to find in jewelry stores.

"These are rough diamonds," Kate said, picking up one of the larger irregular stones and placing it in her palm. "Wes once showed me the difference. See?" She selected what I'd call a store-quality diamond and placed it beside the other.

I studied the two stones for a few seconds. "You said that Ramey hired Wes as a gem buyer, right?"

Kate nodded. "Yeah, he bought from wholesalers mostly in the South, but now and then he'd travel to different places around the country."

"But those were finished diamonds, right, the kind you'd find behind the counter in any jewelry store?"

She nodded again.

"So, what was Wes doing with a bagful of cut and uncut diamonds in his personal filing cabinet?"

Kate's face flushed. She turned away and stared out the window for a moment. "I found something else." She walked over to the filing cabinet, slid the bottom drawer open, and lifted out a folder. She handed it to me. "I don't know what this means, if anything."

I opened the folder, pulled out several loose sheets of paper, and flipped through them. Some were written in English and some were in what appeared to be Spanish. I divided the papers into two small stacks. The English papers were all from the country of Guyana and appeared to be receipts or some other sort of paperwork. They definitely had something to do with diamonds. There were columns of figures showing number counts of stones, carat weights, and values in US dollars.

I only knew a few words of Spanish, my favorite being "*Corona la cerveza mas fina*," but I did recognize the words *República Bolivariana de Venezuela* printed on the Spanish documents. More columns of figures, but written in Spanish. Right then I would've bet my boots these papers were speaking the same lingo as their English compadres.

I looked at Kate. "You got a map of South America around somewhere?"

For a second Kate stared at me like I'd gone loco, then her eyes lit up. She pointed across the room to a chest of drawers, atop which stood a globe of the world. "Will that do?"

It didn't take us long to verify that Venezuela bordered both Guyana and Brazil, just as Dr. Garrett had mentioned. That's where Rachel Todd's plane supposedly disappeared over the Canaima National Park a couple of weeks after Robert Ramey's boat capsized. A bag of diamonds, paperwork in two languages relating to diamonds, a missing-and-presumed-dead missionary to Venezuela—it looked like things were beginning to add up.

"This could be big, Katie girl," Frank said as he finished going through the paperwork spread on his desktop. He picked up the Crown Royal bag and shook it like a kid with a bag of prized marbles. "You do realize that this doesn't look good for Wes and the others?"

Kate bit her lower lip and nodded. "Yes, but I need to know the truth, Uncle Frank. I haven't slept well since Dr. Garrett told us he didn't think Rachel had a brother. I just need to find out the truth about Wes, whatever it is."

"You already know about the trouble he was in as a kid," Frank said.

Kate sighed. "Yes, but people can change."

Frank glanced across the desk at me. I gave my head a slight shake.

Kate almost came out of her chair. Her brows arched as she locked eyes with me. "And just what on earth does that headshake mean?"

"Nothing," I stammered. Damn, I was hoping she hadn't noticed. I looked forward to telling Kate about Travis Hurt and Rachel like I would a case of the clap.

"Mac found out Garrett might have been correct about Eric and Rachel not being related," Frank said, digging my hole a little deeper.

Kate crossed her arms and pursed her lips. Her stare bore through me like a laser. "Mac?"

My mind scrambled for a way out. Fortunately, Frank came to my rescue.

"Whoa, Katie. I told Mac not to discuss what he learned in Texas yet, so the blame is on me. He needs to make another quick trip to verify that the information he found is on the up and up. There's no sense in any of us assuming things until we know for sure, right?"

Kate redirected the laser at Frank. After a moment she let out a deep breath. Her shoulders relaxed, and her hands rested in her lap. "I suppose, if you think it's best." She turned back to me. "What trip?"

"Atlanta," I said. "I need to check out some stuff about Robert Ramey. You're welcome to come with me." I hoped the invitation would be enough to appease her.

"When?"

"Wednesday," I said, pulling the day out of my magician's hat. I hadn't even found out if Ramey's mother was still living, but I was on the spot and had to tell Kate something.

She frowned. "Dang, I can't. The cobia tournament starts Wednesday. And with the Easter holiday coming up I'll be working tomorrow through the weekend."

"Then it's settled," Frank said. "Mac, you head to Atlanta Wednesday and see what you can turn up on Ramey. Katie, you try not to worry your pretty little head until we can verify a few more things. When *we* know, *you'll* know. That's a promise."

Frank jiggled the bag of diamonds again. "Meanwhile, I'll check with a friend of mine who's retired FBI. He just might be able to tell us what we've got here."

CHAPTER 11

I headed back to St. George as soon as our meeting ended. Kate said she had a few more things to attend to and would be home later. I didn't ask what the "things" were. Kate was definitely giving me the cold shoulder, and I didn't want to complicate matters. She'd changed lately, and I didn't much care for the direction the changes seemed headed. There was one thing I was sure of. Despite the negative info we'd learned, Kate still carried a torch for Wes Harrison. I could only hope that torch wouldn't burn whatever bridge was still connecting us.

Back home, I spent the early evening doing my homework via the Internet on Mrs. Edmond Randolph Ramey, née Darla June Spence. To my good fortune several articles from the online *Atlanta Journal-Constitution* showed she was very much among the living, occasionally still participating in various social and charitable events, and entertaining in her upscale Buckhead neighborhood home. Hell, the old lady's address and phone number were even listed on Whitepages.com, along with a generalized map showing directions to her home.

I whispered a prayer to the Internet gods and dialed the number. A woman with a pleasant Southern accent answered. I identified myself and asked if I was speaking with Mrs. Edmond Ramey, though the voice sounded much younger than a woman who I figured must be on the backside of eighty.

No, she wasn't Mrs. Ramey; her name was Alice Spence, Mrs. Ramey's niece and live-in caretaker. She seemed friendly enough, so I took a chance and popped the question. Would Mrs. Ramey feel up to seeing me regarding her late son and a possible new development in the accident? Perhaps tomorrow or Wednesday, or whenever would be convenient for her?

Alice, as she insisted I call her, asked me to hold. A couple of minutes later she returned with the good news that Aunt Darla would be pleased to see me. Would noonish tomorrow be convenient?

How easy was that? An hour of computer research, one phone call, and I was in like Flynn. This PI business might not turn out to be such a bad second career after all.

~~~

Atlanta's about three hundred miles from St. George, but I counted on seven hours to get there, allowing for the city's infamous traffic and tracking down the exact location of the Ramey home. After talking with Alice Spence I'd gone to MapQuest and printed out more detailed directions to the Ramey house. I also surfed over to Google Maps and downloaded a couple of satellite shots of the house and property. I'd done the same thing with the Harpers' home and Barfield Fisheries last year while working on Maddie's case. You never knew if or when they might come in handy.

I drove through Tallahassee, on north to Thomasville, Georgia, and picked up Interstate 75 at Tifton. A few boring hours later I'd passed through downtown and midtown Atlanta to where Interstates 75 and 85 converge. Somehow I managed to find the correct Peachtree Road that took me through the heart of the Buckhead district.

I passed close by the Governor's Mansion, skirted Chastain Park, and found Powers Ferry Road. It was a beautiful area, winding through wooded hills studded with fancy estates of Atlanta's elite old-money families. Following the map, I soon came to Ramey Way, which led through an open wrought iron gate and down a concrete and brick drive to the Ramey house.

"Mansion" would be a more fitting word. I'm no expert on houses, but I guess you could call this one a cross between a Southern plantation and a Victorian. The house was mostly beige brick trimmed with matching native stone. A pair of stout columns stood sentry on either side of the wide stone steps leading to the front entrance. Big porches with elaborate railings spanned the length of the first two stories. The third story was dominated by huge stone dormers at either end. Four brick chimneys rose above the slate-tiled roof. Silver spoon, top to bottom.

I checked my watch. About ten minutes early, but close enough for a three-hundred-mile trip. I pulled to the side of the drive, parked, and grabbed the manila envelope with the photos I'd brought. The front door was a massive eight-footer with leaded glass and ornate antique brass handles. I took a breath and punched the brass doorbell, almost afraid to smudge it.

The last note of the Westminster chime was fading when the door swung open. The attractive woman who answered took a quick step back, eyes wide and brows arched. After a second she relaxed and flashed a smile. "Oh, you must be Mac," she said, breathing a little heavy. "I'm sorry, I'm expecting a package today and I thought you might be the FedEx man." She patted her forehead with a small towel and extended her hand, palm down.

Recognizing the voice dripping with Southern charm, I took her hand, wondering if I should shake or kiss it. I gave the palm a gentle squeeze. "And you must be Alice. Sorry, I'm a few minutes early."

"Nonsense. Please, come in." She stood aside and motioned me in with a graceful sweep of a well-toned arm. "Forgive my appearance," she said, brushing a stray strand of hair from her eyes, "I was shredding fat with Jillian Michaels when the bell rang."

Forgive? Alice Spence was some looker. Early thirties, I guessed, and not a wrinkle in sight. Her strawberry-blonde hair was pulled back in a tight ponytail, and her face with the high cheekbones, big green eyes, and full lips was Hollywood-caliber. And just where the hell was the fat she was trying to shred? The black V-neck leotard and white leggings didn't do a thing to hide her knockout figure. I stepped past her into a foyer the size of a large living room in an average house.

Alice led the way into a great room that would've made the cover of *Southern Living* proud. I'll spare the details, but think Tara of *Gone with the Wind* fame, before the Yankees arrived. We stopped under a massive crystal chandelier hanging from the high ceiling. Alice motioned to a corner near a stone fireplace where a couple of overstuffed beige leather chairs, a huge matching sofa, and floor lamps were arranged around a fancy carved coffee table.

"Make yourself comfortable over here while I go see if Aunt Darla is ready. And please excuse her if she seems a bit distracted. The poor dear is showing some early signs of dementia, bless her heart. Meanwhile, would you care for something to drink, Mac? Coffee, sweet tea, a Coke perhaps?"

"Coffee would be fine, thanks. Black, no sugar."

Alice excused herself and turned to go. I chose a chair and watched as she sashayed out of sight through an arched doorway and down a hall. I began rehashing how I was going to approach Mrs. Ramey with the news that one of the men who'd disappeared with her late son years ago might still be alive. It had all seemed much more straightforward last night when I'd rehearsed it several times before falling asleep. Now, my confidence was shot. I'd felt more at ease leading assaults against the mujahedeen during the Battle of Fallujah.

Footsteps on the marble tile floor snapped me back to attention. I glanced up and stood as Alice came into view, now wearing a loose-fitting Georgia Tech sweatshirt over black jeans. "Ah, a Yellow Jackets fan, I see."

She smiled. "Guilty as charged. Rabid fan. I also happen to be a proud alumnus. Not to brag, but I graduated with a master's in business administration from Tech."

Just then a slim elderly woman with stylish gray hair wearing a light-blue pantsuit appeared behind Alice. She was a handsome lady, probably quite the looker herself in her younger days, and her back was straight as an arrow despite using a cane.

"Aunt Darla, this is Mac McClellan, the gentleman who called last evening about Cousin Bobby."

The old woman craned her neck and looked me over. After a few seconds her gray eyes seemed to light up and her lips broke into a smile. She offered a pale hand with blue veins and age spots. "Nice to meet you, Mac. Were you a friend of Bobby's? I'm afraid I don't remember faces quite as well as I used to."

I took her hand and gave it a gentle shake. "Pleasure to meet you, ma'am."

"No, Aunt Darla, Mac didn't know Cousin Bobby," Alice said before I could answer Mrs. Ramey's question. "He's here because he might have some new information for us about the accident, remember?"

Mrs. Ramey touched her cheek. "Oh, you're that private investigator from . . . where was it now?"

"Florida, Mrs. Ramey. I—"

The clacking of footsteps and rattling of dishes cut me off. A portly black woman with graying hair wearing a black dress with white collar and apron walked into the room. She carried a tray with a silver coffeepot and what I guessed was a real china tea set.

"Thank you, Miss Lettie," Alice said. "Just set it on the table and we'll help ourselves."

"Yes, ma'am." Miss Lettie took care not to upset anything as she placed the loaded tray on the coffee table. "Y'all need anything else, just holler."

After Alice poured tea for Mrs. Ramey and coffee for herself and me, we got down to business. I spent several minutes giving them a brief rundown of the case, emphasizing Kate's encounter with Wes Harrison at O'Malley's, especially their eye contact. Deciding it was best not to offer Alice or Mrs. Ramey any more info than necessary, I didn't mention that Kate and Harrison had been an item, just that they had been friends. I was also careful not to reveal Kohler's real identity, or that I'd learned that he and Rachel weren't brother and sister.

When I finished, Mrs. Ramey looked confused. Knowing the old lady wasn't as sharp as she once was, I figured Alice was my best bet to pick up anything that might be useful to the case.

I reached for the coffeepot to top off my cup. "Are you familiar with any of the names I mentioned, besides your cousin, of course?"

Alice set her cup and saucer on the table. "Yes. In those days I stayed at Bobby's home in Sandestin quite often, during spring break and summers mostly. In fact, the house is still in the family. We try to get down there whenever we can. My aunt says it makes her feel closer to Bobby." She turned and smiled at Mrs. Ramey. "Isn't that right, Aunt Darla?"

Above the rim of her teacup Mrs. Ramey's eyes darted in Alice's direction at the sound of her name. "Hmm?"

Alice reached over and patted her aunt's knee. Either Alice had drifted off-topic or was evading my question. A little reminder was in order.

"You were saying you remembered some of the people I mentioned."

"Oh, pardon me," Alice said, touching the base of her throat. "Yes, I remember Eric quite well. He was the manager of Bobby's store in Destin. Bobby would sometimes treat me to earrings or other jewelry when I was visiting. Eric was always so very friendly and helpful.

"And I remember meeting Eric's sister Rachel at one of Bobby's parties. We got to be quite friendly in the short time I knew her. She was a missionary pilot, of all things. Can you believe it? Such a pretty, petite girl; it was hard to imagine her flying an airplane all over the jungles of South America by herself like that."

"Did you ever hear from Rachel after your cousin's accident?"

Alice's lips pressed together. "No, now that you mention it. I believe she was in South America when it happened. I don't recall her coming back for the memorial service. I suppose she was trying to keep busy with her mission work. There was really nothing she could've done back in Florida anyway."

"What about Kate Bell?"

Alice hesitated and then shook her head. "Sorry, no, not that I remember. Was she a friend of Bobby's? I suppose I might have seen her at a party. Bobby used to entertain quite often."

I ignored Alice's question. "Wes Harrison?"

Alice's eyelids fluttered and she blushed. She looked away for an instant, like she was trying to gather herself. "Yes. Actually, Wes and I dated a few times."

I almost dropped the cup when I heard that.

"I was still a student at Tech, and . . . well, he was such a charmer and so much fun to be with. Wes seemed quite worldly at the time, being older and from California and all." Alice paused a moment. "Now may I ask *you* a question, Mac?"

"Sure."

"What makes you believe that Wes might still be alive, other than this Kate woman claiming she saw him at the theater?"

I took a sip of coffee while I thought it out. "I know Kate very well, and she swears up and down the man she saw was Wes Harrison." I mentioned again how Kate was sure he'd recognized her and turned away when they made eye contact.

"But surely she can't be certain it was Wes just because the man had different-colored eyes," Alice said. "There must be lots of people with eyes like that."

"Actually, not as many as you might think. But it's not only the eye color, Alice. Kate's absolutely certain the man recognized her and deliberately broke eye contact. I believe her."

Alice frowned. "I'm sorry, but it still sounds rather far-fetched to me."

"We do have other information that I'm not at liberty to divulge right now," I said, reaching for the manila envelope resting on my lap. I took out the beach photo and handed it across the coffee table to Alice. "Can you identify these people for me?"

Alice studied the photo for a moment. "This is Wes," she said, pointing with her index finger, "Eric, and that's Rachel standing to his left. The other woman I'm not sure of." She handed the photo to her aunt. "I may have seen her somewhere, but I couldn't swear to it."

"That's Kate Bell."

"Sorry, I don't recall meeting her," Alice said.

"They made such a lovely young couple," Mrs. Ramey said, smiling down at the photo.

My eyes widened. "Wes Harrison and Kate Bell?"

Mrs. Ramey looked at me with her head tilted slightly and her brow furrowed. "Oh my, no, dear." She gave a little chuckle. "Eric and my Bobby."

I felt the hair on the back of my neck rise. I glanced at Alice.

"It was never a secret that Cousin Bobby was gay, Mac."

～～◯

I waited until I was well south of the Atlanta-area traffic before calling Frank.

"Would you believe our boy Eric or Travis or whatever the hell you want to call him was banging Robert Ramey?" I said when he answered.

"Would you mind running that by me again, Mac?"

"We already know Travis Hurt was bi. Turns out Ramey was gay."

"His mother told you that?"

"Yeah. Which probably explains why Hurt and Rachel were doing the brother-sister act. Hurt didn't want to jeopardize his relationship with Ramey."

"That makes sense," Frank said.

"By the way, Ramey's cousin, Alice, just happened to be romantically involved with Wes Harrison back in the day."

"Slow down, you're losing me."

I gave Frank the gist of what went down at the meeting.

"Damn," was all he said after I'd spelled it out.

"You mind telling me how the hell Kate could've been clueless about what was going on?" I said. "She's not blind and she sure as hell isn't stupid."

"No clue, Mac. From what I know, Ramey spent most of his time at his Atlanta store, and when he was down here to check on his Destin business he mostly rubbed elbows with the Sandestin crowd."

"I'm not buying it. Kate spent a lot of time palling around with Harrison and Kohler."

"Don't forget, this is the Bible Belt, Mac. How good would it have been for Ramey's business if he traipsed all over town crowing about a homosexual relationship with his local store manager, or vice versa?"

Touché. "Okay, that much I'll buy."

"Anything else? I've got a client due here in a couple of minutes."

"Yeah, two guesses who was beneficiary to a million-dollar life insurance policy on Robert Ramey. And here's a hint: his mother wasn't one of them."

"Insurance policy? How did you find out about that?"

"Ramey's mother blurted it out. Alice about had a conniption fit trying to shut her up. Take a guess."

"Eric Kohler?"

"Very good, Sherlock. Looks like Ramey wanted to make sure his lover was well taken care of in the event of his untimely demise."

"Damn."

"And when Eric Kohler went down with the ship, guess who stood to inherit the money?"

"I'm guessing it wasn't his favorite charity."

"Good guess, Frank. I won't mention any names, but her initials are Rachel Todd."

CHAPTER 12

There was no sense in putting off the inevitable, so after I hung up with Frank I called Kate at Gillman's and told her we had a lot to discuss. She invited me over for a late dinner of grilled grouper that evening, provided I do the grilling. Of course I agreed, after I'd swallowed the lump in my throat. Normally I'd jump at any chance to be with Kate, but I couldn't shake the feeling that it would be my cojones sizzling on the Weber along with the fish. I looked forward to telling Kate about Travis Hurt like I would a vasectomy with no anesthesia.

Around eight-fifteen I showered and trimmed my beard and moustache. Figuring I might as well look spiffy at my inquisition, I put on a new pair of Dockers and a matching polo shirt. I stopped by Gulf Groceries & Gifts on the way and bought a bottle of Kate's favorite white wine, Kendall-Jackson chardonnay, and a single red rose. I hoped the meager peace offerings would help defuse the situation when the crapola hit the fan.

The weather was mild for the third week of April, so we decided to eat on the deck. Kate fixed our plates with grilled fillets, potatoes, and tossed salad while I opened the wine and poured her a glass. I'd been sipping Dewar's on the rocks while performing my chefly duties, so I refilled my tumbler before sitting down to eat. I enjoy the taste of good Scotch, but it also bolsters the courage better than wine or beer.

"Okay, you said we'd talk while we eat," Kate said, lifting a forkful of grouper to her mouth.

I took a sip of Dewar's. "Why don't we wait till after? It's not polite to talk with food in your mouth."

Kate's eyes narrowed. "Mac."

I knew that look all too well. "Okay, but you're not going to like it. Promise you won't get pissed at me. I'm only the messenger here."

She set her fork down and picked up her wineglass. "Promise."

Kate didn't sound very convincing. I pushed a bite of potato around my plate with my fork and then picked up the tumbler for another slug. "Remember when Dr. Garrett at Sacred Word Missions told us he didn't think Rachel had a brother or half-brother?"

Kate set the wineglass down. "Of course."

"Turns out he was right. Rachel did grow up in an orphanage like Garrett said, and she was adopted by the Todds when she was thirteen. And by the way, the orphanage *is* in Waxahachie, where Eric said they were from."

It was Kate's turn to play with her food. She stared down at her plate a moment before looking up. "Why on earth would they have pretended to be related?"

I reached across the table and took Kate's hand in mine. "It gets worse. You sure you want to hear this?"

Kate bit her lower lip as she nodded.

I took a deep breath and exhaled. "Okay, here goes. Eric was also living in the same orphanage. Him and Rachel met up and had a thing going. He—"

"Thing?" Kate's jaw clenched and her nostrils flared. "What sort of thing?"

I had to force the words out. "They were having sex."

Kate jerked her hand away from mine and covered her eyes with both palms. "Dang . . . no, not . . . dang, shit! *Shit!*"

"I'm sorry, Kate," I muttered, my throat tightening.

"Eric had sex with a thirteen-year-old girl? I don't believe it."

I blew out another breath. "Actually, it started when she was twelve."

Kate's hands slid up and grabbed a double handful of hair. "Shit!"

I waited while she repeated the first real expletive I could remember her saying. After a few seconds she took a deep breath and let it out slowly. "I'm sorry, Mac. What else did you find out?"

"You're going to need more wine," I said, tilting the bottle to Kate's glass. "Okay. The guy you knew as Eric Kohler wasn't Eric Kohler. His name was Travis Hurt. The real Eric Kohler grew up in the same orphanage with Rachel and Travis. He—"

"Wait, wait!" Kate's hands covered her eyes again. She held them there for a couple of seconds and then looked at me. "What?"

"The Eric you knew was actually Travis Hurt. The real Eric Kohler was killed during the invasion of Iraq about a year after he left the orphanage. Travis Hurt most likely stole Eric Kohler's identity to cover up his criminal record."

In the subdued lighting of the tiki torches I saw Kate's face turn pale. I got up and put an arm around her shoulders. "How could I have been such fool, Mac?" she said. "I really liked the guy. How can anybody be such a bad judge of character?"

I didn't have an answer.

After Kate calmed down I told her everything I'd found out during my Texas trip, including Hurt's bisexual exploits at the orphanage and the possibility that he and Rachel might've been responsible for the fatal fire that made Rachel an instant millionaire and rendered her an orphan for the second time. I also gave her a quick briefing on my Atlanta trip, including Alice Spence's history of dating Wes Harrison whenever she was in Destin. But I did hold back one delicate detail.

By then Kate had slugged down over half the bottle of Kendall-Jackson and was well on her way to getting drunk. I figured now was as good a time as any to deliver the coup de grâce. "While I was at Mrs. Ramey's I showed her and Alice the photo of you and the others on the beach," I said. "Out of the blue Mrs. Ramey commented about how they made such a lovely young couple. At first I thought she meant you and Wes, but it turned out she was talking about Eric and her son."

Kate's mouth fell open, but she didn't say anything. A couple of seconds later she turned the bottle of chardonnay up to her lips, foregoing the glass. After a long swig she wiped her mouth with the back of a hand and repeated her new favorite word, "Shit."

I wished to hell we'd never gone to O'Malley's Theater that night. Harrison, Kohler, and Ramey would all be safely resting in Davy Jones' Locker and none of this crap would be happening. A week went by, and Kate didn't answer or return my calls. The two times she answered the phone when I called Gillman's Marina she hung up as soon as she heard my voice. So much for not killing the messenger.

I missed her. I was willing to apologize and take the blame to make things right between us, even though I hadn't done anything wrong, at least the way I saw things. But she evidently wasn't interested, at least not anytime soon. I'm no psychologist, but she was clearly in denial. I guess I'd blown the image she had of Harrison and Kohler that she'd been clinging to. The torch she was carrying for Wes Harrison was hotter than I'd thought.

The last day of April I received a call from Frank. I'd spent the afternoon surf fishing for pompano but had struck out. Earlier in the week I'd twisted an ankle stumbling down the steps of my trailer, burned a finger while grilling chicken, and had two flat tires on my Silverado. So when the phone rang just as the ten o'clock news was coming on, I figured it couldn't be good news.

"What in the hell did you do to get Katie so upset?" Frank said, loud enough to blow the wax out my ear.

I took a sip of Dewar's. "What's with the shouting, Frank? I told her the truth about what I learned in Waxahachie and Atlanta."

"That's it?"

"Yeah, that's it. When did you talk to her?"

"This morning. She's here at her parents' place for the weekend. Jim and Mary got back from Arizona a couple of days ago."

"So, am I fired?"

"I didn't say that. Just give Katie some space until this blows over."

"Blows over? Hell, Frank, it's been over a decade and she's still gaga over Wes Harrison!"

"Calm down, Mac. I've known Katie all her life. She loves you."

I laughed. "Yeah, tell it to the Marines."

"Katie's always been high-spirited, but she loves you. Believe it."

I topped off my Scotch. "So, do I keep working or what?"

"You're still on the payroll. How are the lessons coming along?"

"Like a three-legged turtle through quicksand."

"Well, keep at it. By the way, I've got some interesting dope on the diamonds and paperwork Katie found."

"Shoot."

"No time right now. I'm meeting with a client in a few minutes. I'll be in touch soon."

I'd just clicked off when somebody rapped on the door.

CHAPTER 13

"Hey, McClellan."

A smiling Dakota stepped past me and inside the camper carrying a small purse tucked under one arm and a brown paper sack in the opposite hand. She found her way to the kitchen nook and set the sack on the counter with a thud.

"Brought you a little present." She dropped the purse on the counter and lifted a bottle of Dewar's out of the sack like a magician pulling a rabbit from a top hat. She held up the bottle. "I believe this is your brand?"

Dakota was dressed a little less conservatively than on her previous visit. Okay, a lot less. She wore a sleeveless button-up blouse knotted in front between her bejeweled belly button and rib cage. No bra; I could tell right off because she'd conveniently left the top three or four buttons undone. The denim shorts weren't quite as tight or short as her beachwear the day I'd met her with J.D. outside The Green Parrot, but they weren't in any danger of falling off without considerable effort, either. Oh, and flip-flops.

I must've stared a little too long. "You like?" She grinned and placed her free hand on a hip that she thrust out just enough for effect.

I gathered myself and pointed to the Scotch. "Yeah, thanks. How'd you know I like Dewar's?"

"I've got my connections. I know a lot about you, McClellan. How about a drink for your guest? Neat."

Just then I noticed her hair. The bleached blonde was now a strawberry blonde, damn near the same color as Alice Spence's hair. "What's with the new hair color?"

Dakota threw back her head and laughed. "A gentleman shouldn't ask a lady about such things, but since I'm hoping you're not a gentleman tonight I'll tell you. I saw a woman at work with the color and I liked it. End of story. Now, how about that drink?"

Who the hell was this young vixen, and what was she up to? I made a mental note to talk to J.D. "Looks to me like you've already had a few."

She frowned. "A couple of beers is all."

"You sure you ought to mess with the hard stuff?"

Dakota's eyes darted below my beltline for a teasing second and then locked on mine. She flashed a smile, and the tip of her tongue jutted between her teeth. "You already checked my ID, McClellan. I'm sure I can handle it."

<hr />

I woke up at daybreak with the damndest hangover I'd had since my first liberty in J'ville when I was a newly assigned PFC rifleman stationed at Camp Lejeune. It was a hell of a way to welcome the merry month of May.

I groaned and grabbed both temples as I sat up on the sofa where I'd spent the night. My mouth tasted like a herd of goats had crapped in it. The first thing that caught my eye was the empty bottle of Dewar's on the coffee table. Dakota and I had damn sure made good use of her gift.

Dakota . . . crap! My mind was in a fog. I stood up, relieved to find my shorts and skivvies were still intact. Then I noticed a phone number scrawled on the back of my right hand, followed by "Call me." I eased toward the bedroom and glanced in. Empty. Dakota and what little clothes she'd scattered about the trailer were gone. The way she was kicking back the Scotch last night, the girl sure had one hell of a strong constitution to be up and out of here this early.

I made it back to the sofa and sat down. For a minute guilt grabbed me. I couldn't remember exactly what had happened or hadn't happened. Gradually the fog lifted and it came back to me. I'd poured her a drink, and we'd sat down opposite each other at the kitchen table to talk. She mostly evaded my questions when I tried to find out more about her personal life and what she planned to do with her future. About the only thing she spilled, besides her last shot of Dewar's, was that her mother had never married her father—"The son of a bitch ran out on us while I was still in diapers"—and that her mother had been in and out of rehab for drugs and alcohol during most of Dakota's high school years. She and J.D. practically grew up together and were more like big brother and little sister than cousins.

One thing seemed certain: Dakota was obviously not harboring any love for her long-lost dad. Maybe that's why she seemed so intent on targeting me. Was she somehow attracted to me as a father figure, or was I just a convenient sugar daddy?

After a few drinks Dakota got all giddy and started pawing at me. My willpower just about bottomed out fending her off, especially after she sashayed around the kitchen kicking the flip-flops across the room and peeling off her clothes piece by piece in an impromptu strip-tease. She got down to her pink panties that barely fit the description and then tried to drag me to the bedroom. I retrieved her blouse and attempted to cover her with it, but she snatched it out of my hands and flung it across the room. I tried to keep my eyes off the vitals, but the combination of Dewar's and testosterone won that battle. The girl had one hell of a nice body, there was no denying that.

I finally gave up mimicking a sea anchor and decided the best course was to follow her into the bedroom. Dakota yanked back the sheets and hit the sack. She reached under the covers and wiggled out of the wisp of pink material and tossed it on the floor at the foot of the bed. She patted the mattress next to her. I slipped off my shoes and climbed in beside her, still wearing my shirt and shorts.

"C'mon, McClellan," she said, slurring the words, "you gotta get naked if you wanna do me."

I won't say I wasn't tempted, because I was. Everything told me to go for it. Dakota wasn't jailbait, but Kate's face kept popping up in my mind.

Dakota kept bugging me to get undressed, so finally I tugged off my shirt. That seemed enough to appease her. She rolled over, draped an arm around my shoulders, and snuggled tight against me. A few seconds later she was asleep.

I went to the bathroom, slugged down a double-shot of Alka-Seltzer, brushed my teeth, and headed for the kitchen to make coffee. There was a rolled-up slip of paper inside the handle of the coffee decanter. I unrolled it. It was a note written in a nice cursive hand:

> *McClellan,*
> *Thanks for the party.*
> *124 S. 31st St. Tell J.D. to keep an eye on it and to be careful.*
> *DO NOT mention my name to him or anyone!*
> *D. xoxo*
> *P.S. Better luck next time?* ☺

Dakota the mystery girl just grew more mysterious.

CHAPTER 14

After I'd choked down a couple of pieces of dry toast with my coffee I fired up the Silverado and headed for Highway 98. South 31st Street was beachside and not far from the city pier if my memory was still intact after all the booze I'd soaked my brain cells with last night. There was little traffic at six-thirty as I headed east on 98, checking street signs as I cruised along. I passed the pier and three blocks later turned left onto 31st.

Along the upper part of the street the houses were mostly concrete block with low roofs and faded paint, older residences of St. George from the 1950s and '60s whose owners had so far resisted selling out to developers lusting after their properties to turn them into modern condos or duplexes. The closer to the beach, the more updated the houses became.

The target address was the last house on the right, one of the nicer beachside homes in the neighborhood. It was a two-story structure with lobster-pink siding, built on stout ten-foot pilings. There was no realtor's sign that I could see. A couple of late-model cars were parked side by side on the concrete slab underneath a large wooden deck that ran the width of the house, the entryway to the main floor of the structure. A smaller deck on the second floor was accessed by a sliding door that probably led to the master bedroom.

I slowed to a crawl and gave the cars a closer look. A Chipola Indians decal was pasted on the back window of a sporty black BMW. Chipola College; the backup ID Dakota had shown me during her first social call to my trailer. College kids driving a Beamer and living in a beachfront house? Somebody in the house either came from rich stock or was somehow making damn good money while attending school.

The pavement ended just beyond the house on a small cul-de-sac where sea oats swayed over small dunes. Beyond the dunes the gulf murmured as low waves of the outgoing tide rolled up the sand and retreated back into the foamy surf. A path led to the beach, where a wire and wooden picket fence on either side cordoned off the dunes from foot traffic. I circled and parked on the far side of the street.

I got out and eased the door shut. This early on a Sunday morning I doubted if anybody in the house would be stirring, but I didn't want to be anyone's alarm clock. With a few exceptions the aqua-colored house next door was the spitting image of 124. It was a rental and appeared to be unoccupied, a perfect cover for my snooping around should anyone ask what the hell I was doing there.

Acting as a potential renter, I pulled a pen and small notebook from my shorts pocket and jotted down the realtor's name and number. I eased my way between the houses pretending to take notes, but I kept sneaking glimpses at 124. Beer cans, wine bottles, plastic cups, and cigarette butts were scattered among lawn chairs between the cars and the front of a storage room and outdoor shower stall. Draped haphazardly over the back of one chair was a white T-shirt. I could make out the letters "ino & Re" in red lettering shadowed with gold. An uncovered barbeque grill had been turned into a big ashtray and trash pit. Slobs. Well-to-do slobs.

Retracing my steps, I turned a couple of pages in the notebook and jotted down the license numbers of the BMW and the other car, a metallic-blue Avalon. The BMW had Georgia plates; the Avalon was local. I'd ask J.D. to run the numbers when I told him about the "anonymous" source who tipped me about this place.

Being as discreet as possible, I worked my way between and down the length of the houses. A flight of stairs led to a small deck off the back of 124's first floor. A couple of lounge chairs and a weathered picnic table dominated the small backyard. True to form, empty wine bottles and beer cans were scattered across the table.

I circled on around my potential rental house and climbed the stairs that led to its matching back deck, hoping I might be able to see something worthwhile from there. Lights were on in one of 124's back rooms, and through a window I noticed a side-by-side refrigerator. On the roof above an adjacent room a power vent was running at high speed; odd for such a cool morning, I thought.

I spent a few more minutes looking through the windows of the unoccupied house just in case someone next door might be checking me out. After jotting down more imaginary notes I headed down the stairs to my pickup.

～

I was having lunch at Carl's Sandwich Shop across from Gillman's Marina around one o'clock when my phone rang. I recognized Frank's number. "This is Mac, go."

"I showed my former FBI buddy the diamonds and paperwork Katie found. He says we're dealing with conflict diamonds here, Mac, no doubt about it."

"I hate to show my ignorance, but what the hell is a conflict diamond?"

"Ever hear of blood diamonds?"

"Like in the movie? Yeah."

"Right. It's more prevalent in African countries like Angola and the Congo. Basically, the natives mine and sell the diamonds on the black market to finance rebel groups involved in armed conflicts or civil wars. In South America it's mostly a matter of human rights abuse, usually slave labor and fraud instead of war. And guess which country is one of the worst of the bunch for looking the other way?"

"Venezuela?"

"Right again. The border area where Venezuela meets Guyana and Brazil is a hotspot for conflict diamonds."

"Almost the exact area where Rachel Todd flew for Sacred Word Missions."

"And again."

"I'm a little confused here, Frank. Why would Venezuela be involved in that crap? Last I heard Chávez had a pretty firm grip on things down there."

"Here's a nutshell of what my friend told me without getting too technical. There's this international organization called the Kimberley Process. Their goal is to see that all diamond-producing countries use legitimate labor sources, oversee production, and certify as legit any and all diamonds being exported for sale. You with me so far, Mac?"

"Yeah."

"Venezuela is one of three South American countries signed on with the Kimberley Process, along with Guyana and Brazil. But Venezuela has developed a nasty habit of being noncompliant with the organization. In fact, for the past two years they've reported a grand total of zero diamond production to the Kimberley Process. That's despite an estimated annual production of somewhere between fifteen to thirty million dollars."

"Wow."

"Yeah, and it just so happens that during the same period Guyana's output increased by almost the same estimated dollar amount."

"Double wow."

"Right. Venezuelan diamonds are being mined and smuggled into Guyana and Brazil using what basically amounts to slave labor—workers from isolated villages in the jungles working for peanuts. So, Venezuela mines the diamonds for practically nothing and fences them to certain crooked authorities in Guyana and Brazil. Then the stones are laundered as legitimate KP diamonds with the proper legal governmental paperwork to satisfy the requirements of the Kimberley organization. Guyana and Brazil then sell the diamonds to the legitimate market and pay Venezuela a hefty kickback that amounts to more money than Venezuela would've made had they used legitimate companies to mine the rough diamonds. It throws a monkey wrench in the entire KP system, and all it takes is altering the paperwork to make it look legit."

"Okay, but how does that fit in with what Kate found in Harrison's filing cabinet?"

"My friend thinks Rachel was in contact with some black marketers, probably in one or more of the remote villages she flew supplies to. She bought the rough stones at cutthroat prices and brought them back into the States. Her being a missionary was a perfect cover, especially before 9/11 when things tightened up."

"And Wes Harrison had the conflict stones cut and then replaced them with some of the legitimate diamonds he was buying for Ramey in the States."

"You're catching on quick, Mac. With Harrison's background in gemology it was an easy matter for him for him to size and match the conflicts for the legit stones once the conflicts were cut and polished."

"And then Harrison or Hurt would sell the legitimate stones for a nifty profit. They must've made quite a bundle. What's the value of the stones Kate found?"

"A few million, according to my friend. That's retail, of course, assuming the rough ones would've been brought up to snuff."

I let out a low whistle. "This is all fine and dandy, Frank, but what exactly does it prove?"

"Here's the clincher: Robert Ramey had been in touch with the FBI office in Atlanta just a couple of months before he disappeared in the gulf. He suspected somebody in his employ was playing hanky-panky with the loose stones coming into his stores."

"Damn, and Wes Harrison was his buyer."

"Not his only buyer, but he was the latest hire in that position. Maybe Harrison and Hurt were starting to get greedy or careless."

"Double damn. So if Harrison and Hurt suspected Ramey was on to them, there's the motive for Ramey to wind up as crab bait."

"Right on the money. Things are heating up, Mac."

"What's next?"

"Find Wes Harrison."

First thing Monday morning I called J.D. He agreed to meet me at Shannon's Café for a coffee break at nine. I got there early and ordered a BLT with an extra side of bacon that I added to the sandwich. I'd just finished eating and was on my third cup of coffee when he walked in.

As he sat down I poured him a cup from the decanter the waitress left on the table.

"Morning, Mac. What's up?" he said as he added a packet of sugar to his mug.

I fished a slip of paper from my shirt pocket and handed it across the table. Earlier I'd copied the address Dakota had jotted down, plus the tag numbers of the two vehicles I'd seen parked there.

"Anonymous tip for you. The person said you should keep an eye on this place, and to be careful. The tag numbers were on the two cars parked there when I drove by. I thought you might want to run the plates and see if anything interesting turns up."

The young sergeant took a sip of coffee and stared at me over the top of his mug. "Who's the source, and just what am I supposed to be watching the house for?"

J.D. was carrying a newfound air of professionalism along with the increased responsibilities and stripes he'd earned last summer. Can't say I wasn't impressed with the kid, but was I detecting just a hint of cockiness?

"I can't reveal contacts or my word won't be worth dirt around here. What's written on the note is all I know, except that it looks like college kids are living in the place. If I knew what you were supposed to be looking for, I'd sure as hell tell you, you know that."

J.D. glanced at the note as he took another sip of coffee. "Thanks," he said as he scooted back the chair and stood. "I got to get back on the job. There's a trainee waiting in the cruiser I'm showing the ropes to."

"What about the plates?"

He shrugged. "I'll let you know." He took a couple of steps and turned. "Hey, Mac, don't let this PI stuff go to your head."

My coffee suddenly tasted bitter as I watched J.D. walk out the door. What the hell was going on here? First Kate turns on me for telling her the truth about Harrison and Kohler, and now J.D. puffs up when I pass along information I figured he'd be glad to get. I'd taken a shower just that morning, and I brush my teeth on a regular basis. For whatever reason, I was becoming a social pariah.

I could count my current friends in St. George on one hand, with a thumb and pinkie to spare: Jerry and Donna Meadows, my seventies-plus landlords, and Dakota Blaire Owens, twenty-one-year-old vixen/seductress/siren who I still was nowhere close to figuring out. Maybe it was time to apply for membership in the St. George Country and Yacht Club, not that they would have me. I didn't play golf, and I still did my boating and fishing in a rented 18-foot runabout.

I wondered if Hannibal Lecter was busy.

CHAPTER 15

I spent the next couple of days concentrating on my PI studies. J.D.'s little snub, or what I took as such, lit a fire under me, and I was determined to keep at it until I had my license framed and hanging on my camper wall. I kept hoping Kate would call, but no such luck. At least my studies kept my mind semi-occupied.

By Friday I was burned out on bookwork, so that morning around ten-thirty I decided to drive out to the local shooting range and hone up my aim with the Smith & Wesson .357 Magnum I'd bought for myself as a Christmas present.

Last summer while working on the Maddie Harper case I'd had a close call with a couple of thugs from up north. They were determined to see that I kept my nose out of the drug-smuggling operation whose tentacles reached way beyond St. George. Luckily, the shotgun I'd bought a few weeks earlier proved to be the winning trump card in that little incident. I decided then that carrying a scattergun around was a bit too obvious, so I did some research. I decided on the S & W, which packed more than enough punch to handle most any situation unless I got the urge to go rhino or elephant hunting. I hadn't bothered yet to get a concealed-weapon permit; figured I'd talk that over with Frank once I had my PI license in hand.

The range was located north of town a couple of miles past the Harper estate, which would now belong to Maddie had she not met an untimely death. I turned left onto the dirt road that led to the range. After maneuvering the half-mile twisting road through a forest of slash pines I pulled to a stop beneath a large patch of shade. I had the place all to myself except for a flock of crows raising hell over something at the edge of the woods downrange on the right. I chose station 7, where a fairly intact body target stood about twenty feet away.

I loaded the S & W and prepared to fire, and then remembered the earplugs in my jeans pocket. I inserted the plugs, took aim, and started firing slow, controlled shots. I emptied the cylinder twice, putting most of the rounds within an eight-inch pattern. Not bad. I was reloading a third time and mentally patting myself on the back for my improved aim when a gunshot split the air to my left. I flinched and nearly hit the deck. It had been several years since Fallujah, but my combat instincts were still kicking in.

I recovered and glanced over to see a tall woman standing at station 2. She was dressed in a tight-fitting black shirt and pants and wore safety goggles and full shooting ear protectors over a black ball cap. She continued to aim a flat-black semiautomatic pistol at her target, popping off shot after shot in quick succession. When the slide locked back after the final round left the chamber, the lady in black turned toward me and pulled off the goggles and ear protectors. My jaw dropped open.

"Hey, McClellan!"

"Dakota? What the hell are you doing here?"

She shrugged. "Same as you. A little target practice to keep the rust off." She glanced in the general direction of the Smith & Wesson that I held around mid-thigh and grinned. "That's a nice piece you're packing."

This was getting a little past weird. I held up the revolver. "Smith & Wesson, .357 Magnum."

Dakota nodded. "Fine cannon. You planning a bear hunt?"

"Only if one comes at me. What're you shooting?"

She lifted her weapon and held it profile with her fingertips. "Glock 19 Gen4; 9 millimeter. Puts multiple rounds downrange with minimum recoil or muzzle flip. A girl has to know how to defend herself these days, you know."

I didn't know what Dakota's game was, but she damn sure seemed to know her firearms. I was familiar enough with Glocks to know they're a reliable top-of-the-line weapon and don't come cheap. How the hell did a student who drives a beat-up early-'90s Corolla find the money to buy a new Glock?

"No school today?" I said as I thumbed open the cylinder of the Smith & Wesson, dumped the live rounds into my palm, and dropped them into my pocket.

"Been there and back."

"Are you stalking me, young lady?"

Dakota laughed. "Jeez, last I heard this is a public range."

I was getting agitated. "Yeah, and you just happened to show up and find me here, right?"

Dakota ejected the magazine and checked the chamber. It was clear she wasn't a newbie when it came to handling firearms, and somehow that grabbed my interest. She slipped the magazine and pistol into her purse that was sitting on the bench at her station. "It must be kismet, McClellan," she said, flashing her Elvis smirk.

"What's with the ninja warrior getup?"

Dakota placed both hands on her hips and struck a model's pose. "You like?"

I had to admit she looked damned enticing in that skintight black outfit, but I didn't want to overdo the compliments and give her any wrong ideas. I nodded. "Very nice."

Dakota smiled and shifted her pose. I zipped the revolver inside its carrying case. "See you around," I said, and headed for my truck.

"McClellan, wait!"

I turned to find that Dakota had taken several quick steps in my direction. The smile was gone, replaced by a look of disappointment. Somehow it didn't strike me as phony. "I thought maybe we could talk some."

For whatever reason, I felt a tug in my gut. Maybe it was because I hadn't exactly been cordial to her lately, or maybe my fatherly instincts were kicking in. I wasn't sure. But Dakota no longer looked like the sultry vamp who'd tried to bed me a few nights before. What I saw, at least in her eyes, was a lonely girl who yearned to fill some void deep inside.

Suddenly an idea hit me as I remembered Frank Hightower's parting words the last time we'd talked: *Find Wes Harrison.* "Tell you what," I said, "how would you like to go to dinner and a movie at O'Malley's with me tonight?"

Dakota cocked her head and grinned. "A date? Maybe. What's playing?"

"*I Married a Witch*, Fredric March and Veronica Lake, 1942."

She arched an eyebrow. "Is there a double entendre somewhere in there, McClellan?"

~⌒⁀⌐

There's the old saying that a criminal always returns to the scene of the crime. I wasn't certain we were dealing with an actual crime or criminal, but Frank had said our next step was to find Wes Harrison. If Harrison had been to O'Malley's once, who's to say he might not frequent the place now and then? What the hell, it was worth a shot.

Dakota lived in a nice above-garage apartment on City Canal Place, named for the waterway that runs behind Gillman's Marina and provides access to St. George Bay and the Gulf of Mexico. It's one of the ritzier neighborhoods in town, shared by a hundred or so full-time residents and a number of out-of-state part-timers. Most of the people living there have private docking on the canal, making boating and fishing about as convenient as you could ask for. Dakota's landlord, a physician whose practice and main residence was in Montgomery, Alabama, had offered her barebones monthly rent for doubling as house and property watcher.

Dakota was waiting in a lawn chair at the foot of her apartment's outside stairs when I drove up at seven-thirty. She waved and hurried to the truck and climbed in before I could act the gentleman by getting out and opening the door for her.

I was pleased to see Dakota wore no visible piercings other than earrings. She'd also dressed more conservatively than her usual garb, although the knee-length yellow and white sundress showed enough cleavage to grab any red-blooded male's attention. But I chalked that up to nature's blessings, not Dakota's intent to flaunt her figure. "You look very nice."

She dropped the white purse that matched her sandals on the

console between us and grabbed the seat belt. I glanced at the purse, wondering if the Glock was in there with the makeup and whatever else women carry in their purses.

The seat belt clicked into place. "Thanks, McClellan, you look pretty hot yourself," she said as she opened her purse.

"No smoking in the truck, please."

Dakota glared at me with narrowed eyes and pulled out a tube of lip gloss. "Who said anything about smoking?"

During the drive to Parkersville I tried to make small talk, but Dakota seemed more interested in the radio than talking. She was evasive when I asked about her studies and where she worked part-time while attending school. After a while she quit fiddling with the search button and glanced at me. "I make you nervous, don't I?"

"No. Well, maybe a little. I guess it's the age thing. I don't want people thinking I'm a cradle robber."

She snickered. "Jeez, you need to chill, McClellan. What the crap do you care what other people think?"

Dakota had a point. She was legal and we were both single. Still, the fact that my daughter Megan was only a few months younger than my "date" still bothered me. "You're right, I shouldn't. But let's just keep things platonic between us, okay?"

She sighed and shook her head like I was pathetic. "Whatever."

～◑

Dakota seemed to enjoy the movie, although she thought the ending—where Jennifer, the beautiful witch, seals her father in a liquor bottle so he can't meddle with her marriage to a human mortal—was a little on the hokey side. While Dakota visited the ladies' room I waited in the lobby and people-watched as the audience filed out. All night I'd kept my eyes peeled for any sign of Wes Harrison or his redheaded companion, but no such luck despite the big Friday evening crowd.

I held the door open for Dakota and an older couple as we were leaving the theater. As Dakota stepped outside and passed beneath the neon marquee, something caught my eye. I hurried down the sidewalk and reached for her arm.

Dakota stopped, glanced at my hand on her forearm, and grinned. "Wow, McClellan, you're actually touching me, and in public no less."

"Never mind that." I motioned toward O'Malley's entrance. "Do me a favor. Walk back under the marquee and stand there a minute."

Dakota stared at me like I had a few loose screws, but she turned and headed back. "Stop," I said when she'd passed under the glow of the neon lights again. "Now, take a couple of steps back this way."

Dakota blew out a breath and rolled her eyes as she took exaggerated baby steps toward me.

"Whoa, stay right there."

She huffed again, louder this time. "I'm not your friggin' Irish setter, McClellan."

Ouch. That little remark brought on a few stares from people still filing out or milling around the theater. But Dakota was right. I'd been ordering her around like I was still a first sergeant in the Marines; I figured I'd better mend my ways, and quick. "I know, and I'm sorry. Okay, would you turn around real slow, pretty please?"

She was now directly beneath the glow of the big O'Malley's neon script that alternately flashed deep orange, white, and green. With every sequence of orange, Dakota's dyed strawberry-blonde hair turned reddish—the same shade as the woman I'd bumped into the night Kate saw Wes Harrison.

CHAPTER 16

All that weekend the scene kept looping through my mind like an annoying video trailer that wouldn't go away: Kate's resurrected Wes Harrison coming into my peripheral vision. At the last second I sidestepped to avoid him and bumped headlong into a redhead with a knockout figure clutching his arm. Could it possibly have been Alice Spence outside O'Malley's Theater that night?

I wracked my brain trying again to remember even a glimpse of a face, but I struck out. I tried to recall how tall the woman was. Her breasts had pressed against my ribcage, putting us close enough to enjoy a great slow dance; that much I was sure of. Unless she'd been wearing some serious high heels, that would put her in the neighborhood of Alice's height.

Dakota wasn't among my suspects, of course, but her height and figure were a good match to compare with Alice's. Rachel Todd had natural red hair, but she was shorter and more petite than Alice, at least she had been when the beach photo of her posing with Kate, Wes, and Eric was taken. There was always the possibility of high heels and a boob job. If Harrison had been transformed under some whiz surgeon's knife, why not Rachel? Or Eric Kohler, aka Travis Hurt, too?

I remembered how startled Alice looked when she answered the door at her aunt's house. She'd even taken a step back from me. Now, the more I thought about it, the flimsier her excuse about thinking I was the FedEx man became. She knew I was supposed to be there in a few minutes. Had she suddenly recognized me as the guy she'd run into under the marquee at O'Malley's and failed to hide her surprise?

And then there was the fact that she had admitted dating Wes Harrison during her frequent visits to the coast before the boating incident.

Alice had also been quick to doubt Kate's word that she'd seen Harrison in O'Malley's lobby.

I'd hated algebra in high school. It ranked right up there with chemistry as my all-time least-favorite subjects. But I did recall one thing I learned during the endless, boring hours I'd spent in algebra class: two negatives equal a positive.

As much as I hated the math, things were starting to add up.

Tuesday afternoon around four I was leaving Walmart in Parkersville, where I'd picked up a couple of boxes of .357 ammo and a few grocery items. As I turned onto the outside lane a black car sped past and whipped into my lane, nearly clipping my front fender.

Damn idiot, probably yakking or texting on the phone, I thought, just as I noticed the decal centered near the bottom of the back window: *Chipola College Indians*, with a brave wearing a bandana and war paint snarling back at me. It was the BMW I'd seen parked at the beach house on 31st Street. Dakota attended Chipola part-time. I figured there must be a connection there somewhere.

I sped up and closed the gap enough to see the reflection of a young woman in the BMW's side-view mirror; the tinted windows kept me from seeing much else besides her shoulder-length hair. I decided to back off and follow for a while, even though the Beamer was heading west and away from St. George. What the hell, none of my groceries were perishable and I had nothing on my plate for the rest of the day. With any luck I might just learn a thing or two that might be of interest to J.D.

Just past the city-limit sign the BMW turned right onto Highway 75, one of several routes running north from the Panhandle coast to the Alabama and Georgia state lines. Highway 75 passed through the small crossroads town of Dobro, located in the northwestern corner of Palmetto County. For years it had been one of the most heavily traveled north-south roads in the area due to the greyhound dog track built in Dobro in the mid-1950s.

Like Frank said, the Florida Panhandle is Bible Belt country, and I'd heard from Jerry and Donna Meadows that a sizeable number of the county's residents had nearly rioted when the track was built. I could believe it, because last year, six decades after the track opened, the Palmetto Royale Casino & Resort was added to the complex. Plans were also in the works to four-lane the highway from the Georgia line to Dobro and then on to the coast. For months the controversial Royale topped the local news, and there was no end to the bitching and moaning from the Bible-thumping crowd.

"Gambling is a sin against God, and Palmetto County will certainly feel His mighty wrath because of its evil ways!" I still remembered that proclamation from one of the holier-than-thou local reverends quoted on the front page of the *Parkersville Independent* one morning. Never mind that the casino/resort produced a couple hundred much-needed jobs and was projected to add hundreds of thousands in tax revenue per year to the county coffers during a struggling economy.

My hackles started to rise thinking how some of those same hypocrite preachers probably held weekly bingo games in their churches. But my real beef with the Bible crowd dated back to Iraq. Since Fallujah I'd lost my taste for God and anyone who spouted off about him. Too many of my Marines bled and died in that cesspool of a city, and despite what the chaplains claimed, the Almighty was nowhere to be found. I was damned sick of hearing all the religious, flag-waving chicken hawks cheering our military on to victory while they sat at home on their sorry fat asses.

The flashing of the BMW's turn signal snapped me out of my road hypnosis. The car made a right into a corner convenience store parking lot. I passed by the store and turned right onto the adjacent road, continued on for another block or so, and pulled over onto the shoulder. I'd have to depend on my rearview or side-view mirrors to spot the Beamer when it left the store.

Less than five minutes passed before I caught sight of the black car crossing the intersection heading north. I checked traffic, hung a U-turn and then a right back onto Highway 75. A red Ford Taurus had crossed before I made my turn and was now between the BMW and my pickup. That was fine with me. I could still easily follow the target car while the Taurus provided cover. Another PI tip I'd read about in Frank's books.

There were two men sitting in the front of the Ford, and for whatever reason the driver had pulled dangerously close to the back bumper of the BMW. Probably a couple of young horny toads trying to flirt with the girl, I figured. A few miles up the road a slender hand and bare forearm rose out of the driver's side window of the Beamer. Something small and white went flying up and back, sparked off the Taurus, and scurried erratically in the road ahead. I slowed and straddled a half-smoked cigarette with a white filter.

When I glanced up, the Taurus had pulled alongside the BMW, and from the wild gesturing going on inside both vehicles I figured the occupants weren't have a social chat. An oncoming semi was closing fast. The Taurus driver laid on the horn and sped ahead as the slender hand appeared from the Beamer's window again and flipped him off. The girl had attitude, that much was certain. Not much common sense, but mucho moxie.

Since leaving Parkersville, billboards enticing visitors to the Dobro Greyhound Race Track and the new Palmetto Royale Casino & Resort dotted the roadside about every mile. Muzzled dogs chasing an ever-elusive rabbit; young ladies sporting tuxes dealing poker and blackjack; one-arm bandits flashing triple cherries, discount overnight packages, and free complimentary drinks—what wasn't to like? There was even a supervised Magic Playland available twenty-four/seven for the kiddies while parents with dollar signs in their eyes hit the jackpot or gambled away their future. Now, only a couple of miles from the junction of Highway 75 and the east-west Highway 22, the billboards came every quarter mile, announcing that fun, games, relaxation, and entertainment were just ahead.

I'd slowed down a little when the Taurus passed the BMW and let another car pass and run cover for me. At the intersection of 75 and 22 the Beamer turned left, and the cover car continued north toward the racetrack entrance just ahead. The light turned red before I could make my turn. I pulled forward enough to watch the BMW travel another eighth-mile or so, signal a right turn, and then disappear behind tall palm trees standing like an oasis in the midst of a forest of native pines. Welcome to the Palmetto Royale Casino & Resort.

⁓

I cruised around the parking lot a couple of times but didn't find the black BMW. There was a guard shack and gate at the head of a road leading to the resort area, but I wasn't in the mood to try to bullshit my way past security. I decided to give up on finding the Beamer and snoop around the casino for a while.

Inside, the Royale was pretty much like all the other casinos I'd seen, meaning the few I'd visited during a couple of weekend trips to Vegas while stationed at Camp Pendleton during my Corps career. Think bright, gaudy, posh, and you've got it nailed. Flashing lights, plenty of glass and mirrors, the clicking of dozens of slot machines, and a steady chorus of voices rising and falling at the tables along with the gamblers' luck.

I stopped by a cashier's window, shelled out ten bucks for a roll of quarters, and headed for the slots. A young brunette decked out in black shorts and a white Hooter's-style T-shirt with a royal flush spread across the front strutted over and took my complimentary "Welcome to the Royale!" drink order. I fed a machine a quarter and punched the spin button while I watched her head for the bar. *Palmetto Royale Casino & Resort* was spelled out in an arch across the upper back in red letters shadowed with gold, with *The hottest game in town!* written in fancy cursive below. My mind spun like the symbols in the slot's window, and then I remembered the T-shirt draped over the lawn chair at the 31st Street beach house.

One of the residents of the house Dakota wanted J.D. to keep an eye on probably worked here, most likely Beamer girl. But this was county territory, out of J.D.'s jurisdiction. Something must be going on at the house that wasn't on the up-and-up, but how would Dakota know about—

I stopped in mid-thought as I glanced across the room at a black-jack table and noticed the dealer, an attractive young woman with red-dish-blonde hair. She was wearing a fancy ruffled white blouse, tight black pants complete with cummerbund and suspenders, and a bow tie. I blinked and looked again. I'm pretty damn sure my mouth fell open when I saw for certain it was Dakota.

So *this* was the mysterious part-time job she was so hesitant to talk about. Without waiting for my complimentary drink I scooped up my quarters and headed Dakota's way. I was still several yards away but close enough to hear her chatting and laughing with the few patrons sitting around her table when she spotted me. Her brow furrowed and her lips pressed together as she gave an almost imperceptible shake of her head.

I returned a slight nod and walked on by toward another row of slot machines lined against the wall about thirty feet behind Dakota's table. Dakota's reaction and my gut convinced me that this wasn't the time or place for a casual social visit, but I was damned near as curious as the proverbial cat.

I'd spent a few fruitless minutes feeding quarters to my current one-armed thief and scoping out the room for any sign of familiar faces or busty redheads when I heard a voice call out, "There you are!"

I turned at the sound of the voice to see the cute brunette approaching, carrying a round tray filled with various cocktails and glasses of beer. She set the tray on the stool next to my machine and lifted a tumbler from the assortment. "Dewar's on the rocks," she said, smiling as she carefully placed my drink and a Palmetto Royale coaster on a small table beside my bandit. "Are we having any luck?"

"Yeah, all bad so far," I said as I grabbed my wallet and handed her an Honest Abe for my "free" drink, which just about evened the score.

She smiled and thanked me and slipped the bill in her shorts pocket. "You just keep on trying, honey, 'cause you look like a winner to me." She patted my arm. "By the way, my name's Brianna." She pointed to a name tag pinned above the 10 of Hearts. Wonder how I'd missed that before? "You just holler if you need anything, anything at all." Then she winked, picked up the tray, and sauntered off.

Anything? Okay, Brianna, I've got a question for you. Just who the hell is Dakota? The ragamuffin, trash-talking beach brawler I first laid eyes on outside The Green Parrot; the sweet-talking tuxedoed charmer dealing cards at the blackjack table; or somebody else altogether?

I sipped the Scotch, remembering one of my parents' favorite TV programs—*To Tell the Truth*—that they used to watch religiously as a young married couple. I'd seen a few grainy black-and-white reruns from the 1950s and '60s game show myself when I was a kid.

As host Bud Collyer would say when the celebrity panelists had finished grilling the three contestants, and the audience was on the edge of their seats with anticipation, "Will the real Dakota Blaire Owens please stand up?"

CHAPTER 17

On the drive home my mind was in a flurry. A month and a half had passed since Kate claimed she saw Wes Harrison in the lobby at O'Malley's. I'd learned a lot about the principals involved in the so-called boating disaster, but I was no closer to proving Wes Harrison was still among the living, or that he had any real motive to have staged the "accident," either by himself or with the phony Eric Kohler. I didn't think for a minute that Robert Ramey was in on any scheme. If my theory was correct, Ramey was the innocent victim here. He'd suspected that someone in his employ was dealing conflict diamonds and contacted the authorities with whatever suspicions or info he had. Somehow Harrison and Hurt got wind of it and made sure Ramey paid the ultimate price to cover their asses.

Rachel Todd's connection and past history with Hurt was interesting and added other possibilities to the case, especially the fact that she became an overnight millionaire when her adoptive parents conveniently perished in a house fire only hours after she'd returned to Pensacola from her holiday visit. And Rachel's supposed untimely demise somewhere in the South American jungles two weeks after the boating incident only thickened the Mulligan stew.

Throw in Kate's discovery of the conflict diamonds and altered paperwork among Harrison's possessions; add Alice Spence—Robert Ramey's cousin and his mother's caretaker—and her romantic ties to Wes Harrison, and the damn stewpot was getting so full it was in danger of spilling over.

And yet, what did I have? Nothing that I could prove and take to the bank. There were too many dots already connected for this whole thing to be coincidental, but my dot-to-dot pen had run out of ink. I needed more.

I had a strong hunch Alice Spence was somehow further involved in this mess other than being Wes Harrison's past flame and Mrs. Ramey's current caretaker. It seemed improbable that a young woman with her looks and education would be whiling away the prime of her life playing nursemaid to a near-invalid elderly aunt. There had to more to Alice than that.

There also had to be more to Dakota Blaire Owens, and I was determined to pay her a visit ASAP.

I also started wondering about a few other things I'd overlooked. If Robert Ramey left his lover Eric Kohler a million-dollar life insurance policy, and Eric's "sister" Rachel Todd was the beneficiary, what the hell happened to that money and the other cool millions sweet Rachel had inherited from the Todds? I'm no lawyer, but I figured that if anyone had laid claim to Rachel Todd's estate they would've had to have access to a will or maybe power of attorney. Otherwise, whatever wealth Rachel had accumulated was probably being held by the state of Florida.

When I got back to my trailer after making the Palmetto Royale Casino half a roll of quarters richer, I booted up my laptop and began digging. God bless Al Gore for creating the Internet! Since Rachel Todd had no known living relatives, I didn't know if a death certificate had been issued for her or not, but I did quickly learn that Florida death records aren't available online. Info on wills, however, is another matter.

After a few minutes of searching I learned that a Florida resident's will is not public record unless it's been filed with the clerk of court of the county in which the decedent resided, which in Rachel's case was Escambia County. Will custodians are required to file a decedent's will with the clerk within ten days after receiving notification of the person's death. Once the person dies and the will is filed with the county clerk, it becomes public record. The only catch is, John Q. Public has to visit the county clerk's office in person and request to view the records.

I got on the horn with Frank right away. "Can you get to the Escambia County Courthouse tomorrow or sometime this week and find out if Rachel Todd has a will on file?"

"And good evening to you too, Mac."

"Sorry, Frank. Look, if Harrison and Hurt pulled off some scheme and Rachel was in on it, it doesn't make sense that they would let the money she inherited from the Todds and Brother Eric sit in the state's coffers, would it? My bet is she made some kind of arrangement so they could get hold of that money later, after things cooled down."

"That sounds reasonable. By the way, how is Katie?"

"Your guess is as good as mine. How about it, can you get to Pensacola and check it out for me?"

Frank let out a long sigh. "Sure. It might take a couple of days. I'll be in touch by the end of the week."

"Thanks, I appreciate it."

"Another 'by the way' for you, Mac. While I'm in Pensacola running errands for my partner, what are you up to?"

"If I can't find what I'm looking for online, I'm headed back to Atlanta."

～⌒

After giving Frank the update, I called Dakota's number but got no answer then or the next morning. It looked like my little visit would have to wait until mystery girl was ready to make herself available again.

Over the next two days I spent several hours searching the Internet for any info I could dig up on Alice Spence. In particular, I wanted a good up-to-date color photo. I found her listed on LinkedIn and Facebook, but the photos were not much use for what I needed. I could've tried "friending" Alice on Facebook to obtain access to her photo page, but I figured that might appear just a wee bit suspicious.

In order to gain access to Alice's LinkedIn page, I created my own account with LinkedIn, listing myself minimally as a retired Marine and an investigative consultant. When I clicked onto Alice's profile I struck pay dirt. She not only held an MBA from Georgia Tech but was also a certified massage therapist and certified personal fitness trainer. Both of these degrees she'd earned from Gwinnett College's Atlanta-area campus. That would help explain Alice's great figure and the exercise outfit she was wearing the day of my visit.

There was a link to a web page next to her massage and fitness trainer listings. I clicked on it and learned that Alice offered scheduled in-house massage and fitness training sessions only; call such-and-such number for an appointment. Living in Atlanta's Buckhead area, I figured she must cater to a real upper-crust clientele. Just for the hell of it I jotted down the number in my notebook. You never know.

There was something even more interesting on Alice's LinkedIn site. She was listed as president and manager of Spence-Ramey Investments, a private investment partnership. I had no idea what a "PIP" was, but it jumped right to the top of my "to find out" list. I immediately searched on Google for "private investment partnerships" and came up with some interesting info. A lot of what I found was legalese Greek to me, but this much seemed clear enough: At the most basic level, a private investment partnership is simply a hedge fund—investors put their money in a fund to be managed, for a fee, by a full-time professional. In the case of Spence-Ramey Investments, that was Alice.

Unlike mutual funds, in exchange for less regulation and oversight from the Securities and Exchange Commission, PIPs aren't allowed to advertise or market themselves to the general public. Instead, they solicit what's known as "accredited investors," which in most cases means having up to ninety-nine investors with a net worth of at least a million bucks each.

I also learned that it's common and generally expected that the manager of a PIP have a substantial amount of his or her own net worth in the fund alongside their investors' money. That's a powerful safeguard against any shenanigans and also a nice incentive for the manager to make sound decisions. The one or two percent management fee and twenty percent of net profits earned off each investor's dollar was probably another nice carrot to entice Alice to eagerly take on the managerial role. It was also a nice coup for Spence-Ramey that PIPs aren't usually required to disclose their activities or holdings to the SEC or public. Alice Spence had certainly put the MBA she earned from Georgia Tech to good use.

I still needed a recent photo of Alice to show around. Remembering my previous online search to find out if Mrs. Ramey was still alive and breathing, I typed in the URL for the *Atlanta Journal-Constitution* and entered "Alice Spence" in the site's search engine.

Bingo! Alice's name popped up under several headings. I clicked on the first one, a feature in the Lifestyles section showcasing upscale homes and their owners in the Greater Atlanta area. A close-up photo of Alice sitting in the very chair I'd sat in near the fireplace appeared on the monitor, the first of seventeen photos. The caption read: *Business woman and certified masseuse/fitness trainer Alice Spence relaxes beside a native stone fireplace in the parlor of the late 19th-Century Buckhead mansion she shares with her widowed aunt, Mrs. Edmond Randolph (Darla) Ramey.*

Damn, I'd almost forgotten just how beautiful Alice was. She wore a big smile and a plunging V-neck royal-blue dress with sleeves just past the elbows. Her legs were crossed in a ladylike fashion, and the dress was hiked up a few inches above the knees, leaving plenty to the active imagination. The strawberry-blonde locks were parted just right of center and cascaded well past her shoulders, framing her cleavage.

Alice was decked out with enough yellow gold to open her own jewelry store. A pair of leaping dolphins on a braided chain hung above her breasts, and more fingers than not sported rings. From the slight tilt of Alice's head, one dangling earring was visible. She wore a braided bracelet on her right wrist and a watch on her left, both gold, of course. I wondered just how much of the bling was courtesy of late Cousin Bobby's generosity that Alice had mentioned.

I quickly scanned through the rest of the photos, tastefully done interior and exterior shots like you'd see in magazines such as *Better Homes and Gardens* or *Southern Living*. Then I downloaded all the photos in the feature to my hard drive. Later I planned to crop and enlarge Alice's photo as much as I could without losing resolution and then print a few copies on photo-quality paper to show Dakota and J.D. and whoever else I could come up with.

I was just about burned-out with all the computer research I'd been doing the past couple of days. It was happy hour. I grabbed a beer and headed outside to my picnic table. Tomorrow I planned to do some fishing, using the photos of Alice Spence and Wes Harrison as bait.

CHAPTER 18

Friday morning after breakfast I discovered I was down to one wrinkled sheet of photo paper, so I headed to the Walmart in Parkersville. I'd just passed the St. George city limit sign when my phone rang.

"Mac, it's Mark Bell. Kate's been in a wreck."

A cold fist squeezed my gut. "Is she okay? What happened?"

"She left after work last night to spend a long weekend with Mom and Dad. Her car ran off the highway and flipped. She's got a concussion and a lot of bumps and bruises, but nothing too serious. It scared the crap out of us, but the doctor says she'll be fine."

"I'm headed your way. Where's the hospital?"

"She's in Parkersville, Mac, room 218. The wreck happened just a couple of miles out of St. George. She made me promise to call you first thing this morning. I think that speaks for itself."

～

When I stepped into Kate's room I forced a smile to hide my shock at her appearance. The left side of her face was swollen, leaving that eye barely a slit. Her lips were puffy, and most of the skin that wasn't hidden by the bandage wrapped around her head was various shades of purple. She was hooked to a monitor and an IV drip. She held a hand out to me. I took it in both of mine and gently pressed it to my cheek. "I love you," I choked out.

"I love you, too," she said, barely moving her lips when she spoke. "You're not upset with me?"

I squeezed her hand and smiled again. "No, I'm just glad you're okay. How do you feel?"

Kate let out a weary sigh. "About like I look, I guess."

"You look fine, considering."

"Liar. I made Mom loan me her compact."

"You're still beautiful to me."

Kate started to laugh, but it quickly turned into a groan. "Thanks, Mac. You need to visit the eye doctor."

I grinned. "I just did. He said I've got twenty-twenty."

Kate suffered through another laugh. She started to say something, but I touched her lips with my index finger. "Don't try to talk. I better run and let you get your beauty rest." I leaned down and gently kissed her forehead. "I'll see you later today, okay?"

"You better," Kate said as a single tear trickled from the corner of her swollen eye.

Kate's parents, a fine-looking, friendly enough couple given the circumstances, took up the vigil in Kate's room while Mark and I headed to the hospital cafeteria to grab a cup of coffee. Mostly, I wanted to ask him a few questions.

"What the hell caused her to run off the road?" I said as we sat in the cafeteria over steaming mugs. Kate was a safe driver. The few times I'd ridden shotgun in her car she'd always kept her eyes on the road, even while we were talking.

"I think something in the front end broke," Mark said, adding a half-pack of sugar to his coffee. "Kate said it felt like the right front wheel suddenly fell off. It dug into the pavement, and the next thing she knew the car was rolling and she ended up in a ditch. Thank God for seat belts and airbags."

"Yeah." I took another sip of coffee as a red flag waved in my head. "Her car's only two years old. Honda makes good stuff. Things don't just fall off of a car that new with low mileage."

Mark finished a bite of the doughnut he'd ordered with his coffee. "Kate mentioned she'd been hearing a clunking noise for a couple of days. She was going to have our uncle's Honda dealership check it out today. That's one reason she was coming home this weekend."

"Damn. If I'd known about it I would've made her take it to the one here in Parkersville right away."

"Don't blame yourself, Mac. She bought the car from our Uncle John for just over cost, and he always gives the family a good discount in his service shop."

"Anybody talk to the sheriff's office or Highway Patrol yet?"

Mark shook his head as he stirred his coffee. "We came here as soon as we got the call."

"Who made the call?"

Another shake of the head. "I don't know. My parents were pretty much in a panic. I don't think we talked about it on the way over. We just wanted to make sure Kate was going to be okay."

"You come in separate cars?"

"No, I drove. Mom and Dad were both pretty shook up."

"Any idea what they did with Kate's car?"

"No, not yet. I guess we'll have it hauled to my uncle's shop when the insurance people are finished with it."

"Not if it's totaled. The insurance company owns it then."

Mark licked some sugary glaze off his fingers. "I hadn't thought about that."

I finished my coffee and stood. "I'm heading to the sheriff's office. You want to come with me?"

Mark held up a finger as he finished swallowing a bite. "I better stick around here in case my parents need me."

"Okay, I'll see you later this afternoon. You still got my number?"

He patted his back pants pocket. "Right here."

"You call me if there's any change or if Kate needs me. Got it?" The Top Sergeant in me was snapping orders again.

"You bet."

"McClellan, long time, no see. I've been expecting you. Grab a seat." Sheriff Bo Pickron motioned to a padded wooden chair at the right-front corner of his cluttered desk. He didn't bother to offer a hand, which was fine by me. Since I'd set foot in Palmetto County a year ago our relationship had been more like coarse sandpaper than smooth glass, although he had deputized me to work undercover for him on Maddie Harper's murder case last summer.

The circumstances leading up to my short tour of duty as a county cop were a bit muddled. Basically, I discovered Maddie's body while fishing, and she just happened to be Pickron's niece. After being implicated in her death, I set out to prove my innocence and find the real killer. Once the sheriff was convinced I had nothing to do with Maddie's death, he figured I might make convenient bait for the real perpetrator. The fact that Pickron and Kate had dated briefly when she first moved to St. George didn't do much to endear him to me either.

I dragged the chair closer to the center of the desk and sat. "What can you tell me about Kate's accident last night?"

Pickron leaned forward and planted his muscular forearms on the desktop with his hands clasped. He was tall and built like an NFL line-backer. His bulldoggish face was topped by a military-style buzz-cut, a holdover from his days as an Army chopper pilot. Pickron had earned the Distinguished Flying Cross during the fiasco in Somalia. As much as I disliked the guy personally, I had to salute his courage under fire. "A passerby called 911. One of my deputies beat the ambulance to the scene. Kate was unconscious but had a good pulse and didn't appear to be bleeding badly. My deputy made sure she didn't move until the EMTs arrived and took over."

"What about her car?"

"Looks like it rolled a couple of times. Last I heard FHP is still working on their reconstruction."

"Where's the car?"

"We've got it impounded while our investigators go over it."

I wasn't surprised to hear somebody other than me thought it strange that a front wheel would just fall off, but I had to ask. "Why?"

"The guy driving the wrecker said it looked like the front right wheel came off. He took a closer look and thinks somebody might've tampered with something. If that's the case, my guys will find out."

"And you'll let me know?"

The sheriff's eyes narrowed, and he let out a breath. "You know, McClellan, you're not real high up on my favorite people list, but since you risked your ass for my niece, I feel like I owe you one. So yeah, I'll let you know what we find."

"I appreciate it," I said as I stood to leave.

"Hey, McClellan."

I stopped short of the door and glanced back.

"Don't make more out of this than what it is. Chances are it'll turn out to be a cut-and-dried mechanical failure. Nothing more."

"Right." I walked out of his office.

"And don't go sticking your nose into county business again," Pickron called as I headed down the hallway.

Despite the sheriff's assurance that he'd keep me in the loop, I didn't trust Bo Pickron any farther than I could throw him, and I damn sure couldn't heave two hundred and fifty pounds of muscle and boneheaded ego very far. So, I made a few inquiries before I left the department. It didn't take long to find out that White's Towing & Salvage had handled the wrecker service for Kate's CR-V last night.

I headed west on Highway 98 to the outskirts of Parkersville where White's was located. A short drive north on Sandy Bayou Road brought me to the tall, slatted chain-link fence surrounding the several acres of White's salvage yard. I drove through the open gate and parked the Silverado between a NAPA delivery truck and a midsixties primer-gray and Bondo Mustang.

A couple of customers were seated on stools at the counter flipping through inventory books. Behind the counter a young man with receding blond hair was chatting on the phone. Near him, a husky older man with slicked-back silver hair looked up from a parts catalog. "Can I help you?"

Ted was embroidered on the nametag sewn above the left breast pocket of his dark-blue work shirt. "I hope so. I'd like to speak with the driver on duty who worked the single-car accident just west of St. George last night. Honda CR-V, metallic green."

Ted's bushy eyebrows arched. "You a cop?"

"No." I reached in my shirt pocket and pulled out one of Frank's cards and handed it to Ted. "I'm with Hightower Investigations," I said, using the best PI voice I could muster. Watching those old Sam Spade flicks does have its rewards. "The driver's family asked us to look into the accident before the insurance hounds come sniffing around."

Ted glanced at the card and handed it back. "The county boys impounded it."

"Yeah, I know. I just want to ask your guy a couple of questions, strictly off the record."

Ted stared me down a few seconds, and then his face relaxed. "Okay, as long as it's off the record. I don't want Bo Pickron on my case."

"Off the record. You got my word."

"Charlie Baumgartner." Ted turned and pointed to the east side of the yard. "He's out yonder near the fence pulling a radiator and fan off a Pontiac. Third row."

I thanked Ted and hurried out the door. It hadn't rained in a week, and my shoes kicked up dust from the crushed-shell parking lot with every step I took. By the time I reached the rows of junked cars the footing had changed to trampled crabgrass, sandspurs, and other weeds. I found Charlie Baumgartner hunched over the engine compartment of a Bonneville Coupe wielding a socket wrench and a long-handled screwdriver. The car was so rusted and faded it was impossible to make out the original body color or what was left of the tattered vinyl roof.

"Muscle car," I called from about ten yards away so I wouldn't startle the guy.

Charlie lifted his upper body out of the engine well, wiped his forehead with the back of the hand holding the socket, and squinted my way. He was around thirty, short and wiry with a shock of unruly red hair sticking out from under a faded Atlanta Braves cap. "Was once. Shame she ended up junked. I had the money, I'd restore her."

"A '72?"

"Yep."

"Thought so. My old man had one when I was a kid. Four-fifty-five?"

"Yep. Only got a two-barrel, though."

"I bet it still ran like a bat out of hell in its day."

Charlie set his tools on a fender and pulled a shop rag out of his back pocket. "I'd drop a four-barrel Holley in her. Nothing 'round here could touch her then."

We sweet-talked another couple of minutes, and then it was time to get down to business. "Ted told me you worked the wreck on 98 near St. George last night."

Charlie found a clean spot on the rag and mopped his forehead. "Yep. Rollover. Hope the lady's doing okay."

"She's doing good. What do you think made the wheel come off?"

Charlie frowned. "You the police?"

That seemed to be a popular question around this place. I pulled the card out and gave Charlie the same spiel I'd used on Ted. "I heard you think somebody might've tinkered with the right front end."

"Who told you that?"

"Sheriff Pickron."

Charlie turned his head and spit. "The wheel didn't come off, it collapsed. I did some checking after I got it on the hauler. There were some deep scrape marks on the lower control arm near the weld that ought not've been there. My guess is somebody fooled with it, maybe took a cold chisel and cracked the weld. That's what I told the deputy. Reckon that's why they had me haul it to impoundment 'stead of here."

But how the hell would a person be able to take a hammer and chisel to Kate's car without somebody hearing the racket? Then it dawned on me. In nice weather Kate often rode her bicycle to work. "You drink beer, Charlie?"

He grinned. "Been known to down a few every now and again."

I reached for my wallet, pulled out an Old Hickory, and handed it to Charlie. "Buy yourself a case on me."

CHAPTER 19

I was walking past the second-floor waiting room headed for 218 when somebody called my name. I turned and saw Frank Hightower standing in the doorway. He motioned for me to follow and took a seat in a corner of the room farthest away from the wall-mounted TV. There were only two other people in the room; a young man flipping through the pages of a dog-eared *Sports Illustrated* magazine, and a portly middle-aged woman watching a black-and-white rerun of an early *Andy Griffith* episode.

"A nurse ran me out of Katie's room a few minutes ago," Frank said. "She said the doctor wants to check on her and then she needs to rest."

"Where's her parents and Mark?"

Frank ran a hand through his thick gray hair and fiddled with the collar of his light-blue dress shirt. "They went to lunch. Jim's a Captain D's addict, can you believe that? The man grew up eating fresh seafood his whole life, and now he prefers that fast food crap. Go figure."

"How was Kate when you saw her?"

"She's putting up a brave front, Mac. I'll tell you, that girl must be hurting something awful, as banged-up as she is."

"Roger that." I glanced at the others in the room and lowered my voice. "It wasn't an accident, Frank. Somebody tried to take Kate out."

His jaw dropped. "What the hell are you talking about?"

"I had a little visit with Bo Pickron this morning. The county's got her car impounded."

"Whoa, slow down, Mac. That doesn't necessarily indicate foul play. There's several reasons why they might've impound—"

"I talked to the guy who worked the wrecker. He said it looks like somebody used a chisel on the control arm. That convinced Pickron to at least have his guys check it out."

Frank clasped his hands together and rested his forearms on his thighs. "Damn."

"Yeah, my sentiments exactly. This crap is getting personal."

"Damn," Frank repeated. "Who would want to hurt Katie? And why?"

"Wes Harrison, for one. Think about it. Kate and Harrison cross paths at O'Malley's. They make eye contact, and despite all the fancy scalpel work, Harrison is pretty damn sure he's been ID'd. Then we start probing around, asking a lot of questions. Harrison knows Kate's the only one who can connect the dots after all these years since him and Kohler supposedly bought the farm. So, he decides to shut her up before his little scam is ruined."

Frank sighed. "I don't know. That's reaching some, don't you think?"

"You got any better scenarios?"

Frank shook his head. His face was pinched, and he looked like he hadn't slept in days. Just then I remembered another link to Harrison and the old gang I'd somehow overlooked. "I spoke too quick, Frank. Kate's not the only one still around with ties to Harrison's past."

He thought for a moment. "Alice Spence?"

"Roger. I'd bet my retirement check she's up to her pretty little neck in this mess somehow."

"Focus on her then, Mac. She just might lead us to Harrison."

"You're reading my mind." I decided to change the subject. "Did you make it to Pensacola?"

Frank sat upright and rubbed at the old scar above his right eyebrow. "Yeah, very interesting."

I waited while Frank kept massaging the scar. "Well?"

"Rachel Todd did leave a will. All legally witnessed and notarized."

"And?"

I waited several seconds, but Frank's thoughts seemed to have drifted off to Never-Never Land. "Christ on a crutch, Frank, come on!"

"She left her entire estate to Sacred Word Missions. The will was filed with the Escambia County Clerk of Court by one Dr. Lawrence Garrett the week after Rachel's plane disappeared. Garrett also happened to be named the will's trustee by Rachel when she drew it up."

"Trustee . . . which means?"

"Which means Garrett had legal control to administer Rachel's estate as he saw fit, under the terms of the will."

"So, by Rachel leaving everything to Sacred Word Missions, Garrett had free rein with her money?"

"There's some legal mumbo-jumbo involved, Mac, but Sacred Word being a not-for-profit organization, that about sums it up. I believe a five-year waiting period is the max, but if good reason was shown that the decedent was exposed to a specific peril of death, that could be waived."

"And a pilot suddenly veering off course and disappearing somewhere in the Amazon jungle would probably stand a good chance of qualifying as a peril of death."

"My money says it would."

"This whole mess is starting to stink."

"How's that?"

"The day Kate and I visited Sacred Word; at first Garrett acted like he barely remembered Rachel. But after we pressed him a little he did a one-eighty and started spouting all kinds of info about her. Now that I think about it, that just didn't fit. Seems to me if an attractive young employee, and a pilot at that, left a few million bucks to your organization *and* made you the trustee, you wouldn't have a very hard time remembering who she was."

Frank chuckled. "I doubt I would."

"There's something else. I remember Garrett saying they didn't give up hope of finding Rachel alive until several weeks after her plane went missing. Yet he filed the will with the clerk of court the week after she disappeared. What's with that?"

Frank shrugged. "I'm not sure, but I believe Florida law states that a will should be filed within ten days of the death."

When Frank said that, I remembered reading something about "ten days" during my research on Florida wills. "Fine and dandy. But the guy claimed they beat the bushes looking for Rachel for weeks. I do know this much—Garrett's starting to smell like last week's garbage."

Kate proved to be a fast healer. On Monday the bandages came off, and by Wednesday most of the bruising had all but disappeared. The hospital discharged her Thursday morning, and she returned to Destin with Mark and their parents to finish recuperating at the family home. I'd spent as much time at Kate's beside during her hospital stay as the nurses would allow and made sure I didn't come across as a nuisance to her folks. By the time the Bells returned home, I'd developed enough rapport with the family to feel comfortable around them and to accept an open invitation to visit as often as I could.

Meanwhile, I'd used the time to mull over and rethink the case and all its details from top to bottom. Sheriff Pickron's investigators determined there was inconclusive evidence that Kate's car had been tampered with. There were the scrape marks that Charlie Baumgartner claimed were made by somebody wielding a cold chisel, but Kate might have previously run over some debris that caused them. The control arm could have been a factory defect. Insufficient evidence of a crime was the department's final determination. The "accident" was most likely the result of a mechanical failure, just as Bo Pickron had predicted. Bullshit. I put my money on Charlie.

My instincts told me that Robert Ramey's sweet cousin Alice was involved one way or another. Her past involvement with Wes Harrison; the surprised look on her face when she'd greeted me at her doorstep in Atlanta; the way she'd quickly dismissed as "far-fetched" Kate's claim that she'd seen Harrison at O'Malley's. Alice Spence was just too damn squeaky-clean for me to swallow.

The evening after Kate left for Destin I dug through the daily newspaper and retrieved a pink flyer insert for a mobile-unit prostate screening that was blank on the back side. Why the hell they picked pink for a prostate ad was beyond me, but I needed a blank sheet of paper and there was no use wasting perfectly good printing paper to scribble on.

Years ago I'd read a mystery novel, probably from the Hardy

Boys. The sleuths had drawn a diagram listing all the pertinent people involved in the case, and by using a sort of connect-the-dots system had nailed down or eliminated the most likely suspects. What the hell, if it was good enough for Frank and Joe Hardy, it was good enough for me.

I opened my catch-all drawer, found a pencil with a good eraser, grabbed a beer from the fridge, and sat at the table. I drew a crude boat inside a big circle in the center of the page and jotted the names Robert Ramey, Wes Harrison, and Eric Kohler/Travis Hurt around the boat. At top center I wrote and circled Rachel Todd; bottom center was Lawrence Garrett. Left of the page was Kate's circle. Mrs. Darla Ramey's and Alice Spence's circles shared the right of the page. Then I started wracking my brain, trying to connect the dots or, in this case, arrows pointing to who was involved with who, and how.

Three beers and an hour later I sat admiring my detective work. Hell, even old Sherlock himself would've been proud of my deductive reasoning. On second thought, probably not.

Kohler/Hurt, Wes Harrison, and Robert Ramey had the obvious connection of working together and, supposedly, dying together. Kohler had a long-standing relationship with his phony half-sister Rachel Todd dating back to their days in the Texas orphanage. He also had a fling with Ramey, and he knew Alice Spence on a friendly but casual basis.

Wes Harrison was romantically involved with Alice Spence and was Kate's main squeeze.

Robert Ramey knew Kohler intimately, knew Harrison from work, and was close to his mother and younger cousin, Alice.

Rachel Todd was lovers with phony half-brother Kohler, knew Harrison and Ramey through Kohler, and was friendly enough with Kate to have had her picture taken at a beach outing with Kate and Harrison and Kohler. She'd also met and befriended Alice Spence at one of Ramey's parties. And, she worked for Lawrence Garrett, making her the only person on the page with a known connection to Garrett.

Kate was in love with Wes Harrison, good friends with Eric Kohler, and had rubbed elbows with Rachel Todd in social settings, although their friendship was casual at best.

Lawrence Garrett was Rachel Todd's boss and had obviously done enough background checking to know about Rachel's time in the orphanage, her adoption by the Todds, as well as her education in Christian mission studies and pilot training. He was also named the trustee of Rachel's will, which left her entire estate to Garrett's Sacred Word Missions—a somewhat baffling event considering Rachel had worked less than two years with Sacred Word when her plane disappeared.

Darla Spence Ramey, widow of Edmond Randolph Ramey, mother of Robert, and "Dear Aunt Darla" to niece Alice Spence, was well aware of her son's relationship with Eric Kohler but had no idea Harrison and Kate were an item. That was about the extent of the elderly woman's knowledge as far as I could figure.

Alice Spence seemed to have been very close to "Cousin Bobby," given the amount of time she spent at his home in Sandestin. She was infatuated with Wes Harrison, who was friends with Eric Kohler and Rachel Todd, but didn't recall ever meeting Kate Bell. Add in her current roles as caretaker to Aunt Darla and president of Spence-Ramey Investments, and the pot was beginning to simmer.

I got up for another beer but decided to change to something stronger. I poured a hefty shot of Dewar's into a tumbler and sat back down at the table. The more I studied the pattern of circles and arrows, the more confused I got. I grabbed my Scotch and the scrambled drawing and headed for the picnic table, hoping the fresh air would clear my head.

The sun had sunk below the shadowy pines, leaving a faint orange glow filtering through the trunks. Far out over the gulf, thunder rumbled. I glanced at the scribbled mess that I'd hoped would help clear things up, but by then it was almost too dark to see. What the hell, it didn't much matter anyway. I wadded up the pink sheet and tossed it at the garbage can with the upended lid on top standing next to the steps of the camper. It banked off the siding and fell into the lid. Ringer—three points for me. Whoopee.

CHAPTER 20

I'd spent a near sleepless night tossing and turning with visions of my crude drawing dancing through my head. Conclusion? Alice Spence. Someway, somehow, she was involved in the Wes Harrison case. The fact that Alice's surname was listed first in Spence-Ramey Investments suggested she'd somehow gained control of the Ramey fortune—probably all legal and aboveboard as Aunt Darla's power of attorney. Alice was too damn savvy to let a legal loophole get in her way.

Kate swore she'd seen Wes Harrison at O'Malley's, and I'd bumped head-on into an attractive redhead that could've been Alice Spence—based on Alice's height and figure and her reaction when she'd opened the door at her aunt's house during my Atlanta visit. If I'd only had the wits to notice her face that night, that little mystery might already be solved. Too late now. Some PI.

Knowing that Dakota worked at the casino gave me a hunch she just might've seen Harrison around the place, maybe Alice too, if she was the redhead I'd bumped into that night. Alice and Harrison *had* been romantically involved, and if he was still alive, who knew? What the hell, the odds weren't good, but it was worth a shot. So I drove by Dakota's place on the chance she might be home. Her old Corolla was parked in the driveway. I climbed the stairs to her garage apartment and rang the doorbell.

"Hey, McClellan." A disheveled, bleary-eyed Dakota dressed in a man's striped button-up shirt raised a hand to stifle a yawn. I assumed she had panties on underneath. "What brings you here so early this fine Friday morning?"

I tapped my watch. "It's after eleven. We need to talk."

Dakota yawned again, this time not bothering to lift a hand. She stepped aside and waved me in. I walked into the kitchen area, modern and well-equipped with stainless steel appliances. Beyond an island was the living room, nicely furnished but a bit messy for my liking.

"I need some coffee," Dakota said, "you want some?"

"Sure, thanks." For some reason I sniffed the air and noticed there wasn't a trace of tobacco smoke. I glanced around for ashtrays but came up empty. For all Dakota's talk and bravado, I'd never detected the odor of cigarettes on her clothes, hair, or breath, and we'd gotten pretty damn up-close and personal.

Dakota made her way to the coffeemaker near the sink. She dumped the old grounds down the garbage disposal, opened a cabinet, and reached for a can of Maxwell House. The shirt hiked halfway up her butt, revealing a skimpy pair of beige panties. "So, what's up?" she said, pouring fresh grounds from the can into the basket.

"You give up smoking?"

She turned to face me with a blank expression and then grinned. "Oh, that. Yeah, you proud of me?"

"Good for you."

Dakota pointed to the manila envelope in my hand. "What you got there?"

"Business. Let's wait for the coffee."

While the coffee dripped, Dakota disappeared through the living room to get dressed, I assumed. She returned just as the coffeemaker gave a final sigh and the beeper sounded. She was wearing the same shirt with a pair of faded denim shorts. The sleep was washed from her eyes, and her hair was brushed and pulled back into a ponytail. Dakota reached for a cup inside the sink, glanced into it, and grabbed a second cup from an overhead cabinet. After pouring the coffee she joined me at the table.

"Thanks," I said, reaching for the cup she'd taken from the cabinet. I took a sip of the strong, hot brew and pushed the envelope across the table. "Ever seen these two before?"

Dakota opened the envelope and pulled out the prints. She sipped her coffee, staring at them a moment. Her eyebrows rose. "Hey, I think this is the lady with the hair," she said, pointing to the photo of Alice Spence.

"The hair?"

"Yeah." Dakota grabbed her ponytail and waved it up and down. "From work, remember? The hair color I liked?"

Now I remembered; the night Dakota showed up at my camper with the bottle of Dewar's and the new hair color; the night we'd wound up in bed together after she'd tried seducing me. "Does she have a name?"

Dakota giggled. "Of course she does, McClellan. Everybody's got a name. I don't know hers, though."

"Crap. Where exactly did you see this 'lady with the hair'?"

"Upstairs. I'd just finished my shift. It was a Friday, so I clocked out and went upstairs to get my paycheck. I saw her coming out of one of the offices down the hall. I remember liking her hair color."

"Was she with anybody?"

Dakota thought a moment. "Don't think so."

"You got any idea who she is? It's important."

Dakota sipped her coffee and stared at me over the cup. "Not by name, but I asked a girl I work with about her because of the hair. She didn't know a name either but said she thought she was one of the big wheels from out of state."

"Big wheels?"

"Yeah, like an owner or investor or something."

"Have you seen her since?"

Dakota shook her head and set down the cup as she swallowed. "Nope, only that once."

"What about the guy?"

Dakota stared at the computer-generated likeness of the resurrected Wes Harrison that Frank had created in his office from Kate's description. I swore I heard her mutter "Faces ID" under her breath. She looked up, searching my eyes. "Where'd you get this?"

"Never mind. Have you seen him or not?"

Dakota blew out a breath, got up, grabbed the coffee decanter, and topped off our cups. "You can be a rude son of a bitch sometimes, you know that, McClellan? You come to my apartment, start grilling me about shit at work, and order me around like I was one of your friggin' Marine flunkies."

She was right and I knew it. Time to lighten up. "I apologize. Sometimes I have trouble shaking off twenty-four years in the Corps. Please, take a good look. Do you recognize the man?"

Dakota's face relaxed a little. She gave Harrison the once-over again. "Maybe."

"Maybe?"

"Look McClellan, this is a computer composite, not a photo, but I'm sure you already know that. I might've seen somebody who sort of looks like him, but I'm not sure."

"How close?"

Dakota studied the printout again. "Well, the facial features are pretty close, but the guy I saw wore his hair combed straight back, not parted like this. And it was a little longer."

Bingo. The young Wes Harrison had worn his blond locks slicked straight back. Maybe since Kate had seen him that night at O'Malley's he'd reverted to his old hairstyle to change his appearance.

"And the eyes are wrong."

"How so?"

"The color, mainly." Dakota tapped the printout with a turquoise nail. "These are freaky. The man I saw had brown eyes."

"You sure?"

Dakota huffed. "He's a good-looking guy, McClellan. Believe me, women notice such things."

On a lark I covered my eyes. "What color are mine?"

"Blue, sometimes bluish-gray, depends on what you're wearing."

I moved my hand away and grinned. "Good answer. One more question?"

"Okay."

"Name?"

"No."

"Where'd you see him?"

"That's two, but I'll answer anyway. In the resort area, coming out of an office near the pool complex. They've got this great indoor-outdoor pool. I like to swim, so, hey, sometimes I take advantage of it after work."

"They let the employees do that?"

Dakota flashed a coy smile. "Nobody's complained about it yet."

I saw Dakota's point. Who the hell would bitch about eye candy like her dressing up the pool area? Talk about great free advertisement. "One more thing, pretty please?"

Dakota pursed her lips. "What?"

I reached across the table and tapped the printouts. "These are for you. The names I have are Alice Spence and Wes Harrison, but don't go letting that slip to anyone. Would you keep an eye out for these people and let me know if you see or hear anything about them?"

"Jeez, McClellan, now I'm your friggin' watchdog?"

<hr />

Saturday morning just after daylight I drove to Gillman's Marina, loaded my rental boat with bait, tackle, and plenty of beer, and headed out the canal to do a little fishing and a lot of thinking. I eased out the mouth of the canal past the seawall, crossed the sandbar, and gunned the motor. I hadn't been on the water in a while. The sky was clear, and there was barely a ripple on the surface. It felt good to smell the salt air and feel the fresh sea breeze on my face.

I crossed St. George Bay and anchored at The Stumps, the remnants of an old pine forest that had been cut off from Five-Mile Island during a hurricane many years before. I'd found Brett Barfield's sunken runabout there last summer, which had proven instrumental in solving Maddie Harper's murder. It was also a hell of a good fishing spot when conditions were right.

The light wind was out of the east, so I anchored at the western edge of the dead forest, baited my hook with a live shrimp, and cast toward shore along the edge of the stumps rising out of the water like black ghosts. No more than a minute passed before the bobber twisted slightly and then disappeared. I waited a couple of seconds and set the hook. It was touch and go for a minute until I managed to work the fish clear of the stumps and toward the boat. A couple more minutes of tug-of-war, and a nice three-and-a half- to four-pound speckled trout slapped the side of the boat. I slipped the net under the speck, brought it aboard, unhooked it, and dropped it in the live well. Less than fifteen minutes at The Stumps, and supper was already caught. I popped open a Bud to celebrate. After netting another shrimp from my aerated bucket, I baited up and cast again, hoping for gravy.

In the next half hour I caught two more keeper specks and drank a second beer before I decided to retire the rod and reel for the day. I wasn't a meat hog; I'd give the other two fish to Jerry and Donna when I got back to the campground.

I poured myself a cup of coffee from the thermos I'd packed and unwrapped a Jimmy Dean's sausage and egg biscuit I'd microwaved just before leaving my camper. Propping my legs on the gunnels, I ate breakfast while my thoughts drifted back to Alice Spence.

If Dakota's friend at work was right, Alice's investment company might have at least some interest in the Palmetto Royale Casino & Resort. Throw in the fact that Dakota might have seen our Wes Harrison character around the place, and things were really beginning to get interesting.

I don't know why I hadn't thought about it before, but I needed to access county records and look up the owners of the casino and resort. I'd been too occupied working on the drug-smuggling case last year to give the casino much thought, other than hearing the Bible-thumpers raising holy hell about it. Chances were I could get the info online, but I needed to stock up on groceries anyway, so I decided to wait until Monday for the courthouse to open.

The diamonds Kate found in Harrison's filing cabinet were also bugging me. Frank Hightower's FBI buddy was sure they were conflict diamonds smuggled into the country from South America. That pointed a finger directly at Rachel Todd, who would've had easy access to black-market contacts in the outlying villages she flew supplies to. The bagful of diamonds was in Harrison's possession when the so-called boating accident went down, so it was almost a sure bet that Rachel was passing the smuggled stones along to him and/or Kohler.

But why would Kohler and Harrison just walk away from those diamonds if they faked their own deaths? Had it been a simple oversight to move them before they staged the accident? How the hell does somebody forget about a bagful of diamonds potentially worth a few million bucks? Did Harrison plan to sneak back to the apartment later to retrieve them when things quieted down, only to find Kate had given up the lease and moved them? If so, it would've been awful damn risky to break into Kate's parents' house to search for them. Maybe they'd made enough of a killing already to even bother with the Crown Royal bag of rocks. Not likely in my book, not for that greedy bunch.

I finished the coffee and biscuit, weighed anchor, and headed home.

After finishing my supper of grilled speckled trout and potato logs, I poured myself a Scotch and booted up my laptop. I did a Google search for "Georgia Power of Attorney" and spent the better part of an hour learning what I could. After I'd finished, my best guess was that Darla Ramey had probably signed, as "principal," what's called a "Durable Power of Attorney," with niece Alice Spence designated as "agent." If so, that would give Alice full control of her aunt's estate with the legal power to act on her behalf in any matter granted by the document. With Mrs. Ramey's diminishing mental state, my money said Alice probably had Dear Aunt Darla designate unlimited power to her.

My research also showed that such a Durable Power of Attorney didn't necessarily have to be filed with the county clerk of court; however, if any property transfers occurred, it would then be a matter of public record and filed with the clerk of court. Another guess—

Alice Spence now had legal ownership of the Ramey's swanky Buckhead mansion and possibly all their business interests as well.

I poured myself another Scotch. There was a decision to be made. Either I could spend who-knows-how-many fruitless hours on the Internet and phone trying to find the info I needed from the Fulton County Clerk of Court, or I could make another trip to Atlanta and do it in person. By the time I drained my second drink I decided to head for Atlanta sometime in the next few days. With a nice buzz coming on, I grinned, wondering how sweet Alice would react to a surprise visit.

CHAPTER 21

I left for Atlanta just after daylight Tuesday, more convinced than ever that my ducks were starting to swim in a row. The previous morning I'd struck pay dirt during my visit to the courthouse in Parkersville. Spence-Ramey Investments was listed as one of the "Tenants in Common" for the Palmetto Royale Casino & Resort, along with Dobro Greyhound Racing, Inc., and Garrett Realty and Development Corporation.

I nearly shouted out a "hallelujah" right there in the clerk of court's office when I read this last-named partner in the venture; however, the Garrett listed as CEO of the corporation was a Mr. David Jarrod Garrett from Miami, Florida. Still, the fact that the surnames Spence-Ramey and Garrett were listed as co-owners of the same enterprise was enough for me to fire off a call to Frank as soon as I left the courthouse. He promised to check into the two Garretts' backgrounds and see if he could dig up any relationship or ties between them.

I hoped to hell there was. Now I had a possible connection between the names Spence and Garrett, and the crude drawing of circles and arrows I'd made was beginning to make some sense after all. I was chomping at the bit to hear what Alice had to say now that I had concrete proof she had business interests in Palmetto County. That bump-in I'd had at O'Malley's was starting to feel more familiar, too.

I stopped for lunch at a Hardee's off Interstate 75 and made downtown Atlanta just after one. I turned left onto Martin Luther King Jr. Drive, made another left three blocks later at Pryor Street, and found a parking spot near the Fulton County Courthouse.

Less than thirty minutes later, with the invaluable help of Shauna, a savvy young African American clerk, I stepped outside into the

Georgia sunshine with the info I'd been seeking. Mrs. Edmond Randolph Ramey had signed a watertight "Durable Power of Attorney Effective Immediately" document, naming Alice Spence as agent. As far as I could tell, this gave Alice unlimited legal right to act on her aunt's behalf in all matters. And, for the kicker, Alice was also now legal and sole owner of the Ramey Buckhead estate. Most likely for tax purposes, was Shauna's best guess, thereby saving tens of thousands in taxes had Mrs. Ramey waited to bequeath the property to her niece upon her passing.

I climbed into my Silverado, and while waiting for the air conditioner to chase some of the heat out the half-opened windows, double-checked the directions to the Ramey house from the map I'd printed out for my previous trip. Confident of my route, I drove back to the freeway and headed north.

There was a three-car accident that had traffic crawling for a couple of miles, and it was nearing three o'clock by the time I turned onto Ramey Way and passed through the open wrought iron gate. The driveway ended in a wide circle. I followed it around and parked along the side facing back the way I'd come. I got out and climbed the steps. I hadn't really thought about what I was going to say to Alice. I figured I'd just wing it.

I pushed the doorbell and listened to the strains of the Westminster chime resonating inside. About halfway through, the big glass-paneled door swung open. Standing there was Miss Lettie, the maid, or was "housekeeper" the more politically correct term these days? Inside the house I heard faint voices, probably from a TV.

"Yes, sir, can I help you?"

I offered my hand. "Hi, Miss Lettie, I'm Mac McClellan. I was here a few weeks ago to see Alice and Mrs. Ramey, remember?"

She gave my hand a tentative shake as the big dark eyes in the round face studied me for a minute. "Yes, sir, believe I do. Sorry, but they not here right now."

I glanced at my watch. "Oh . . . when do you expect them back?"

Lettie frowned. "Don't know for sure. They in Florida, been gone a week now. Miss Alice said she'll call and let me know when they coming back."

Damn, there went my element of surprise to catch Alice off her guard and see if she might let something slip. "Are they staying at the house in Sandestin?"

Lettie glanced over her shoulder a second. She looked a little impatient, like she had something important to get back to. Probably a soap opera or talk show. "Yes, sir, far's I know."

"Well, thanks for your time."

"Yes, sir." The door shut in my face.

I walked toward my truck but then decided to take a little detour around the back of the house. I recognized some of the objects from the outside photos I'd seen in the *Atlanta Journal-Constitution* feature on Alice and the Ramey home. I made my way to the swimming pool area. Nearby, a big statue of Neptune carrying his trident and riding three horses stood in the center of a circulating fountain. Water spouted from the horses' flared nostrils. I glanced around at the rest of the area. Something seemed out of place, but I couldn't pinpoint it.

From the corner of my eye I saw a window curtain peel to one side and Miss Lettie's disapproving face staring out at me. I gave a quick wave and about-faced for my pickup.

~~~

Back home, I found a folded slip of paper wedged between the door and the frame. I unlocked the door, switched on a light, and unfolded the white square: *Call me. D.*

I glanced at the clock on the microwave above the stove. Ten after ten. I opened a beer, slumped onto the sofa in the living area, and dialed Dakota's number.

"Where you been, McClellan? I tried calling you all afternoon."

"Atlanta. I didn't hear my phone ring. Probably a lousy signal. What's up?"

"I saw the hair lady, that Alice somebody."

"Spence."

"Yeah, whatever. Anyway, my shift ended at two, so I decided to hang out at the pool for a couple of hours. I was coming out of the dressing room, and there she was on the other side of the pool heading for the offices."

"You sure it was her?"

Dakota huffed. "I've got twenty-ten, McClellan. I'm sure. Guess what else?" She sounded like a schoolgirl who couldn't wait to spill a secret.

"She was with our Wes Harrison?"

"You wish. No, but I got a photo of her. I was working on my tan when she came walking out of the office, so I grabbed my phone and snapped a couple of shots."

The fatigue from my trip suddenly lifted. Not only was Alice Spence a part-owner of the casino/resort, but here was possible proof that she might be taking a hands-on role in running the place. "That's great. Anybody notice you?"

"I don't think so. There was this old geezer nearby that tried to hit on me earlier, but if he saw me he probably thought I was just checking my messages or whatever."

"Good. These people might be up to something on the shady side of the law, so you be careful snooping around. I don't want you getting hurt."

"Jeez, McClellan, you're tugging at my heartstrings. Don't worry, I'm a big girl. I can take care of myself."

That I didn't doubt for a second. "When can I see the photos?"

"Hang up. I'm sending them now."

It only took a minute for Dakota to send the two photos to my phone. The first was sort of blurry but looked a lot like Alice in profile. There was no doubting the second shot. For some reason Alice had glanced over her shoulder toward the pool, and Dakota had nailed it. Alice's eyes seemed to be focused on something or someone to Dakota's left, so the chance that she'd spotted Dakota taking the shot seemed slim. I was still studying the photos when my phone rang. Dakota again.

"McClellan, you got the local news on?" She sounded somewhere between excited and agitated.

"No, why?"

"Turn on Channel 7, now!"

I grabbed the remote and pressed the "on" button. It was already tuned to *News Team 7 at Ten*, Palmetto County's local NBC affiliate based in Parkersville. The Ken and Barbie anchors had on their serious faces and were repeating the evening's top story, a drug bust in nearby St. George by the St. George police. A residence located at 124 South 31st Street had been under surveillance for the past few weeks. Local authorities obtained a search warrant and made their move just after six this evening. Inside, officers found evidence of a methamphetamine lab, along with other illegal drugs and paraphernalia.

Arrested at the scene were Caitlin Alexandra Medlin, twenty-two, of Chamblee, Georgia, whose parents reportedly owned the beach-front house; and Whit Tanner Coleman, also twenty-two, of Marianna, Florida. An arrest warrant had been issued for Summer Leigh Tyson, twenty, of the residence, originally from Hollywood, Florida. Other possible arrests were pending.

I watched the young female on-scene reporter interviewing Chief Brian Tolliver, but my mind kept wandering to the night a few weeks ago when Dakota left the note at my camper for me to pass along to J.D. How the hell had she known? My attention snapped back to the footage as a young, dark-haired woman in handcuffs was escorted to a patrol cruiser. Her head was bowed and her face was turned away from the camera, so I couldn't be certain, but she damn sure resembled the Beamer girl I'd followed to the Palmetto Royale. That answered one question.

"What the hell's going on, Dakota?" I said when the story wrapped.

"What do you mean?"

"You leave me a note telling J.D. to watch that place. While I'm at the gun range you just happen to show up dressed like a ninja warrior firing a Glock like you were born with it in your fist. That girl they just arrested almost runs my ass off the road, so I follow her to the casino where I find you working a table. What's your game?"

There was silence for several seconds, unusual considering Dakota's usually sharp, witty comebacks. "I got no friggin' game, McClellan," she finally snapped, reverting to the beach-brawling, tough-girl attitude I'd first encountered outside The Green Parrot.

I was pissed. No way was she playing straight. "Are you a cop?" Damn, now *I* was saying it.

There was no answer, and then no connection.

Around seven-thirty the next morning tires crunched on the gravel drive outside my camper. I glanced through the window by the dinette table and saw Sergeant J.D. Owens unlimbering his lanky frame from the blue-and-white cruiser parked behind my Silverado.

"Want some coffee?" I said, opening the door before he could knock.

"Yes, sir, thanks."

I filled another cup and joined him at the table. J.D. grabbed a sugar packet from the bowl and dumped it into his coffee. "Did you hear about the raid last night?"

"Yeah, caught it on the ten o'clock news."

He stirred his coffee and glanced at me. "That's why I never got back to you about the tags you wanted me to run. We been watching the place since you tipped me off."

I nodded. "Anything else you can tell me about the bust, off the record?"

J.D. blew on his coffee and took a sip. "That Medlin girl we arrested graduated last semester from Chipola. Now she's working at the Palmetto Royale. She's assistant manager of the gym and also works at the spa as a masseuse."

J.D. must've read the surprise on my face. He held up a hand. "Hey, it's all on the up-and-up, Mac. We checked it out. She's got a degree and all."

"From where?"

He hesitated, brow furrowed. "Some college up in Georgia; I can't remember the name."

I took a quick sip of the strong black coffee, trying not to let the excitement I felt inside register on my face. Chamblee, where Beamer girl hailed from, was only a few miles from Alice Spence's Buckhead neighborhood. Alice held fitness and massage therapist degrees from Atlanta's Gwinnett College branch. It wasn't too much of a stretch that Beamer girl had somehow connected with Alice through her web pages and landed work at the Palmetto Royale Casino & Resort. But why the meth lab and the other drugs? How did that fit into the picture?

"You know your cousin Dakota works at the casino?"

J.D. flushed a little. "Yeah, she told me a while back."

"Does she know the Medlin girl?"

"No, I already asked her that."

"Anything on the other two, that Coleman guy or the missing girl?"

"Whit Coleman is Caitlin Medlin's boyfriend, from what we could find out. He's got no connection to the casino as far as we know. But get this: he's a student at Chipola, majoring in criminal justice."

"No crap?"

"Yeah. And that Tyson girl we're looking for? She's a student at Chipola too, full-time. She's up here from south Florida on some sort of scholarship, studying to be a teacher."

"What about her parents?"

"She was raised by a single mother who works as a hairdresser. The father hasn't been in the picture for years."

"Does the Tyson girl belong to the Avalon?"

"Yes, sir, it's registered in her name."

"Does she work?"

"Not that we could find out."

"How the hell does a twenty-year-old student with no job afford a late-model Avalon?"

J.D. shrugged. "Selling drugs? I don't know, unless she's got some rich relatives back home." He glanced at his watch and stood up. "I gotta run; I'm on duty at eight. Thanks for the coffee."

"Welcome. Hey, one more question."

"Yes, sir?"

"Dakota's a student at Chipola, right?"

"Yes, sir, part-time, I think."

"What's she studying?"

J.D.'s brow wrinkled. "You know what? I never asked her."

Later that morning I called Frank, ready to bring him up to speed on everything that had gone down the past couple of days. No answer at the office or on his cell, so I left a message for him to call me when he got the chance. I was also eager to know if he'd found any connection between Lawrence and David Garrett.

That evening I called Kate on her cell phone. She'd been recuperating at her parents' home for about a week now, and we'd talked three or four times. But with my trip to Atlanta and the meth lab bust, time had gotten away from me. I hoped she wasn't pissed that I hadn't checked in for a couple of days.

She wasn't. In fact, she was in great spirits. She'd seen her family physician that morning and had been given a clean bill of health to return to her job, providing she took things easy and didn't overexert herself. Kate had talked with Linda Gillman in the afternoon and had made arrangements to be back on the job the following Monday. She planned on spending Thursday and Friday in Destin and returning to St. George Saturday evening. At Kate's invite I jumped at the chance to grill a couple of steaks at her place to celebrate her return.

Thursday morning I got up at daylight, made coffee, and walked to the campground store. I fed the *Parkersville Independent* paper box four quarters and retraced my steps. I sat down at the kitchen table and unfolded the paper. When I saw the front-page headline I almost choked on my coffee:

Wanted Woman's Car Discovered in South Florida Canal.

CHAPTER 22

I t was a brief article with few details, arriving as late-breaking news and giving the local newsroom just enough time to throw together a quick piece to make the morning deadline. Thursday night around nine o'clock a driver traveling east on the Everglades Parkway had spotted the red glow of taillights just beneath the surface of the swampy waters that skirt much of both sides of the four-lane highway. The passerby called 911. Florida Highway Patrol troopers responded and investigated. A wrecker was called to the scene, and a blue late-model Toyota Avalon was hauled from the water. There was front-end damage and airbags had deployed. Both front doors were ajar, but there was no sign of a driver or passengers. A search for the possible victim or victims was underway.

Records showed the automobile was registered to Summer Leigh Tyson, twenty, of Hollywood, Florida, currently residing in the Panhandle town of St. George. Authorities stated that an outstanding arrest warrant for drug charges had recently been issued for Miss Tyson. End of story.

A black-and-white photo of Summer accompanied the article, a posed head-and-shoulders shot probably taken from a high school yearbook. She was a very pretty young lady with large, bright eyes and shoulder-length dark hair.

I booted up my computer and did some quick research. Better known as Alligator Alley, the Everglades Parkway runs almost due west to east across the southern end of Florida, from Naples on the Gulf of Mexico to near Ft. Lauderdale on the Atlantic. The western portion crosses Big Cypress Swamp, and the central and eastern parts traverse the northern reaches of Florida's famed Everglades. Given that the road is an almost straight shot of eighty miles, accidents are common due to excessive speed, soft shoulders, and the nearby proximity of the swamps. Run-ins with the abundant wildlife crossing from one side to the other are all too common.

I poured myself another cup of coffee and reread the newspaper article. Two scenarios kept popping up in my mind. First, poor Summer, scared and on the lam, had swerved off the road trying to avoid a gator or deer or some other critter and wound up in the swamp. There, perhaps knocked unconscious from the collision and not wearing a seat belt, she'd possibly drowned and floated out one of the doors opened by the impact, likely becoming gator bait.

Because the airbags had deployed, my second theory was that Summer had purposely damaged the car and staged the accident, catching a pre-planned ride with a cohort who might've followed her all the way from St. George or had agreed to meet her at the scene of the "accident." From there they were most likely headed for some small airport where Summer would use a fake ID and passport, charter a plane, and sky out to some safe haven in the Caribbean until things settled down. Chances were good that she was already soaking up rays on some island paradise while sipping a fancy cocktail decorated with a tiny umbrella.

That is, of course, if she wasn't now being digested in the belly of a bull gator according to scenario one.

My gut told me the gators got cheated out of one hell of a tasty meal this time.

The boss man called just after eight with some more interesting news. David Jarrod Garrett was Lawrence Garrett's nephew, son of Lawrence's late older brother from whom he'd inherited the realty and development business. Puzzle pieces were beginning to lock into place. My drawing of circles and arrows was now making way too many connections to be coincidental. I wished like hell I hadn't thrown the damn thing away.

I brought Frank up to date on my new info, including the Atlanta trip and the recent drug bust and arrests. He promised to keep digging on his end. "Oh, one more thing," I said before we ended the conversation.

"What's that?"

"Where are the diamonds Kate found?"

"At the bank in my safe deposit box. I didn't think it would be wise for Katie to have them around."

"Good thinking. What about your FBI friend? Is he okay with this?"

"No problem there, Mac. He's been retired for a couple of years. He said he'd keep it under wraps and help out any way he can if we need him. He did say we'd need to turn the diamonds and paperwork over to the Feds after this shindig is over. With the finders-keepers law, Katie might be entitled to the cut diamonds, but the roughs are a no-no."

"Good. By the way, we might need those rocks for collateral."

"Collateral? What . . . never mind. I'm not even going to ask."

I laughed. "You'll be the first to know, Frank."

Friday morning's *Independent* updated the Summer Tyson story with an interesting twist. Divers braving the alligator- and moccasin-infested swamps had discovered a handbag belonging to Ms. Tyson. A shoe found in the same general area was also thought to belong to the missing woman. The search was continuing.

Meanwhile, authorities at Miami International and other area airports had been alerted, but so far no boarding passengers fitting the young woman's description had turned up. She'd also failed to contact her mother at home, and local reporters described the hardworking single mother as "distraught." Maybe I was wrong, but if the accident was staged it would've been easy enough to toss the handbag and shoe into the drink to add more weight to the theory that Summer had drowned or been taken by gators. I was still betting that Summer was relaxing on some Caribbean beach rather than turning to mush inside the innards of a some overgrown water lizard.

Also making the front-page news was a story stating that Caitlin Medlin and Whit Coleman had appeared before a judge and both had been released on bail. Twenty-five thousand and fifteen thousand dollars respectively. Neither individual had a prior arrest record. Though Medlin and Coleman denied others were involved, local authorities were continuing the investigation and search for additional, unnamed suspects.

Saturday morning I drove to the Piggly Wiggly supermarket in Parkersville and bought a couple of two-inch-thick filets mignons and a nice bottle of Kendall-Jackson Cabernet Sauvignon, Kate's favorite red wine. I also picked up a fancy bouquet of mixed flowers I thought she'd like. I wanted her welcome home to be special.

Kate called at five o'clock to let me know she was home and asked me to come over around six. That would give her enough time to rest and clean up for what we both hoped would be an enjoyable evening together.

I was there at six sharp, steaks, wine, and flowers in hand. Kate thanked me for the flowers and wine, and greeted me with a light kiss. I decided that had more to do with residual pain than a less-than-enthusiastic welcome. She'd lost a few pounds—something she didn't need. She could use a little fattening up, I decided. The steaks, double-baked potatoes, salad, and wine would be a nice way to begin. There was still some light bruising on her forehead above the left eye and on her left cheek. But the swelling was gone and she looked great to me.

Kate must've been reading my mind. "I'm still a little sore, Mac," she said as we sat on the back deck enjoying a glass of wine while waiting for the coals to reach cooking temp. She smiled and squeezed my arm. "Please don't take this the wrong way, but I'm afraid any hanky-panky will have to wait a few more days, dang it."

I couldn't resist. I leaned in close to Kate's face and focused on her mouth. "There's more than one way to skin a cat, you know."

"What on earth?" she said, pretending to look shocked. The gentle squeeze on my arm turned into a hard pinch. "You are incorrigible, MacArthur McClellan."

After supper we sat together on the glider enjoying the cool evening air on the deck and listening to the waves breaking on the beach several blocks away. I switched to Dewar's on the rocks while Kate was sipping the last of the wine. I'd hoped it wouldn't happen, but somehow our conversation took a detour to the case. I gave Kate a quick rehash of the latest information Frank and I had dug up. "Oh, I almost forgot." I set my Scotch on a table beside the glider and got up. "Be right back."

I hurried out to my truck and grabbed the Thursday and Friday editions of the *Parkersville Independent* and handed them to Kate when I returned. "I thought you might like to read these later."

Kate glanced at the papers for a moment and suddenly drew in a sharp breath. She jumped up and flipped on the outside light, staring at the paper under the yellow glow of the insect bulb. I was by her side in a flash. She pointed to the photo of Summer Tyson. "Dang, Mac, this looks like the brunette in the fight that J.D. broke up behind The Green Parrot!"

⁓❍

Any doubts that Dakota hadn't been playing straight with me were gone now. Kate was certain the girl on the beach cat-fighting with the "scruffy blonde" was the missing Summer Leigh Tyson. I resisted the urge to drive over to Dakota's apartment for a face-to-face confrontation and headed for home instead. I didn't feel up to talking to her tonight anyway. Didn't want to spoil the nice evening I'd just spent with Kate. But I damn sure intended to have a friendly little chat with her ASAP.

I followed 15th Street around the big curve where it changes directions from running north to east, passed the Methodist church, and turned left onto the gravel road that runs through Gulf Pines Campground. Being Memorial Day weekend, the campground was packed. Several groups were still gathered around campfires. I pulled into my drive and parked the Silverado. Grabbing the zippered case holding the .357 that had become my constant traveling companion, I headed across the yard toward my Grey Wolf. I stood on the first step while I fiddled with the keys in the dark. The streetlight in front of my site had burned out almost two weeks ago, and Jerry still hadn't gotten around to having it replaced. I made a mental note to see him about it in the morning.

Finally I found the right key and was just about to slip it into the deadbolt when the noise of crunching gravel and a car's purring engine distracted me. In my peripheral vision I noticed there were no head-lights; somebody making their way to their campsite and trying not to disturb the neighbors, I figured. Nice gesture. Just then the keys slipped from my grasp, and as I bent over to retrieve them gunfire erupted!

Three quick rounds buzzed over my head and slammed into the camper. Instinctively I flattened myself against Mother Earth and rolled under the trailer, using what precious little cover the darkness and metal steps afforded. In a second I had the case unzipped and the Smith & Wesson in hand, pointing at the disappearing vehicle, which was now hauling ass down the gravel road toward the entrance I'd driven through moments before.

Still no lights on the vehicle, not even a tag light. My combat training kicked in, and my finger tightened on the trigger. At the last possible instant I released the squeeze. No sense taking the chance of putting a round through a tent or RV or somebody out for a late-eve-ning stroll. Taking several deep breaths to squelch the adrenaline rush, I lay there a couple more minutes just in case there might be another shooter nearby waiting to take a crack at me.

Lights were turning on all around the campground as people stuck their heads out of RVs and tents to see what the hell all the commotion was about. Two men were arguing about whether it was gunshots or fire-works they'd heard. Somebody else said it might've been a car backfiring. Nobody seemed to know exactly where the sound had come from.

I stayed where I was and fished my phone out of the right front pocket of my shorts. I punched J.D.'s personal cell number that I had programmed into my phone. He answered on the second ring. "It's

Mac. Somebody just tried to take me out in front of my camper. Three shots."

"I'm on 98 near Gulf Grocery. I'll be there in five. Are you hurt?"

"Negative," I said, just as I noticed a stinging sensation in my front left shoulder, like a pissed-off wasp had nailed me. "Check that. I might've taken a fragment in the shoulder. Don't call the EMTs; it's nothing but a scratch. Jerry and Donna don't need this turning into a circus. Just get over here. No flashers or siren, okay?"

"Okay, but I gotta call it in."

"I know. Just say a camper complained about somebody shooting off fireworks close by. Can you do that?"

"Yes, sir, on my way."

CHAPTER 23

Several of my temporary neighbors milled around Sergeant J.D. Owens's cruiser as I explained to the officer that a carload of joy-riding kids had hurled cherry bombs toward me from their car and then sped away. Just pranksters out for some Saturday night fun, I said. No damage done, and the kids had been careful to toss them a safe enough distance from me. "Probably just trying to see if they could make some old fart mess his pants," I said, drawing some laughs from the crowd.

J.D. had his clipboard out, dutifully writing down the report in the beam of the penlight clenched between his teeth. After a few minutes the people dispersed. J.D. asked Jerry Meadows, who'd walked over from the office to check out the commotion, to stay. "You need to get that light replaced soon, Mr. Meadows," J.D. said. "It's a hazard. Any others out that you know of?"

Jerry nodded. "The one over by 76," he said, pointing across several rows of sites to the opposite end of the campground. "And the one by 12's been flickering; I think it's about ready to go, too. Been meaning to change 'em, but it's hard to keep up with everything needs doing these days. I'll get a crew out here first thing Monday."

"Yes, sir," J.D. said, "that'll do fine."

After Jerry left we glanced around to make sure nobody was watching. We approached the camper door, J.D. carrying the clipboard to give the impression he was still filling out his report.

"There were three quick shots," I repeated quietly. "Sounded like a large-caliber handgun, maybe a .45 or .357. Whoever it was meant business."

A bullet had punched through the door about two-thirds up and near the left edge. Two more, almost side by side and lower, had cut through the camper wall between the door and the window to the left. As I turned the key to open the deadbolt J.D. let out a low whistle. "From that distance you're lucky to be alive, Mac. You said you were hit?"

Inside, I switched on a light and pointed to the front of my upper left shoulder where a small irregular patch of blood stained my dark-blue polo shirt. I lifted the short sleeve above my shoulder, exposing a small purplish puncture wound encircled with dried blood. "Fragment from one of the rounds, I guess. Not too deep. I'll clean it up later."

A quick look around showed that the bullet through the door had traveled across the interior and smashed into the cabinet above the kitchen sink, taking out my spice rack and lodging inside a canister filled with sugar. I dug my hand into the sugar, felt around, and retrieved the mangled bullet. "Looks like a .45 to me," I said, handing it to J.D. "You better hang on to this in case we need it for evidence later."

The other two rounds had punched through at just the correct angle to turn the toaster next to the stove into scrap metal. Two jagged holes scarred the wall behind. J.D. took a quick trip out back and reported that both rounds had passed through the outer wall. Good thing there was nothing but pine trees behind my site.

I unplugged the microwave and toaster to lessen the chance of an electrical fire. All the other lights and sockets in the camper checked out okay. "I'll patch the holes with caulk first thing in the morning," I said. "That should take care of any neighbors who might come snooping around."

J.D. promised to have a car patrol the campground and Kate's place several times throughout the night. After he left I poured myself a hefty shot of The Dalmore, the twelve-year-old single-malt I keep on hand for extra-special occasions. Surviving a drive-by ambush sure as hell qualified in my book.

When I finished the Scotch I poured myself another and headed for the bathroom. I stripped off the shirt and poured rubbing alcohol over the small puncture, then probed the wound with tweezers. It hurt like hell, but I gritted my teeth and kept at it. Finally, I got a firm grip on the fragment and yanked it out.

It was no larger than a fingernail clipping, but my digging had started the damn thing bleeding again. I stopped the bleeding with a wad of toilet paper, doused the area with more alcohol, squeezed some antibiotic ointment on a thick square of gauze, and pressed it over the wound. Then I secured the bandage with tape. Good as new except for the pain.

I stayed awake keeping watch and drinking twelve-year-old painkiller in the darkened camper for a couple of hours. I finally allowed myself to stretch out on the sofa, the Smith & Wesson within easy reach, sans zippered case. I'd already decided I wouldn't be caught with my zipper down again, or in this case, up.

My thoughts turned to Kate. She wasn't safe here in St. George. Somebody had screwed with her car and come close to killing her, and now they'd targeted me. Much as I missed her, I had to convince Kate to go back to her parents' place until this crap was resolved one way or another. I knew she would pitch a fit, but this time The Fabulous Moolah would just have to leave the ring and let somebody else pin the opponent.

I was up with the sun and had the bullet holes smoothly caulked before the campground began stirring. At seven-thirty I called Kate and invited myself over for breakfast, promising I'd cook up my self-proclaimed world-famous Mexican omelet. Who could resist that offer?

I was there before eight with all the fixings. Kate had coffee ready when I arrived. She sat at the kitchen table and we made small talk while I concocted my masterpiece. When we'd finished eating we poured ourselves another cup of coffee and sat at the picnic table on the shaded deck out back.

"What on earth? No way, Mac, I can't," Kate said when I brought up the subject of her moving back in with her parents until the case was wrapped. "I've got the new CR-V payments and the rent on this place, not to mention my job."

"I can help you out if it's the money you're worried about."

Kate huffed and her eyes bore into mine. "Sorry, Mac, but I'm not playing *that* game."

The Fabulous Moolah was being stubborn. "Look, that wreck you had was no accident. Who's to say it won't happen again?"

Kate looked away and sipped her coffee. "I'll take my chances."

I set my cup on the table, turned on the bench, and lifted my shirtsleeve to reveal the bandage. "Somebody tried to kill me last night outside my trailer. Three shots and I barely got nicked. I'm lucky as hell to be sitting here right now. If I hadn't dropped my keys just before they fired, I wouldn't be."

The color drained from Kate's face and her jaw trembled. She sloshed coffee as she set her cup down and covered her face with both hands. "What have I done, Mac?" she said. "What in the world have I done?"

I slipped my arm around her shoulders. "You haven't done anything wrong. You just happened to notice Wes Harrison at O'Malley's that night and reacted to it. What were you supposed to do, pretend you didn't see somebody who you thought was long dead?"

"I wish now I had," she said, sniffling, her face still covered.

With my free hand I eased Kate's hands away from her face and kissed her cheek. "It's too late for wishing. It is what it is. You need to go back home to your parents until this is over. You'll be safer there, and I won't have to worry so much."

Kate nodded as she wiped at her eyes. "But what about my job?"

"Give Linda or Gary a call today and tell them you need to take a leave of absence for a while. They'll understand. School lets out next week. There'll be plenty of teenagers looking for work."

A few tears trickled down Kate's cheeks. "What if they fire me?"

Kate had never looked or sounded so vulnerable since I'd known her. I guess this whole mess had caught up to her. I forced a little laugh to lighten the mood. "They won't fire you. You're way too valuable to them. That place would fall apart without you. Hundred-to-one odds say I'm right."

Even though it was Memorial Day weekend and the official beginning of the marina's busy season, Linda Gillman told Kate to take all the time she needed and to not worry, just as I'd predicted. Her job would be waiting when she was ready to come back to work. I felt like Nostradamus. That afternoon I helped Kate pack for an extended stay with her parents and spent the night on the sofa at her place just to be on the safe side. We kept the outside floodlights on, I slept with one eye open, and the night passed uneventfully.

The next day was Memorial Day. Hoping to beat the beach-going traffic, we got up early to load Kate's new Honda. We were on our way by seven with Kate in the lead and me tailgating her in my Silverado to make sure no vehicles got between us. After stopping in Panama City Beach for breakfast, we hit the road again and arrived at the Bells' home in Destin around eleven.

During her previous stay at her parents' home after leaving the hospital, Kate—with Frank's support—had informed them about Wes Harrison and the case we were working on. Jim and Mary Bell had tried their best to persuade their hardheaded daughter to stay in Destin, to no avail. They were pleased that I'd had the fortitude and patience to convince Moolah she would be safer at home with them rather than exposing herself to unnecessary risks in St. George. Brownie points for me.

Pleading that I was still full from breakfast, I declined an invitation to stay for lunch, said my good-byes, and headed for downtown Destin and a meeting I'd arranged with Frank during the drive over. "How quick can you get your hands on the diamonds Kate found?" I said when we were seated inside his office.

Frank took off the glasses he'd been using to read the newspaper. "Anytime, as long as the bank's open; meaning tomorrow morning at the soonest. Why?"

"Spence-Ramey Investments. How would you like to buy your way into the company as an investor?"

"And just why would I want to do that?"

"Spence-Ramey is part-owner of the casino and resort. Alice Spence has been seen there at least twice coming out of their offices. If you were an investor you could sit in on the meetings and maybe get some inside info on what they're up to. You might even run into our elusive Mr. Harrison. My source thinks she may have seen him around there, too."

"Just who is this source, Mac?"

"Will you be pissed if I don't say? She works at the casino, and I don't want her to wind up in the grinder if something slips."

"No, but how do you know she can be trusted?"

"My manly intuition says so."

Frank's eyes narrowed. "So I just walk up, knock on Alice Spence's office door, hand her the bag of diamonds, and say I want in? You know they'll have me checked out."

"How hard would it be for you to assume an alias with the help of your buddies at the sheriff's department?"

Frank massaged the bridge of his nose. "It could be arranged. ID, background, the works."

"Good. So, you tell Alice Spence you're a widower who's retired from the Okaloosa Sheriff's Department and looking for a way to invest your life's savings. Once they find that checks out chances are it'll stop there, especially if you warn your contacts at the department not to mention the PI business."

"And what happens if they somehow do find out I'm a PI? You've been flashing my card around, remember?"

"You'll have an alias. But if they were to find out, my guess is they'll say, 'Sorry, Mr. Doe, but we don't feel you're a good fit for our company.' I doubt they'll want to stir up the shit stew by messing with an ex-cop who's snooping around."

"My life savings can't be a bagful of diamonds."

"No, but I think I know where I can get the money if we put the rocks up as collateral."

Frank snorted. "And just where might that be?"

"Sheriff Bocephus Pickron."

"Are you nuts, Mac? Where the hell would a small county sheriff's office get that kind of money, even if he was to agree to the deal?"

"Remember the drug bust at Barfield Fisheries last summer? I'd wager after the Feds took their cut on the trucks transporting across state lines, there was enough in confiscated property for the county to more than cover the million you'd need to buy into Spence-Ramey. Besides, Pickron owes me and he knows it. Don't forget that Maddie Harper was his niece."

"What happens to the diamonds if Pickron agrees to put up the million and I do buy in? How are we going to get our hands on the cash to pay Pickron back?"

"The diamonds are unclaimed property, right? Besides your retired FBI buddy and us, nobody knows they exist except for the old Destin gang, if they're even still alive. None of them are likely to come forward to make a claim. You might be able to recoup the million by selling your partnership to a third party. If not, Pickron could keep the diamonds. I'm sure he could find a use for them."

"You're forgetting Katie. She might very well have a claim to some of the cut stones eventually."

"I'll have a talk with her. My guess is she'll be willing to go along with the program if it helps solve this mess."

Frank scratched at his chin stubble. "It just might fly. When do we move?"

I got up to leave. "I'll let you know after I have a little face-to-face with Bocephus."

CHAPTER 24

Back in St. George and with Kate safely tucked away at her parents' house, I decided it was time for a little vacation. Bo Pickron could wait a few days. With the huge crowd down for the holiday I knew he'd be busy, and I had other priorities. I leafed through the phone book, found the listings for Palmetto Royale Casino & Resort and called the resort's reservation desk.

"Yes, sir, we do have a few rooms still available," a sweet voice informed me. I damn near dropped the phone when she told me it would cost two hundred and fifty bucks a night. What the hell; if there was a chance to find out more about Alice Spence and Wes Harrison, and possibly who had tried to take out Kate and me, it was worth it. The cost did include full use of the facilities, a complimentary half-hour massage at the spa, *and* a continental breakfast each morning. Who could pass up all that for a few measly bucks? Thank the powers that be for plastic.

I booked the room for that Thursday, Friday, and Saturday under my middle name, Andrew. I'd have to take my chances on McClellan because this little thousand-dollar R&R was going on my Visa card. I made a mental note to enjoy breakfast to the max each morning during my stay.

I spent the last day of May and the first of June relaxing and fishing off the bay side of Five-Mile Island. Thursday around noon I drove to the airport north of Parkersville, parked the Silverado in the overnight garage, and rented a gray four-door Ford Fusion. With some time to kill I drove around awhile, getting used to the feel of the new wheels, and then headed for the Palmetto Royale.

Normal check-in time at the resort was two o'clock. I arrived a half-hour early, but my room was already available. I listed my ex-wife's North Carolina home as my address. What the hell, that was the least Jill could contribute to the cause. After all, the divorce had been her idea, and she'd wound up with what would've been our retirement paradise on the New River outside Jacksonville. Not that I'm bitter or anything. At least she'd agreed to keep her slippery paws off my retirement pay.

I handed the desk clerk my charge card and took the elevator up to the third floor. I followed the signs to Room 321, inserted the key card, and let myself in. The room was plenty swanky and sparkling clean. There were two queen-size beds, a good-size refrigerator, microwave, coffee-maker with all the fixings, and a flat-screen television damn near as wide as the sofa in my camper. Twenty dollars' worth of casino chips rested on one of the bed pillows beside some foil-wrapped chocolates. All in all, not too shabby a deal, not to mention the outside balcony overlooking the fancy indoor-outdoor pool with its waterfalls and hot tubs.

After unpacking my bag I grabbed the chips and headed for the casino, about a five-minute walk across the large parking lot. Hoping to find Dakota on the job, I strolled through the casino to the blackjack tables. She wasn't on duty that I could see, and I didn't want to take the chance of putting her in jeopardy by asking any of the employees if they knew when she was due in.

I enjoyed a beer, busted out of a couple quick games of blackjack, and walked back to the resort sans chips. Back in my room I put on my swimsuit and a T-shirt, grabbed a couple of plush towels from the bath-room, and headed for the pool.

At the tiki bar, located where the pool morphs from indoor to outdoor, I bought a Michelob from a cute brunette bartender. Past the tiki bar and just inside the indoor pool area, two side-by-side doors were marked "Office" by a lighted sign on the wall between them. Beyond the office the resort's cavernous shopping mall surrounded the huge indoor pool. It was a great location to people-watch.

I took the beer and chose a spot outside by the pool where I could keep an eye on anyone walking in or out of the office doors. After spreading one of the towels on the wide tile border surrounding the pool, I shed my T-shirt and deck shoes and stuffed my valuables inside the shoes. Then I headed for the deep end of the pool where three diving boards of various heights were located.

After a death-defying dive off the medium board for a quick dip to cool off, I climbed out of the pool and toweled off. I sat there for several minutes drinking beer, basking in the sun, and taking in the view. Several guests were sunbathing on chaise longues. Nearby, two bronzed young women relaxing side by side on their stomachs had undone the straps of their bikini tops, offering an enticing eyeful to any alert viewer. At the shallow end of the pool, separated by a colorful rope and floats, several kids were fighting with water noodles and batting beach balls back and forth.

I finished the beer, folded and rolled the second towel into a pillow, and lay down to soak up some rays. At some point I drifted off to sleep and dreamed I was back in Iraq listening to the distant rumble of artillery. Friendlies, I knew, our own batteries firing a mission in support of some unit to our north. The sound was strangely comforting.

I bolted awake when thunder crashed from a lightning strike way too close for comfort. Cold raindrops pelted my body as I grabbed my gear and hustled to the shelter of the tiki bar. I checked my watch. Damn, ten to five. My little nap had lasted longer than I thought. I took a seat on a stool at the bar and slipped on my shirt. I ordered another beer from the young brunette who was decked out in white shorts and a Hawaiian-style shirt with the tails knotted around her tanned midriff. The clothing suited her; it looked like there might be a branch or two of Polynesian in her family tree. *Dillon* was pinned above her left breast pocket. Dillon? Where the hell did parents come up with these names for their daughters these days?

Dillon brought the Michelob along with a frosted mug and some napkins. I declined the mug, handed her an Alexander Hamilton, and told her to keep the change. What the hell, it couldn't hurt to make a friend around here. "Thank you," she said, and flashed a wide smile full of pearly whites that gleamed against her bronzed face. She offered a hand. "I'm Dillon."

"Andrew," I said, taking the soft hand and returning a light squeeze.

Dillon leaned closer and said in a low voice meant only for me, "The second one is on the house." She winked and pointed to her watch. "Happy hour begins at five. Close enough."

From my stool I had a fairly clear view of the office doors directly to my front across from the bar. The only obstacle was a boisterous hulk of a man with thick gray-white hair, a ruddy face, and a bulbous nose lined with purplish veins. He was probably around fifty and looked alarmingly similar to former president Bill Clinton before heart surgery forced him to trim off the excess poundage. He was smoking a big cigar and flirting with Dillon and a couple of women around my age who sat a few stools away. He kept offering to buy the pair drinks, and they kept refusing. At one point I thought I heard him say something about getting them a free upgrade on their room. With the cigar and the sweet talk, the comparison to Willy J. was getting downright uncanny.

I finished the beer, and when Dillon glanced my way I smiled and pointed at the bottle. She brought my free Michelob, and I laid an Honest Abe on the bar for her. She thanked me with another flash of teeth. "Who's Mr. Friendly behind you?" I said, casually lifting a finger off the bar and pointing at Dillon's midriff, which stood between me and my former commander-in-chief's double. I was pleasantly surprised to see that her belly button wasn't sporting jewelry.

"Oh, him." Dillon puffed out a breath. She leaned a little closer and lowered her voice. "That's Mr. Garrett."

I almost spit out the mouthful of beer I'd just taken. "David Garrett?" I regretted mentioning Garrett's first name as soon as it left my mouth. Another rookie mistake.

Dillon shrugged. "Maybe, I'm not sure. He's one of the owners of the place or something like that. I've heard there's supposed to be a big corporate meeting here sometime this weekend." She leaned in so close that I could feel her breath on my face when she whispered, "He's a real pain in the you-know-what. He just arrived this morning, and he's already pinched me on the butt twice when I turned my back to him."

I looked at Garrett again and tried to visualize Dr. Lawrence Garrett's face. The hair and ruddy complexions were similar, but I wouldn't bet the family jewels they were related. "Why didn't you slap the taste out of his mouth?"

Dillon frowned. "Don't I wish." She sighed. "I'm a single mom with a little boy to raise, and I can't afford to lose this job."

Hearing that, my dislike for Garrett grew tenfold. Dillon couldn't be much older than my Megan, and to think she had to put up with the crap that pompous bigwig was dishing out really pissed me off. I felt like walking over and decking the SOB, but the news I'd just learned about the meeting forced me to back off. If Garrett was in town, there was a good chance the other big shots would make a show, too. This could turn out to be an interesting weekend.

I ordered three more brews to go. When Dillon brought them I handed her a twenty, thanked her for the great service, and headed to my room.

⁓

Back in my room I put two of the beers in the fridge and carried the other out to the balcony overlooking the pool. The weather had cleared, and the automatic lights around the pool complex were coming on. I scoped out the surroundings again, and this time found that I could see a portion of the tiki bar from my vantage point. Garrett was still there, chatting up a bottled blonde sitting to his right. The pair he'd been schmoozing earlier had vanished.

I spread a towel over one of the wet chairs and punched in Frank's cell number. When he answered I filled him in on what was up and asked if he could get over here this weekend to help me out.

"Sorry, Mac, but I'm on surveillance for a couple more days. Looks like you're on your own for now."

"Let me guess: another feline straying on her tomcat?"

"Close. This time it's the tom on the prowl."

"Christ, Frank, don't you ever get tired of being a voyeur-for-hire?"

"Don't knock it. Cheating spouses are most PI's bread and butter.

Without them we'd go hungry. Did you talk to Sheriff Pickron about the rocks?"

"Not yet. He'll be so busy with this holiday crowd I figured he wouldn't give me the time of day, much less a million bucks."

Frank laughed. "Sounds just like his old man."

"Well, enjoy your exciting weekend at the peep show."

"You too. Let me know how it goes. And watch your tail."

Just then a shapely blonde sporting a white string bikini that left almost nothing to the imagination sauntered to the pool's edge and stuck a toe in the water. "Will do, Frank. I promise I'll keep my eyes peeled."

Thirty minutes later I was showered and dressed and headed for the Polynesian Royale, a restaurant located on the opposite side of the indoor pool from the tiki bar. A nonchalant glance toward the bar told me Garrett was gone. Two perky blondes in Dillon-wear were now waiting on a growing number of patrons. They could've passed for twins, if they weren't.

A few feet from the restaurant entrance somebody touched the back of my arm. I spun around with my arm cocked and saw Dillon flinch back.

"Sorry, Andrew, I didn't mean to startle you!"

I let out a breath and lowered my hands. "Me too. What's up?"

Dillon gave a quick sideways nod of her head and moved away from the entrance to one of several benches lined against the wall where the lighting was more subdued. I followed her, and we took a seat on either end so we wouldn't give the appearance of being a couple. She glanced around until she seemed satisfied we weren't being watched. "I thought you should know that Mr. Garrett asked me if I knew you." She said this without looking my way.

"And?"

"He thought we seemed awfully friendly, but I told him no, that I'd never seen you before this afternoon when you showed up at the bar. I don't know what business it is of his, anyway."

"Did he give you any idea why he might be interested in me?"

"No, that's all he said. I didn't mention your name or anything."

"Did he ask?"

Dillon leaned forward, resting her hands on the bench's edge and scuffed at the walkway with a Nike. "Yes, but I told him I didn't know."

"Thanks, let's keep it that way, okay?"

She kept her eyes to the front. "Sure. Are you . . . with the police or something?"

There was that question again. "No. Why?"

In my peripheral vision I could see she seemed on edge. "Nothing, really."

Dillon's answer was less than convincing. I scanned around and casually slipped one of Frank's business cards from my pants pocket. I set it on the bench next to my thigh. "My number's on the back of this card. If you feel like talking, give me a call sometime when you're sure it's safe." I knew I was taking a risk, but my gut told me she knew something that she wanted to get off her chest.

From the corner of my eye I noticed Dillon's lips tweak into a smile, and I could sense she was trying hard not to look my way. "Are you hitting on me, Andrew?"

I stood and started toward the restaurant without making eye contact. "I wish. See you around."

❦

The next morning I skipped the gratis continental breakfast the hotel offered and instead ordered eggs, grits, and country ham at the Royale Café a few doors down from the Polynesian Royale. I figured the more locations I covered, the better my chances were of spotting someone who might be involved in the case, namely Alice, Wes, or possibly even Eric Kohler or Rachel Todd. The food was first-rate, but unfortunately nobody of interest made an appearance.

Back in my room, I'd just finished brushing my teeth when my cell phone rang out the Marines' Hymn that my son Mike had programmed in for me. I answered quickly, guessing it was probably Kate.

"Andrew? Or should I call you Mac?"

"Morning, Dillon. Let's keep it Andrew between us for now. It's my middle name."

"Fine. I called Mr. Hightower to check up on you."

"Then I guess you figured out that I'm not at the resort for a vacation."

"Yes. I hope you don't mind."

I finished pouring a cup of coffee from the pot I'd started before brushing my teeth. "Not at all; I would've done the same thing. Did I pass the test?"

"Yes, he told me you were in the Marines and all, and that I could trust you."

I decided to be blunt. "Good, but can I trust you? You know I put my butt in a sling when I left you that card."

"Yes, I know. That's why I called. I think we should talk."

I took another sip and swallowed. "Okay, shoot."

"I'd rather not talk over the phone. Can you ... come to my house?"

Dillon sounded hesitant, and the thought of an ambush toyed with my mind. This could easily be a setup, but what the hell. If she was on the up and up, then she'd taken a big risk by tipping me off about Garrett outside the restaurant last night. If she really had something for me, I figured it was worth the risk. Nothing ventured, nothing gained, and all that other philosophical BS. "Sure. When and where?"

There was silence for a moment. Maybe Dillon was having second thoughts about getting involved or setting me up. "I live in Parkersville with my aunt and son." She gave me the address and her cell phone number. "Can you be here at eleven? I have to be at work by two this afternoon."

I assured her I'd be there and started to end the call when she stopped me in mid-sentence.

"Andrew? Please make sure nobody follows you here."

On the drive down to Parkersville, Dillon's parting words kept running through my mind. There were two ways I could take it. Either she was really scared that someone from the Palmetto Royale would find out we were talking, or she was throwing me one hell of a curveball. If she lived with her aunt and little boy like she said, then I probably had nothing to worry about. On the other hand, what if there was no aunt or son? What if she'd agreed to be the lure in exchange for a nice payoff from Garrett or Alice and company? Then my ass truly would be in a sling. Either way, I'd decided to show up packing my S & W.

I damn near wore out the Fusion's rear- and side-view mirrors by the time I pulled into Dillon's empty driveway and parked in front of the attached garage. It was a typical house of brick and siding located in a typical middle-class neighborhood with similar houses up and down the street. I breathed a little easier. If this was to be an ambush, whoever chose the location could've done a hell of a lot better. I grabbed the manila envelope with the photos of the old Destin gang that I'd brought along for my stay at the Palmetto Royale. As I exited the rental I tucked the .357 Magnum in the back of my Dockers and made sure my pull-over shirt covered it. They say one can never be too careful, a lesson I've learned the hard way.

I rang the bell, and Dillon quickly opened the door. She took an anxious glance around and practically jerked me inside. I reached behind me, but my adrenaline stopped pumping when I saw a curly-haired youngster maybe a year old propelling himself across the hard-wood floor in one of those little tyke walkers. My fatherly instincts said that Dillon was who she claimed to be, and that this was no setup.

"Did anybody follow you?"

I let out the deep breath I'd taken when I'd rang the doorbell. "No. I checked my mirrors the whole way and made a lot of unnecessary turns instead of driving straight here. We're safe."

Dillon let out a big sigh and seemed to relax a little. "Thanks for coming." She took a peek out the window, locked the deadbolt, and then intercepted her son and lifted him from the walker. "I made coffee. Let's talk in the kitchen."

I didn't ask, but I assumed the aunt wasn't home as I followed Dillon and watched as she buckled the kid into a high chair and spread a handful of Cheerios across the tray.

"Andrew, meet Tyler. Tyler, meet Andrew."

I held out a finger, and the boy wrapped a chubby fist around it. "Delighted to make your acquaintance, Tyler."

Dillon laughed and looked even more relaxed. She told me to have a seat at the table while she poured the coffee. I sat facing the double windows above the sink and watched her pad barefoot across the kitchen tile to the coffeepot. She was dressed in faded jeans and an oversized man's shirt with all the buttons in their proper place except the collar button. Somewhere beneath all that fabric I knew lurked a very nice figure, but I admired Dillon for her motherly modesty.

She seemed a little hesitant to dive right into the topic she'd called me about. Instead, she sidestepped the issue with small talk about growing up in Lompoc, California, and attending Cal State-Fullerton where she'd graduated with a BA in sociology. While home during a semester break she'd met her future husband, an airman stationed at nearby Vandenberg Air Force Base. A whirlwind romance led to marriage. A few months later, soon after the budding family was transferred to Eglin AFB in the Florida Panhandle, Tyler was born. Eglin wasn't far from Frank's home stomping grounds, and it was the source of a good portion of his cheating-spouse business.

Tyler was only three months old when his daddy announced he was in love with another woman and wanted out of the marriage. Luckily for the new mother and baby, Dillon had an aunt living in Parkersville. She welcomed the two into her home until Dillon could get back on her feet. Dillon went right to work with plans to save enough money to return home to California and begin a new life for herself and Tyler. The divorce was just recently finalized, but the Air Force had quickly docked hubby's pay for back child support. Throw in the salary and tips from her job at the Palmetto Royale, and Dillon was doing all right for herself. End of story.

I sensed that Dillon was hungry for companionship and the chance to talk to someone of the adult variety other than her aunt. I appreciated that, but this wasn't a social call. I made a show of looking at my watch. "I'm glad you and Tyler have landed on your feet, but we both know you didn't ask me here so we could swap bios. You said you had to be at work by two, so we better get down to business."

Dillon got up and refilled our cups and sat back down. She stared into her coffee for a moment before looking up. "I think someone is dealing drugs at the resort."

My eyes lit up. I took a sip of coffee and set the cup down. "What makes you think that?"

"Just talk from some of the employees at the resort. And I've seen certain people coming out of rooms where they had no business being."

That was an interesting scenario, but it didn't prove anything and I told her so.

Dillon shook her head and stared into her cup again. "I've smelled odors . . . my husband was involved with meth and marijuana and other junk while we were stationed at Eglin, so I'm pretty sure something's going on."

"If you think something's up, why don't you just quit and look for another job? There's no sense putting yourself in a risky situation."

Dillon looked away. "Have you checked the job market around here? It sucks. I couldn't make half of what I'm making at the Royale anywhere else." She turned her head and faced me with searching eyes. "Besides, it might be too late. This one girl approached me."

I waited a few seconds. "About what?"

She sniffled. "She said I could make some extra money, more money than the resort was paying me, if . . ."

"If what?"

She shook her head. "I think whoever's behind the drugs has been pressuring certain employees, mostly attractive girls, to help them push their junk."

"You got any idea who's behind this?"

Dillon shook a few more Cheerios from the box onto Tyler's tray. "No, not for sure. I mean, I've seen a couple of people, but I really can't mention any names."

I waited again, but Dillon wasn't offering. "Is Caitlin Medlin one of these people?"

Her jaw tightened, and she focused on the Cheerios box like she was reading a best-selling novel. "I really can't mention any names. It's not safe."

"How so?"

She let out a breath. "This girl asked me to flirt with the customers, find out who might be interested in what they were selling. I told her I didn't want to get involved, that I didn't want any trouble because of Tyler and all." Dillon dabbed at her eyes with her fingertips. "She told me it would be a shame if my son was taken away from me for being found with drugs in my possession." Tears trickled down her cheeks. "Can you help us?"

So that was their game. Put the squeeze on single moms or others in vulnerable situations who stood to lose more than a job if they didn't cooperate. Either help push their junk or risk being framed for refusing to get involved. I got up and tore a paper towel from a roll on the counter near the sink and handed it to Dillon. "You think the owners might be involved in this drug stuff?"

Dillon shook her head again. "I don't think so. I mean, from what I hear they're making a lot of money. Why would they risk losing their business over something illegal like that?"

Good answer. This girl had a savvy head on her shoulders.

Dillon sniffed and drew in a ragged breath. "There's something else you should know."

I waited.

"Back in college, I was busted for possession of marijuana."

"With intent to distribute?"

She shook her head. "No, we were at a big fraternity party and suddenly the cops came busting in. The word was that somebody working undercover tipped off the police. It was my first offense, so I had to appear in court and pay a small fine."

"No probation?"

"No."

"Then you're clean. I wouldn't worry about it."

She sighed. "I can't help but worry, because of my son. I mean, if somebody planted something on me and it was found, I might lose him."

"They're probably bluffing just to increase business," I said, hoping to ease her mind. I opened the envelope, pulled out the photos and handed them to Dillon. "Have you seen any of these people around the resort or casino?"

She spread the photos on the table and studied them a moment. "Yes." She turned the photo of Alice so that it was facing me. "This is Ms. Spence. She's one of the main owners or whatever; at least that's what I've heard."

I pointed to Wes Harrison's likeness. "What about him?"

Dillon's eyes narrowed as she gave the composite another look-see. "That could be Mr. Weston, only his hair is different and he doesn't have those funny-looking eyes."

"Does this Mr. Weston have a first name?"

Dillon turned her head and gently blew her nose into the paper towel. "I only know him as Mr. Weston. I mean, I don't really know him or anything. I've just seen him around a couple of times."

"Have you ever seen the two of them together?"

Dillon sucked on her lower lip. "I'm not sure, but I think so. Coming out of the office a few weeks ago just as my shift started. I'm pretty sure it was them."

It was a long shot, but I showed her the old beach photo of Kate and the others. She didn't recognize any of them.

"Can you help us, Andrew? Please, I don't have anyone at work I can discuss this with. And I can't tell my aunt. She'd go straight to the police, and the owners would find out and I'd lose my job for sure."

I reached across the table and placed a hand on her arm. "I'll see what I can do. For the time being don't trust anybody, period. You never know who might be working as a snitch to cover whose butt. Just go to work, do your job, and come home."

She wiped her nose and nodded.

The clock had caught up with us. Dillon had to get ready for work and drop Tyler off at daycare on the way. Tyler grabbed my finger and we shook good-bye as I got up to leave. Dillon unbuckled her son and carried him on a hip as she walked me to the door. I unlocked the deadbolt and started to turn the doorknob and then stopped. I looked straight into her eyes.

"It's real important that you don't talk about this to anybody," I said. "Not your aunt and especially nobody at work. Just go about your business as usual and act like nothing has happened. And try to avoid contact with any of the employees you don't trust. Meanwhile, I'll see what I can do, but this thing is probably bigger than anything we can handle by ourselves."

Dillon bit her lower lip and nodded as Tyler pawed at her breasts. "Mommy will feed you in a minute," she said.

Lucky guy. "And if you see me around, we don't know each other from Adam's second cousin. Not even eye contact. Got it?"

"Yes."

Suddenly Dillon wrapped her free hand around the back of my neck, pulled my face toward hers, and planted a kiss on my cheek. "Thank you, Andrew," she said as she closed the door behind me and locked the deadbolt.

CHAPTER 25

After leaving Dillon's house I drove around Parkersville a while and then turned east on Highway 98 toward St. George, chewing on what we'd just talked about. Like Dillon said, it wouldn't make sense for Alice or Wes to jeopardize their perfectly legitimate casino/resort business by allowing drugs to be dealt on the grounds. Why risk screwing up a very profitable and booming business for a few extra bucks such an operation might bring in? And why the hell would they have chanced having "Mr. Weston" fingered as Wes Harrison if it resulted in a police investigation? They were too sharp for that; at least I knew Alice was. My guess was that Alice was doing everything in her power to nip Caitlin Medlin's business in the bud before the cops got wind of it.

On the other hand, Ms. Medlin and her cohorts, Whit Coleman and Summer Tyson, were neck-deep in the drug crapola. This little entrepreneurial endeavor had their names written all over it. Also, Coleman and Tyson were both students at Chipola, another fertile ground for pushing their goodies.

My brain was starting to hurt. I figured I'd take my mind off things long enough to drive by the camper and make sure it was still in one piece. The campground was packed, and the Grey Wolf looked fine from the outside, so I drove on by and headed back to the Palmetto Royale. I hadn't used my complimentary half-hour massage yet, and after my meeting with Dillon I figured a little muscle-kneading might help me unwind and clear my mind while I thought about what my next step would be. I definitely needed to contact Frank and bring him up to date, but figured I'd wait until later that night. It might help liven up his evening.

On the way to the resort I called Kate on her cell phone. She and her mother were at the beach soaking up rays and were just about ready to head home. Things were going fine, but she was still a little miffed about being held prisoner at her parents' house, as she so delicately put it. Kate invited me to visit and have dinner with the Bells on Sunday, and I accepted. I didn't mention the little vacation I was taking at the Palmetto Royale. No sense in giving Kate cause to worry, or getting her more riled up than she already was, whichever the case might be.

It was around three-thirty when I got back to my room. I showered and then called the spa to see if I'd need an appointment for the massage, or if they took walk-ins. The young lady I spoke with assured me that I would be accommodated with a pleasurable experience at my convenience. Fancy words, but I took them to mean they accepted walk-ins. So, with my gratis certificate in hand I headed for the elevator.

The spa and gym were located in a wing of the hotel at the end of a long corridor past the offices. The outdoor pool area was crowded with swimmers and sunbathers. At the tiki bar I saw Dillon and a tall young man on duty. Dillon was serving a cocktail with a fancy looped straw to one of the few customers gathered around the bar. Either she didn't notice me as I passed, or she was heeding my warning not to make so much as eye contact with me.

Walking by the office doors I hesitated and glanced through the glass panes. An older couple stood at the counter talking to a young man wearing a resort polo shirt. I could also see a couple of disembodied heads behind the counter that obviously belonged to other employees busy at their desks, but nothing much else.

Pushing open the corridor's glass doors, I noticed the high ceiling was made of glass panels, and it was nearly as bright as the outdoors. Palms and other tropical plants grew along the borders of the stone walkway. Parrots and cockatiels and smaller colorful birds chirped and squawked and flitted about the lush foliage, and I wondered how the establishment kept the feathery critters from crapping on the customers. Maybe they didn't.

I followed the signs to the spa and entered through double glass doors. A well-toned, attractive woman around thirty dressed in a tight

Palmetto Royale T and white shorts greeted me with a practiced smile. Christ, did they ever hire any other types around here?

"Good afternoon, sir! How may I help you?"

I checked the name tag: Maryann. What the hell happened to her parents' imagination? "Hi," I said and handed her the certificate. "I thought I might try a massage."

Maryann glanced at the certificate and dropped it in a basket on the counter. "Certainly, Mr. McClellan." She handed me a flyer from a loose stack beside the basket. "It'll be just a few minutes. Why don't you have a seat over there and make yourself comfortable. In the meantime, would you like a complimentary drink?"

What the hell; I decided to go for broke. "Dewar's on the rocks?"

Another big smile from Maryann. "Certainly." She picked up a receiver, punched in a number, and said, "Dewar's on the rocks, please," and hung up. "We'll be right with you, Mr. McClellan."

A couple of minutes later another smiling resort clone appeared through a side door. She sashayed over and placed a tumbler of Scotch and a couple of napkins on the table beside my chair. I didn't bother to check her name tag. "There we go!"

I already had a five-spot ready and laid it on the small tray she was carrying. All these comps were breaking my bank.

"Thank you so much," she said. "Please let me know if I can get you anything else." With that, she retraced her path through the door.

I leaned back in the plush chair and sipped my drink while I looked at the flyer Maryann had given me:

You will soon enjoy thirty minutes of relaxing Swedish Massage Therapy, compliments of the Palmetto Royale Casino & Resort. We are certain you will find it an enjoyable and beneficial experience.

For a nominal fee our highly trained professionals offer the following healthful massage techniques to help ensure your stay at the Palmetto Royale is the most rewarding and pleasurable possible.

The flyer went on to list Aromatherapy, Hot Stone, Deep Tissue, Shiatsu, Thai, Reflexology, and other massages, with a description of each. Prices varied according to the technique and time involved. The one that grabbed my attention was the Royale Deluxe, described only as *The most intense, pleasurable and satisfying experience we offer.* I was half-tempted to give that one a try, but at two hundred bucks for an hour my imagination would have to do.

I'd just knocked back the last of the Dewar's when Maryann announced that they were ready for me. I followed her through a door and down a long hallway with several rooms on either side. We stopped at Room 7. Lucky me. Maryann tapped lightly on the door, and a tall blonde goddess appeared. What else should I have expected? She stood there smiling and looking me over with big blue almond-shaped eyes. She was decked out in a white halter and shorts. Oh, and a pair of white sandals that my eyes finally worked their way down to.

"Isabella, this is Mr. McClellan. He's here for our complimentary massage."

Isabella offered her hand. She had long slender fingers, perfect for a concert pianist. With digits like those I figured she could make some really beautiful body music. I took the hand and was surprised by the firm grip. I guess it comes with the territory. She arched an eyebrow. "Must I call you Mr. McClellan?"

I caught my breath. "Andrew will do just fine."

Isabella smiled. "Welcome, Andrew."

Isabella spoke very good English, but there was definitely an accent that I didn't quite recognize. My best guess was Latina. That probably accounted for the dark complexion that didn't appear to be the result of baking for hours under the sun.

Maryann made some sort of throaty noise to get my attention. "I'll leave you two now. Would you care for another drink, Mr. McClellan?"

"No thanks, I'm fine."

Maryann put on her smile. "If you change your mind or need anything at all, just let Isabella know. She'll take good care of you." With that, she left the room and closed the door behind her.

Before I could wonder what was coming next, Isabella opened a stainless steel cabinet, grabbed a plush white towel from a shelf, and handed it to me. "I will step out of the room for a moment while you undress to where you feel comfortable. You may lie on this table when you are ready." Good English, but a bit stodgy. She pointed to a stout table with thick padding covered in what looked to be genuine leather dyed a deep burgundy. "What kind of music do you wish, Andrew?"

Music? I hadn't thought of music as being part of the massage experience. "Why don't you choose," I said. Before I realized it, the sound of soft jazz was flowing from surround-sound speakers, and Isabella had disappeared through a door at the far wall.

I stood in the center of the room holding the towel. During my twenty-four-year career in the Marine Corps I came under enemy fire many times, but I don't recall ever being as nervous as I was right then. What the hell, it wasn't like I hadn't been naked in front of people a thousand times before. I kicked off my deck shoes, pulled my shirt over my head, and dropped my shorts. I debated and then decided that keeping my skivvies on would show Isabella that I had a touch of decorum. I draped my clothes across a chair and set my shoes on the floor beside it. Then I hopped onto the table, stretched out on my back, and covered myself with the large towel. After a couple of deep breaths I was able to relax a little, knowing everything from my shoulders to mid-calves was safely concealed.

A moment later the door opened and a smiling Isabella approached carrying a clear bottle that I assumed contained massage oil. She asked if I would please turn over on my stomach and place my face in the cradle at the head of the table. As I started to move she reached for the towel and turned her head away, for the sake of my modesty, I guessed.

I relaxed as best I could as Isabella folded the towel down past my waist. When she saw my skivvies she made a little "tsk-tsk" with her tongue. "Do you wish to keep these on, Andrew?"

My pulse was starting to pick up speed. "Does it matter?"

"I will not be able to do the massage as well, but it is up to you."

"Go ahead," I said, meaning for her to begin the massage. In a flash the towel was gone and my skivvies off in one smooth motion, leaving me basking in all my glory.

"I see you have scars," she said, lightly touching the exit wound from an AK-47 on the back of my left shoulder and then the shrapnel wound on my left calf. "I will be most careful to work around these."

Isabella draped the towel across me and folded it back somewhere in the vicinity of my butt crack. For the next several minutes she put those practiced hands of hers to work, stroking and kneading my shoulders and back, massaging the oil deep into my pores. Several times she discovered knots in my muscles and attacked them with deep pressure and well-placed karate chops. A bonus, I guess, and damn, it hurt so good.

Then she turned her attention to the backs of my legs, rubbing and stroking and squeezing her way down my thighs and calves to my feet. Next, she grabbed each leg in turn, lifting and stretching and kneading the tightness from them.

The old gluteus maximus awaited. Isabella warmed another squirt of oil between her palms and went to work. I tightened up like an over-wound clock spring. "Andrew, you must relax to get the benefit," Isabella said with a slight giggle.

I took a deep breath, exhaled like a pinpricked balloon, and relaxed. At least I tried to. The feel of Isabella's hands rubbing and squeezing my butt, and those slender fingers gliding along my crack and drifting dangerously close to the family jewels made relaxing all but impossible. She giggled again. "I will need two hours to make you relax."

When she was finished, Isabella gave my rear a playful slap. "You may turn over now, please. Do not worry, I will not look." She held the towel up and turned her head. I flipped over onto my back, and she dropped the towel across my body and then folded it from top and bottom until only my nether region was covered. I hadn't been so relaxed since my company spearheaded the assault into the Julan District during the fight for Fallujah in November of '04.

Isabella grabbed the oil and went to work on my thighs, stroking and kneading her way down both legs and even tweaking my toes. I'd had the advantage of not being able to see Isabella perform her magic while I was sprawled on my stomach, but now my eyes joined the adventure. I felt myself stir as she leaned over me, those smooth, strong hands gliding up and down my thighs, and her breasts jiggling enticingly in the process. A couple of times she came close but somehow managed not to allow them to brush against me. I turned my eyes away and tried to concentrate on the jazz. This was one time I sure as hell hoped I wouldn't rise to the occasion.

The situation was in grave doubt by the time Isabella folded the towel to one side, exposing my inner thigh. The family heirlooms were barely covered as she worked the muscles around my groin. I felt a throb and clenched my jaw tight to avoid snapping to attention. Isabella's eyes met mine and she smiled. "You are having a very hard time relaxing, Andrew," she said, and winked.

Isabella finally moved away from the danger zone and completed my relaxing and beneficial complimentary massage by working over my arms, shoulders, and neck. After a quick rubdown with a clean towel to remove any excess traces of oil, she excused herself so I could get dressed in the privacy of my own presence.

As soon as the door shut I grabbed my skivvies and set a new personal record for throwing on my clothes. Safely covered, I collapsed into a chair and waited. In a few minutes Isabella returned. She was wearing a bathrobe and carrying a round serving tray with two rock glasses half-filled with ice and what I guessed was Scotch.

She smiled and handed me one of the drinks. "Maryann said this is . . . how do you say . . . on the house." She chose the chair next to mine, sat with her legs tucked underneath, and turned to face me. "I hope you do not mind that I join you. You are my last customer today, and Maryann said it would be proper."

I took "proper" to mean okay or all right. "Be my guest." I was beginning to wonder if this whole massage routine was strictly on the up-and-up, no pun intended.

Isabella took a sip of her drink and swirled the ice around the glass. "You are here with your wife and family, Andrew?"

"No, it's just little ol' me. I've been divorced for a while now."

She arched one eyebrow again. "I see. I too was married long ago, but I was very young and it did not work out well."

What were you, twelve? I wondered. "I'm sorry to hear that."

Isabella sighed. "Yes, it is very sad when love does not last. Where is your home, Andrew?"

"North Carolina." I wasn't really lying. I was born in the Tar Heel State and had lived the majority of my life there. I decided to play along a while longer. "Where do you hail from, Isabella?"

She looked a little confused for a moment and then touched the hollow of her throat. "My home? I am from the city of San Jose del Cabo. You have heard of it?"

"I think so. It's on the Baja Peninsula, in Mexico, right?"

Isabella seemed pleased. "Sí, yes. I see you are a student of geography."

I smiled. "Let's just say I get by. So, how did you wind up in the States?"

Isabella sipped her drink and shifted in the chair. The top of her robe parted, but she was quick to raise a hand to close it. "I am here as a student at the university in Tallahassee. I wish to earn my degree in fitness management."

"Ah, a Florida State Seminole."

She smiled and raised an arm and gave the tomahawk chop. "Yes, go 'Noles!"

I laughed with her and then glanced at my watch. "Sorry, but I need to get going."

Isabella's lips formed a pout. "You must?"

"Yeah, I've got an appointment."

"With a lady friend?"

I gulped down the rest of my Scotch and gave her a wink. "It's business." I stood and handed the glass to Isabella and reached for my wallet.

Isabella got up and set the glasses on the tray in the chair next to her. She placed a hand on my forearm. "Thank you, Andrew. I do not often have the chance for talk. You must come again and try one of our finer massages. It will relieve you of all your tension, and I know you will enjoy it very much."

I tossed a twenty on the tray. "I might just do that. Can I ask for you?"

She smiled. "I will be very sad if you do not."

CHAPTER 26

That evening I was at the Polynesian Royale feasting on a medium-rare rib eye and roasted potatoes when Alice Spence walked up to my table. "Hello, Mac, imagine meeting you here!"

I managed to finish swallowing a bite of steak without requiring the Heimlich maneuver. She was wearing a teal suit with a knee-length skirt and a belted jacket with a loose, ruffled collar. A small matching purse was clutched in her left hand. Even dressed for business, Alice was stunning. I stood, and we shook hands and exchanged the usual pleasantries. "Have a seat," I said, motioning to the chair across from me. She took me up on the offer, and I remembered my manners just in time to hurry around the table and hold the chair for her. "Can I order something for you?" My mind was racing trying to come up with an excuse for what I was doing here.

"I can't stay long, but a drink would be nice." She waggled a perfectly manicured finger at my Dewar's. Her nail polish matched the suit. "What are you having?"

"Scotch."

"Then I'll join you."

I got the waitress's attention and ordered a Dewar's on the rocks for Alice and a double for me. Meanwhile, the old lightbulb flashed on and I had my excuse. I just hoped Alice would buy it.

"So, what brings you to the Palmetto Royale, Mac?"

I took a sip of Scotch to wet my whistle. "My ex-wife," I said. "Actually, my ex and her fiancé. They were planning on spending a long weekend at the resort. We were supposed to meet to talk over some family matters. Money and the kids and that kind of boring stuff. I thought I'd make it convenient and get a room here for a couple of days and do a little relaxing myself. But it looks like I've been stood up."

Alice smiled and swept a strawberry-blonde strand from her eyes. "How nice the two of you can get along so well."

"Yeah, just one big happy family."

She caught the sarcasm in my voice and offered a little laugh. "And I suppose you want to know why I'm here?"

"The thought crossed my mind."

The waitress brought our drinks. Alice took a sip of Dewar's, held the glass to one side, and smiled. She took another little taste and set the glass down. "It just so happens I own an investment company, and the Palmetto Royale is part of our portfolio. We're having a board meeting tomorrow here at the resort. Surprised?"

I figured that last word was a test. "A woman of your education and talent? Not at all."

Alice sipped more Scotch and put on yet another smile. "Miss Lettie told me you dropped by the house last week. I'm sorry I missed you."

Oops, another red flag. I decided I'd try a little schmoozing of my own to cover my tail. "I'm sorry I missed you, too. I was in the area on business for Frank Hightower and thought I'd take a chance and drop by to say hello. I was hoping you could suggest a nice restaurant and do me the honor of joining me for dinner."

"Aren't you ever the charmer? But tell me, do you always go snooping around people's backyards when you find out they're not home?"

I felt like somebody had jerked my swimsuit down around my ankles and left me standing butt-naked on a crowded beach. "Miss Lettie ratted on me, huh?"

"Of course she did."

My mind was whirring. "Okay, I stand guilty as charged. To be honest, I couldn't quite get you off my mind after we met, so I searched online for your name and found the lifestyles feature the *Journal-Constitution* ran on you and your mansion. I know I should've asked Lettie's permission, but since you weren't home I thought I'd go ahead and take a firsthand look at some of the scenery I saw in the article. You have a very beautiful place."

Alice pursed her lips and then her face relaxed. I had a hunch she wasn't buying much, if any, of the BS explanation I was feeding her. "I suppose I should be flattered, shouldn't I? But what about Kate . . . Bell, isn't it? I thought you two were an item."

"We're friends, that's all."

A good imitation of the Mona Lisa spread across Alice's face. "I see." She took another drink and glanced at her gold wristwatch. "I hate to run, Mac, but I have a meeting in ten minutes. It was certainly nice seeing you again. Thank you for the drink." She grabbed her purse and made a move to stand, and then hesitated. "Oh, and if you're ever in Atlanta on business again, try calling first."

I started to get up to help Alice with the chair, but her back was to me before my knees straightened out.

As soon as I got back to my room I gave Frank a call. "How's lover-boy doing?"

"I'm parked a half block down the street from his girlfriend's house as we talk. According to his wife he's supposed to be on duty tonight."

"Some duty. I just had an interesting conversation with Alice Spence."

"Yeah?"

"Yeah. I was having supper and she walked right up to my table. Quite a coincidence, huh?"

"I'd say you're a marked man."

"No argument here. I fed Alice a cock-and-bull story about meeting my ex-wife and her fiancé at the resort this weekend to settle some family matters. She played along like she believed me, but I wouldn't bet my last three-dollar bill on it. Alice volunteered that she owns an investment company, and the Palmetto Royale is one of their properties. She also said she was here because they're holding a board meeting tomorrow. That little tidbit checks out with what my new contact said."

"New contact?"

"Yeah. I'll get to that in a minute. Guess who else I happened to run into?"

"Wes Harrison?"

"No, but I'll get to him later, too. David Garrett."

"You're kidding?"

"Nope. He just happened to be sitting across from me at this tiki bar out by the pool where I stopped for a beer. He was half plastered and kept hitting on a couple of women and making a general ass of himself. I asked the girl tending bar if she knew who he was, and she said his name was Garrett, and that she'd heard he was one of the owners of the place."

"And this bartender just happens to be your new contact."

"Still sharp as a tack, Frank."

"What makes you think you can trust her, Mac? She could be in on it and working to set you up."

"That crossed my mind until we met this morning at her house. She's a single mother living with her aunt and little boy in Parkersville. She ID'd Alice immediately from the photos, and she's heard through the grapevine that Alice is the big cheese at the Palmetto Royale. She also recognized Wes Harrison from the composite you worked up. She knows him as Mr. Weston, no known first name. She said the hairstyle was wrong and that he didn't have the funny-looking eyes, but she was pretty sure it was him. And, she saw Alice and Harrison coming out of the resort office together a couple of weeks ago."

"Wait a minute. Weston? Isn't that—"

"Yeah, it's Harrison's real first name. The guy's either not very inventive or he's flat-out stupid."

"Okay, Mac, so we know that Alice, by her own admission, owns a big slice of the Palmetto Royale, and that they're holding a board meeting there this weekend. That's SOP for practically all corporate-owned businesses. And we already knew Garrett is in on the deal, so it makes perfect sense for him to be there, too. Wes Harrison may or may not be in the picture. 'Pretty sure' doesn't constitute a positive ID.

It seems like all your new contact has accomplished is to back up facts that you received directly from Alice."

"There's more, Frank, and I'll cut right to the bone. My contact thinks somebody is dealing drugs from the resort. She said that whoever's running the show is recruiting certain people, mostly good-looking young women, to help sell their wares."

"You don't think Spence and Harrison are involved, do you?"

"No way, this is small potatoes. They stand to lose too much to risk that. My girl thinks the perps are employees at the resort trying to make some extra money on the side using the Royale's clientele. Not bad waters to go fishing in with all the money and other niceties flowing around this place."

"And just where did this contact of yours come up with all this information? I doubt the resort has it listed in their brochure under 'activities' or 'things not to miss during your stay.'"

"One of the girls involved in dealing tried to get my contact to enlist. My girl's a single mother and wanted no part of it. She told me meth just happens to be on the menu, along with other junk. Does that ring any bells?"

"Yeah, the raid on that house in St. George your other contact tipped you off about. They turned up a meth lab, right?"

"Right. And don't forget that the Tyson girl who went missing was a student driving a fancy car with no apparent job to pay for it. My guess is she was shopping her wares at college."

"Hmm. As Arte Johnson used to say, 'Verrry in-ter-est-ing.'"

"Who?"

"Never mind, he was before your time. Where do we go from here?"

"My contact wants my help. She's afraid to get involved or go to the cops because of her son and the risk of losing her job. I told her I'd see what I could do, meaning you and me."

"I can't get away, so you're on your own for now, Mac. Do what you can, but watch your backside."

"Gee, thanks for the support. By the way, did I happen to mention the complimentary massage that came as part of my three-day package?"

"No, but I'd bet good money that you're about to."

"My masseuse was this tall blue-eyed blonde from Mexico with magic fingers. She was dressed to kill, and I was sure she was going to put the make on me, but it turns out she was legit. Afterward, she showed up in a bathrobe with drinks, and we sat and talked a while. She's a student at FSU working on a degree in fitness management. Nice girl."

"And your point is?"

"You should give it a try, Frank. It'll do you a world of good, work out all those kinks you've been accumulating while watching the peep show. Ask for Isabella and request the Royale Deluxe massage. And be sure to tell her I sent you."

"Good night, Mac."

∼⌒

I was sitting in the Royale Café the next morning having a late breakfast when I felt my cell phone vibrate. I was at a small corner table for two with no one else close by, so I answered instead of letting the call go to voice mail.

"Mac, it's J.D. Dakota just got arrested at the casino."

I nearly dropped my fork. "What?"

"I said Dakota just got—"

"Yeah, I heard you. Arrested for what?"

"Suspicion of murder."

"Murder? Christ. Come on, J.D., spit it out." J.D. Owens was a fine young officer, but he had a tendency to drag things out now and then.

"Remember that Medlin girl, the one who lives in the house on 31st Street that we busted?"

"Yeah?"

"They found her dead in the sand dunes near the house around one-thirty this morning."

"Damn. Who found her?"

"A couple of teenagers. They'd gone up in the dunes to make out and found her there."

Scratch one night of hot and horny teen romantic action. "Why do they think Dakota had anything to do with it?"

"We found her knife near the body just after daylight while we were searching the area."

"How do they know it's her knife?"

J.D. let out a heavy breath. "Because I gave it to her for Christmas when we were kids. It's got her initials inscribed on the handle and her prints are all over it."

"Lock blade?"

"No, it's just a small Buck with two blades."

"They think Dakota stabbed the girl to death with a pocketknife?" It wasn't impossible, but it wouldn't be an easy thing to do, especially if the victim was putting up any kind of a fight. In that case the attacker would likely have cuts on the hands or fingers, too.

"No, she wasn't stabbed. The victim was clubbed on the back of the head and then her carotid artery was cut. She bled to death."

My appetite was gone, but I signaled the waitress with my empty coffee cup. "Sounds like a professional hit. You don't think Dakota did it, do you?"

"No way, Mac, but with the knife and all, the evidence points to her."

"What's the 'all' you're talking about, J.D.?"

J.D. let out a long breath. "Dakota and Caitlin Medlin both worked at the casino, and the word is that they didn't get along very well."

What the hell was with Dakota? First she gets into a public brawl with Summer Tyson behind The Green Parrott, and now she's accused of murdering Summer's roomie. The waitress arrived with the coffeepot and refilled my cup. I waited until she headed for another table across the room. "What about Caitlin Medlin's boyfriend, what's-his-name? Have you questioned him?" I was having a sudden brain fart and couldn't come up with the name.

"Whit Coleman. We're looking for him. He quit going to his classes at Chipola before the semester ended, and his parents haven't heard from him in over a week."

"Looks like you guys are on the ball."

"Yeah, Chief Tolliver says a rolling stone gathers no moss, whatever that means. There's something that doesn't make much sense though, Mac. About two hours ago FHP found Caitlin Medlin's BMW just inside the woods on the west side of Highway 75 about ten miles south of the casino. It wasn't locked and the keys were still in the ignition. The county's towing it in."

That put the old brain cells into motion. "Maybe somebody stopped her car and killed her there, and then planted the body in the dunes."

"I thought about that, but there was a whole bunch of blood around the body. The coroner said she bled to death at the scene."

"Okay, what if they knocked her unconscious along the highway and then moved the body to the dunes and killed her there?"

"I reckon that's possible. I'll ask the chief about it."

"You do that, J.D. Where are they holding Dakota?"

"The county jail in Parkersville. Sheriff Pickron was the arresting officer."

That was strange. I knew the sheriff's department had a couple of deputies patrolling the northern part of Palmetto County at all times since the casino opened. Why would Bo Pickron drive all the way out to Dobro to make the arrest? The sheriff had a touch of glory-hog in him, but this seemed a little over the top even for Bocephus. A question that had been bugging me for quite a while kept running through my mind, and I intended to get the answer ASAP.

"Thanks, J.D. Keep me posted."

CHAPTER 27

"What is it now, McClellan?" Sheriff Bo Pickron didn't bother to get up from behind his desk, or extend a friendly hand, for that matter. He did motion to one of the chairs on either side of his messy desk. I pulled one toward the middle and took a seat.

"You're like a festering boil on my ass," he said.

Good analogy; I'm the boil, he's the ass. "I heard you made an arrest at the casino this morning."

"From Sergeant J.D. Owens, I'd wager."

"Maybe."

Pickron's two hundred and fifty pounds made the plush swivel chair groan as he rocked back and took a swig from a bottle of Diet Coke. He swallowed, and a smirk crawled across his bulldoggish mug. "And what business is that of yours?"

"Dakota is J.D.'s cousin, but I guess you already know that. I'm a friend of hers."

"And that's supposed to impress me . . . why?"

"You know Dakota didn't have a damn thing to do with killing Caitlin Medlin."

A wry grin replaced the smirk. "Dakota's knife was found at the murder scene, and she and the Medlin girl have a history of bad blood between them. I talked to several employees at the casino who'll swear to it. That's plenty enough evidence for a murder charge."

"Did you bother to look into the fact that Miss Medlin's car was found in the woods along the highway heading south from the casino? Or that Whit Coleman has been missing for over a week? Where is he? They were shacked up together, you know."

"Yeah, yeah, I'm aware of all that."

"Look, Sheriff, did you ever consider the possibility that somebody might've accosted the girl on the highway and knocked her senseless, then moved her to the dunes where they did the butcher job and left her to bleed out and die? Or are you too damn hardheaded to look past the fact that Dakota's pocketknife was found at the scene? Where's the blunt object? And why would she be so careless as to leave her knife near the body? Sounds like a plant job to me."

Pickron's grin morphed into a frown. He sat up and rested his beefy forearms on the desk and pointed a finger at me. "That still doesn't let the Owens girl off the hook. She could've pulled off exactly what you just said. From what I hear she's a pretty tough character. And how many times do I have to tell you to keep your nose out of county business, McClellan? If you want to tell me how to do my job, I suggest you run for sheriff next election."

I felt like jerking the big SOB over the table and pounding the crap out of him, but sanity prevailed. "Maybe I'll do just that." There was no sense in beating my head against a brick wall any longer. I got up to leave, but then the thought my mind had been haggling over stopped me in my tracks. I turned and pointed a finger at him. "You look me straight in the eye and answer one question for me, Pickron. And I want you to swear on Maddie's memory that it'll be the truth."

Pickron looked flustered when I mentioned his late niece's name, and then his face lost all expression. "I don't owe you a damn thing, McClellan, remember that. But because you turned up Maddie's killer, I'll be straight with you."

"I appreciate that." I locked eyes with his and tried to see through them into his soul, assuming he had one. "Man-to-man—is Dakota Owens working undercover with your department?"

Pickron clenched his jaw and flushed a deep shade of red, and for a split-second I thought he was going to come out of that chair and pound me to a pulp. Then he remembered to breathe and relaxed a little. "Yes."

Dakota's third-floor cell was at the far end of a corridor with several empty cells between her and the rest of the female prisoners being housed in the county slammer. Dakota was curled into the fetal position on one of the lower bunks with her face to the wall. She was in typical prison garb: loose-fitting orange shirt and pants and white ankle socks. The Adidas running shoes I'd seen her wearing before were under the bunk. The gruff, stocky woman jailer turned the key and slid the barred door open. "Sheriff says ya got ten minutes, startin' now," she grunted out, pointing at the watch strapped to her thick wrist. Miss Congeniality, in the flesh.

The watch must've been digital. I couldn't imagine her possessing the IQ necessary to figure out what Mickey's pointing hands meant. I thanked Attila the Hunness as she slammed the door shut and locked it. What a class act. Bocephus should consider promoting her to his personal secretary to replace the twenty-something model manning the desk outside his office.

There was a groan as Dakota slowly rolled over and sat up. She was bent at the waist and staring down at the concrete floor, both hands gripping the edge of the bunk for support. Her hair covered her face and looked like it could stand a good brushing. "What the hell are *you* doing here, McClellan? Rob a bank or something?"

Her voice sounded different, more a forced mumble than her usual sharp and lively tongue. When Dakota slowly lifted her head to look at me I saw why. "Christ, looks like Caitlin Medlin put up one hell of a fight while you were killing her." There was a stitched inch-and-a-half-long cut on top of a big eggplant lump above Dakota's right eye. Her lower lip was split and also stitched. The left side of her jaw was bruised and swollen. Somebody had done a bang-up job of pounding the crap out of her, and I'd bet my next three retirement checks it wasn't the late drug czaress.

Dakota forced her battered lips into what I took for a smile. "Yeah, she's one badass bitch all right." She coughed and grabbed her rib cage. That was enough for me. I stepped to the bunk and took hold of the bottom hem of her shirt. She slapped my hand away. "Get your paws off me, McClellan. You already had your chance."

"Please, let me take a look," I said in the kindest, most fatherly voice I could muster.

Dakota winced as she flashed her Elvis snarl, and then sighed and let me lift the blouse up to just below her breasts. Her rib cage was heavily taped. I gently lowered the orange top to her lap. "Broken?"

"Couple cracked is all."

I was pissed. "Who the hell did this?"

"A doctor."

I couldn't hold back a quick laugh. Dakota was one tough cookie. You could beat the crap out of her, but not her spirit or sense of humor. "Very funny. Who beat you?"

Another snarl, followed by a shake of the head. "None of your friggin' business."

I dropped to a knee so Dakota wouldn't have to keep looking up at me. Before I could ask my next question, she said, "Jeez, McClellan, are you fixing to propose?"

I laughed again. Dakota did too and grabbed her ribs as payment. I reached out and gently put my fingertips under her chin until she was looking into my eyes. "Maybe, if I was fifteen years younger. Look, let's drop the tough girl act, okay? I know you're a deputy and that you've been working undercover."

She turned her face away. "That's a real hoot. You always into the Scotch this early?"

"I just came from Sheriff Pickron's office. He told me."

Dakota kept her head turned for a minute. When she finally looked back and faced me, there was a trace of moisture in her eyes. "Well, I guess that makes us kindred spirits of a sort, doesn't it, McClellan?"

"How so?"

"Last summer. Sheriff Pickron deputized you, and you worked undercover for him on Maddie Harper's case."

"So, you know about that."

"Yeah, I was already with the department, part time until I finished my training. Pickron let me in on it because I was trying to get info on Brett's customers."

"Then you also know he wound up firing me."

"Good thing. You're too friggin' hotheaded to be a cop."

My mind kick-started into motion. "Why did you come on to me the way you did?"

Dakota gave that throaty growling sound I'd first heard outside The Green Parrot. "Don't flatter yourself. It was all part of the job."

"You always go around trying to seduce people as part of your job?"

She gave a half-hearted smile. "Well, you're not all that hard to look at, McClellan. I figured a few perks while doing my duty wouldn't hurt."

I grinned. "Thanks, I think."

"You're welcome."

"So, the job at the casino was a cover for an investigation."

"You're sharp as a scalpel, McClellan."

"What led you there?"

Dakota ran her fingers along her swollen jaw like she was testing for loose teeth. "Remember the night I asked you to keep an eye out for J.D.?"

I nodded.

"J.D.'s a good cop, but he gets careless sometimes. I was at his house having supper one night and found some printouts he'd left out on the counter in an envelope that had your name on it. I recognized the guy you call Wes Harrison. I'd seen him around the pool a couple of times. Do the math."

"But why were you working at the casino in the first place?" Heavy clomping echoed from the corridor, growing louder with each step. My ten minutes had flown by way too fast, especially since my watch showed I had two left. But who's counting? "Attila's coming."

"Somebody working at the resort made an anonymous call to the department a while back, something about drugs being pushed."

Dillon flashed through my mind.

"Sheriff Pickron needed somebody there who would fit in. I had the background, so I was it."

Just then the lock clinked. The door slid open, and Attila growled, "Time's up."

I leaned in close and whispered, "Who beat you?"

Dakota shook her head. "Later. Be careful, they're on to you."

～～⤳

As soon as I left Dakota's cell I headed straight for Pickron's office. The good sheriff wasn't exactly thrilled to see me again so soon, but when I left after a heated twenty-minute visit I had most of the answers I was after.

Returning home around midnight from her shift at the casino, Dakota had been jumped from behind outside her apartment. The assailants (she thought there were two) quickly pulled a laundry bag or something similar over her head and shoulders and proceeded to pummel the shit out of her. Being a black belt in karate probably saved her life. She fought back and got off a few lucky kicks and was finally able to work free of the hood. Fortunately, just before losing consciousness she managed to draw the Glock from its hidden holster tucked in her waistband, and the assailants beat feet. She passed out and woke up a little before dawn and called the sheriff's department for help. A deputy patrolling the unincorporated area outside of St. George quickly arrived on the scene, with the sheriff himself not far behind.

They transported Dakota to the emergency room at Parkersville Memorial. After a thorough examination and x-rays, a doctor stitched her cuts and wrapped her ribs. She was battered and bruised but otherwise in no danger physically.

After being treated at the hospital, Dakota told the sheriff that someone had opened the combination lock on her locker at the casino during her shift. When she opened her purse to get her car keys, she noticed the purse had been messed with. Her pocketknife, which she always placed next to her wallet as an alarm, was missing. It didn't take an Einstein to figure out somebody had used the knife to set her up for the murder.

If Dakota had been found beaten to death and the murder of Caitlin Medlin was pinned on her, the authorities might've figured it was a revenge killing. Dakota, with her tough-girl reputation and history of run-ins with Medlin, would've taken the heat. The cops would've been looking for someone in Medlin's circle of friends who figured an eye for an eye. Her live-in boyfriend—the missing Whit Coleman—in particular.

Dakota agreed to gut it out and show up for her nine o'clock shift wearing sunglasses and a hat and makeup to hide her face as much as possible. Pickron was waiting when she arrived at the casino and made a big show of arresting her just outside the casino's entrance. Dakota was handcuffed, read her rights, and placed in the back of a deputy's car. She was then transported to the county jail where she was being held in protective custody safely away from the other inmates or another try on her life.

Meanwhile, Sheriff Pickron interviewed several employees of the Palmetto Royale, asking all the right questions and conveniently letting it slip more than once that Dakota had been charged with the murder of Caitlin Medlin.

Driving back to the Palmetto Royale, Dakota's whispered warning kept running through my mind: "Be careful, they're on to you." Just who the hell were the "they" Dakota meant? The goons who hammered her? Alice Spence and Wes Harrison, or David Garrett? The drug pushers? I scratched the latter off my list, since somebody had already snuffed out Ms. Medlin, and most likely Whit Coleman, too. The others involved in Caitlin's enterprise were most likely running scared or hiding.

I was tired and beginning to lose focus on the case, and mentally tried to tie some loose ends together as I turned onto Highway 75 and headed north. I had to assume that Wes Harrison was alive and well and somehow hooked up with Alice Spence. There was fairly hard evidence attesting to that. Harrison had been one of the principals fencing the illegal diamonds that Rachel Todd smuggled into the country, and he and Alice had a history.

Robert Ramey was long dead, I was convinced of that. And there was no real evidence I'd uncovered that showed Rachel Todd or Travis Hurt, aka Eric Kohler, were still in the picture. Sacred Word Missions, with Dr. Lawrence Garrett designated as trustee, had inherited Rachel's money after her supposed death in the jungles of South America. Garrett's nephew David was a current partner in the ownership of the casino and resort. What could be clearer? I needed Watson, IBM's supercomputer *Jeopardy* champion, to unscramble this mess.

Then again, maybe not. Maybe I was trying to overcomplicate things with too many parameters. Maybe it was time to trim away all the fat and get down to the lean. Somebody had rigged Kate's car to crash, and somebody had tried to kill me in a drive-by shooting. None of this had begun until the night Kate and I exited O'Malley's Theater after watching *Dead Man Walking*. There, Kate had seen Wes Harrison, a ghost from her past, and I had bumped headlong into the woman with him, a woman with a knockout body and reddish hair, like Alice Spence. Throw in Alice's look of surprise when I showed up at her Buckhead mansion that day, and the theory of Alice being Harrison's date at O'Malley's that night wasn't such a long shot at all.

The mysterious Mr. Weston had been seen with Ms. Spence at the Palmetto Royale by an eyewitness, namely Dillon. Dakota had also seen the two there, though not together.

That had to be it. All roads led to "they" being none other than Wes Harrison and Alice Spence. For the moment, anyway, Watson could relax.

CHAPTER 28

Dakota's warning gave me reservations about returning to the Palmetto Royale, but I couldn't leave my stuff there. I parked the rental and made sure my revolver was tucked safely in the back of my Dockers as I headed back to my room. There was no one in the hallway. I drew the .357 and slid the key card through the slot, then threw the door open in case someone was hiding behind it. It bounced off the stop, and I caught it with my free hand as it came back at me.

I eased the door shut, turned the deadbolt to cover my back, and did a quick but thorough search of my room, including the outside balcony. It reminded me of clearing buildings in Iraq, only this place was much swankier and I had no backup. When I knew all was clear, the adrenaline rush slowed and I breathed easier. For a moment I considered packing and leaving, but what the hell, the room was paid for, so I figured I might as well stay the night.

It was only a few minutes past three, but I was on vacation, so I grabbed a beer from a six-pack I had stored in the fridge. I stepped out to the balcony with the Smith & Wesson tucked inside my waistband, just in case. There was an older couple sitting out a few balconies away to my left, and I returned their friendly wave. The pool area was crowded, and from what I could see the tiki bar was doing a brisk business on this sunny Saturday afternoon. I wondered if Dillon was on duty. For some reason I missed her company.

Frank says any PI worth his salt would never be caught without having a good pair of binoculars handy, and when I saw a woman with reddish-blonde hair wearing a tight green dress saunter past the tiki bar and into the mall, I felt like kicking myself in the butt. I was pretty damn sure it was Alice Spence, and she'd been accompanied by a big man with thick whitish hair. David Garrett, maybe, but I wasn't sure. I was tossing around the idea of following them when my cell phone rang. I hurried inside to answer it so the neighbors wouldn't hear.

"McClellan, I've only got a minute, so listen up." Dakota sounded like she was speaking through clenched teeth, which was understandable considering the beating she'd taken. "Caitlin Medlin and her crew were pushing ice and weed and other crap to select customers around the Royale. Whit Coleman and Summer Tyson were covering Chipola and other places."

"Ice?"

Dakota let out an annoyed breath. "Crystal meth. Not only did they have a meth lab in the house, but they were also shaking and baking the shit. It's a wonder they didn't blow the friggin' neighborhood to kingdom come."

"Shaking and baking?"

"Never mind, McClellan, just listen. They had Medlin snuffed out before she could bargain with the DA's office. They couldn't risk having a police investigation ruin their legit casino operation."

"Who exactly is 'they'?"

"I think you've got that pretty much figured out."

"What about Coleman?"

"My nickel says he's dead, too."

"Summer Tyson?"

"Like I said, she was working the college scene with Coleman. When the bust went down she had the good sense to get while the getting was good."

"The little catfight you two had behind The Green Parrot—what was that about?"

"I suspected Tyson was dealing at Chipola and I needed an excuse to be able to approach her there. I knew she was dating a guy I'd gone with in high school, so I put the heat on her to lay off *my* boyfriend. Then I conveniently picked a fight in a public place when the two of them were together."

"Dakota the tough girl."

"Yeah. Now keep quiet for a minute and listen. I managed to get into Alice Spence's office and went through some of her files. Before you ask, I picked a couple of locks. Your Wes Harrison is now Russell Weston. He's a silent partner and spends most of his time in the Caymans. He's a real wheeler-dealer with some pretty sticky fingers. Him and Spence have a friggin' shitload of money stashed in banks on Grand Cayman. We're talking millions here, mostly legit from what I could tell. They've done a lot of investing in the Caribbean over the last decade; nightclubs, casinos, restaurants, real estate, a lot of crap. They also have a home on Grand Cayman, more like a walled compound on several acres."

"Why did—"

"No time for Twenty Questions, McClellan. I got careless and overlooked a security camera in Spence's office that was hidden on a bookshelf. By the time I noticed the friggin' thing it was too late. I got out of there, but I'm sure that's how they fingered me, and why they sicced the dogs on me. I think those bad boys who jumped me are pros down from Hotlanta. These people aren't fooling around, so watch your ass. And don't let Sheriff Pickron know I called you or he'll have mine. Gotta go."

After talking with Dakota my mind was spinning. I was in over my head, so I called Frank and brought him up to speed on my rather eventful Saturday.

"It looks like we can shelve the idea of me buying into Alice's little enterprise," he said. "Things are moving way too fast for that. Pack up and get out of there and lay low, Mac. My guess is that Wes Harrison is not a very happy investor at this point. Pickron knows something's up now. Let him and the department handle this."

Frank was right, and I fully intended to follow his advice. With Caitlin Medlin out of the picture, the drug dealing was pretty much a nonissue at this point. But the odds were sweet that the Palmetto

Royale stood to get a nasty black eye by proxy from Caitlin's little business venture. If that happened Wes Harrison could be in deep shit. Plus, there were goons on the loose, probably the same goons who'd already tried to silence both Kate and me and take out Dakota. Saving my bacon was way up there on my current list of priorities.

But first there was something I had to do. I changed into shorts and a fresh polo shirt and packed my things. Then I tore a sheet of notepaper from the pad on the telephone stand beside the bed and jotted down a quick note:

Leave here as soon as you can and don't come back to work until you hear from me. The cavalry is on the way.

If Dillon was working the tiki bar, I hoped she would understand the message I intended to slip her. If she wasn't there, I'd call her on my way back to St. George. I set the suitcase by the door and then secured the Smith & Wesson in the back of my waistband under my shirt. I hoped it wouldn't be too obvious, but I sure as hell wasn't going anywhere without it. Then I headed for the elevator.

My luck was holding. Dillon was working with a pale-skinned, freckled young woman sporting a lip ring and eggplant-colored hair streaked with fuchsia. The bar was still crowded, but I found an empty stool in the area Dillon was serving. My back was to the office doors. I didn't care for that, but at least I'd be able to see anyone walking past the bar and heading in the direction of the office.

It was a couple of minutes before Dillon noticed me sitting there. There was a quick widening of her eyes, but she quickly recovered. She flashed a businesslike smile as she walked over. "Hi, there. What can I get for you?"

I ordered a Michelob, and as Dillon turned and walked away I pulled three dollar bills from my wallet, and the Alexander Hamilton that I'd folded over the note. In a minute Dillon returned with the beer, a frosted mug, and some napkins. "Here we are," she said, flashing her pearly whites.

I declined the mug and smiled. "Thanks." I pushed the three singles across the bar. She scooped them up and started to turn away. "Wait, this is for you, honey," I said, holding the folded ten-spot out to her. I placed the bill into her waiting hand, gave it a gentle squeeze, and winked. "For your friendly smile." I hoped like hell Dillon would get the message that I was flirting with her.

She returned the smile, thanked me, and slipped the ten into her short's pocket without looking, then went about her business. I nursed the Michelob and kept my eyes peeled for anyone I might recognize. A man sitting to my left tried to strike up a conversation, but I wasn't in a talking mood, and he soon turned his attention to the person at his other side.

About halfway through the beer I felt something hard press into the small of my back a little to the right of my revolver. A head leaned over my left shoulder just out of my peripheral vision, and a gruff voice muttered quietly, "Turn around real slow and come with me."

I straightened my back and polished off the beer in four gulps. I figured I could use all the liquid bravado I could get, but I knew one beer damn sure wasn't going to help much. For a second I considered my chances might be better settling this with the guy right there at the bar, but if things turned nasty I didn't want any innocents getting shot. This wasn't their fight.

As I stood I glanced and saw Dillon with her back to me. Damn, scratch one slim chance of getting rescued. I did a one-eighty as ordered, and the guy turned with me like a dancing partner, keeping just out of my sight with what I figured was his gun hand still pressing against my back. He slapped my shoulder with his free hand and laughed like we were old friends and said, "We better go check on Phil before he gets into any more trouble." And then me and my new old buddy walked away from the bar toward the office.

∼✑

When I came to, it was dark and my head hurt like holy hell. It took a minute or so before I realized I was sitting in a chair with my hands tied behind me and lashed tightly to the back spindles. There was a ribbon of light on the floor underneath a door across the room to my left front, and I thought I heard murmuring voices coming from that direction. Given the current circumstances, I didn't figure Isabella was getting ready to make a grand entrance into the room and treat me to a Royale Deluxe, although I sure as hell could've used one right then. After a few minutes the voices stopped.

My head finally cleared enough that I remembered my dancing partner had led me past the office doors where he relieved me of the .357. We continued down the long corridor with all the tropical plants and squawking birds to a door somewhere on the left side of the spa building. He rapped twice on the door, and that's when I'd made my big move.

I rammed an elbow into the guy's solar plexus and heard the air rush from his lungs. I spun around and saw he was bent over double, so I jerked my knee up, cracking him hard in the face, and watched him tumble backward flat on his back. I was trying to retrieve the S & W when my running lights went out.

I sat there for several more minutes as my senses slowly returned. My chivalrous intentions to warn Dillon had landed me up to my neck in shit stew. I glanced around the room but saw no windows. I guessed it was sometime Saturday night. I remembered that I was supposed to visit Kate in Destin on Sunday. She was going to be highly pissed when I stood her up, especially with no phone call to explain why.

Phone call. My cell phone had been in the right front pocket of my shorts. I moved my feet and found they weren't tied. A modicum of good news, as Sherlock Holmes or Watson might have put it. I wiggled my right leg back and forth but couldn't detect anything in the pocket. It didn't really matter at that point with my hands bound behind me. The luck I'd felt when I found Dillon at the tiki bar and managed to slip her the note had wasted little time turning around to bite me on the ass.

My eyes finally adjusted to the darkness some, and I could see shadowy objects. There were filing cabinets and shelving of some kind lining a couple of walls. A utility desk stood before me, and the shelves behind it were lined with books and big binders. To my right was a metal door. I could make out the round knob, but no trace of light shone through any of the edges. Most likely it led outside and was probably the door I'd been hauled through when my noble escape attempt had royally flopped. I jerked when a telephone sitting on the desk rang. Somebody picked up from another room during the third ring.

Another half hour or so dragged by. I spent it generally feeling sorry for myself and mentally kicking my ass for being so damn careless. Some private eye I'd turned out to be. I should've vacated the premises ASAP, but for some reason I'd felt an obligation, maybe even a duty, to warn Dillon first. After all, what Marine worth his salt would leave a person who had trusted him in a lurch? Semper Fi, do or die, oooraahhh! Shit. I did what I did because I had to. Simple as that.

The back of my head still throbbed like somebody had nailed me with a two-by-four or baseball bat, which they probably had, à la Caitlin Medlin. But why hadn't they finished the job? After thinking for a minute, it was an easy enough question to deduce. They were waiting until things quieted down around the resort before transporting me elsewhere to slit my throat or blow my brains out or however they planned to do me in. After all, why splatter blood or brains or both all over their shiny new facilities for the cops to find after the big vamoose back to the Caymans?

This pleasant thought was still bouncing around my head when I heard footsteps clacking toward the door with the strip of light at the bottom. The handle turned, and then a rush of light nearly blinded me as someone opened the door and flipped on a switch. I lowered my eyes and blinked against the glare as footsteps clattered into the room. A few seconds later I glanced up, squinting directly into the beautiful green eyes of Alice Spence. She was wearing the same jade party dress I'd seen from my balcony earlier in the day, or at least I assumed this was still Saturday. Only now I saw the front and was treated to a plunging neckline that balanced nicely with the mid-thigh length. And standing beside Alice in the flesh was none other than the late Weston Russell Harrison, or the very much alive Russell Weston. Take your pick.

"You just couldn't leave well enough alone, could you, Mac?" Alice said with a smirk spread across her full lips.

I mustered up a smirk of my own. "You know what they say: a day without Alice is like a day without sunshine."

"You should learn to mind your own business."

"Well, when somebody tries to kill a close friend of mine, and then me, I tend to make it my business. And now you've gotten careless and let an employee's two-bit sideshow threaten to bring down your empire. By the way, how was your board meeting?"

The smirk stayed in place. "Great. Business is booming and our profit margin is up nicely for the quarter."

I nodded. "I guess those smuggled diamonds are still paying big dividends after all these years."

Harrison stepped over and slugged me in the jaw. The room spun for a minute and then gradually slowed to a stop. All in all, it was quite an introduction. "Not bad for an immovable target," I said, after checking with my tongue to make sure none of my teeth had abandoned ship. "Did you tie up those Mexican girls back during high school before you beat them, too? Or did you just schmooze them into obeying you with your irresistible natural charm?"

He made another move for me, but Alice reached out and grabbed his arm. "Uh-uh, leave him alone." She moved the few feet to the desk and like an agile feline perched herself on the desktop. Crossing those well-toned legs of hers at the knees, she flashed me a teasing up-skirt peek. Placing a hand on the desk on either side of her thighs, she leaned slightly forward, accentuating her cleavage. Even though Alice was probably going to have me killed in the not-too-distant future, she was still one hell of a sexy, good-looking woman.

"And how did your meeting with your ex-wife and her fiancé turn out, Mac? Did you get all those pressing family matters resolved?" Alice said, slowly swinging her crossover leg back and forth.

I shook my head. "Turns out I was right about them standing me up. I think they decided to go to the French Riviera instead." I ran my tongue around my mouth again and spit out a little blood, both for show and to dirty-up her shiny tile floor. "Tell me something, Alice," I said, nodding toward Harrison. "You're obviously a savvy businesswoman and probably have more money than you could ever spend in ten lifetimes, so why stay hooked up with this loser all these years?"

The smirk changed into an adoring smile as her gaze shifted to Harrison. He looked really pissed. Her eyes lingered for a moment and then moved back to me. "Love . . . money . . . the thrills. All of the above?"

The honey-eyed look Alice laid on Harrison told me she was still as infatuated with the guy now as when she'd been a love-struck college girl. In Alice's case, the old adage about good girls being attracted to bad boys was chiseled into her stony heart. I put my smirk back on. "Speaking of love, I need to call my girlfriend. We're supposed to have dinner together tomorrow. Could I borrow your phone a minute?"

Alice's lips formed a phony pout. "Why, Mac, just last night you told me you had the hots for *me*. I'm soooo hurt."

"So I lied. You're one gorgeous woman, Alice, but I wouldn't touch you with his stick," I said, tilting my head at Harrison again. "Whatever it is you have, I sure as hell don't want to catch it."

Alice damn near levitated off the desk and slapped me hard across the cheek. At least she had the courtesy to choose the side Harrison hadn't used. She moved her face close to mine and put on a nasty sneer that seemed to come as natural as breathing to her. "You don't realize just how much trouble you're in, Mac. I'd strongly suggest you keep the smart remarks to yourself."

I forced a laugh. "Is keeping my trap shut going to make any difference? And yeah, I do realize the trouble I'm in. Let's see, Caitlin Medlin, Whit Coleman, uh, who else? Robert Ramey, Eric Kohler, Rachel Todd, maybe?"

Harrison shot Alice a glance when I mentioned their old cohorts, but she kept a poker face.

"Oh, by the way, you might want to consider hiring a new set of goons after this. Those two clowns together couldn't take out that girl you set up for Caitlin Medlin's murder."

"How did you know about that?" It was the first time I'd heard Harrison speak. His voice was higher-pitched than I would've imagined for a man his size.

Alice flashed him a stern look. "Shut up, Wes."

I grinned. "Yeah, shut up, Wes. By the way, shouldn't you be hauling ass out of the country right about now? I hear the cops are looking for you. Last I heard, murder for hire is still a crime in this country."

Harrison clenched his fists and turned red, but Alice kept him heeled. "You're bluffing, McClellan," he snarled. "You can't pin that on us."

"By the way, nice brown eyes you got there, Harrison. Colored contacts?"

No answer, but I decided to keep goading him, hoping it would stall the inevitable for a while. "Didn't it bother you just a little when your hired guns tried to take out Kate Bell by rigging her car to crash? You two had been pretty damn close, at least she thought so."

"Kate was okay, but nothing special, just a convenient piece of tail."

My jaw clenched, but I kept my poker face. "How about Travis Hurt?"

Harrison looked confused. "Who?"

"You know, Rachel Todd's brother, or was it lover? Or lover *and* brother?"

Harrison's brow wrinkled even tighter. "What?"

I had a nice pot of confusion stew started, so I decided to add a few more ingredients. "Why don't you ask Alice? Or didn't you know Eric Kohler was banging your boss, Ramey?"

Harrison's jaw dropped, and he turned to Alice. "What the hell is he talking about?"

I jumped in before Alice could answer. "You're a real rocket scientist, Harrison. I thought you and Kohler were best buds. Looks to me like the old Destin gang kept you in the dark about a lot of crap. Maybe they figured you were too stupid to handle all the details."

Alice walked over and slapped me twice with alternating hands. Ouch. "Shut your *fucking* mouth, Mac! Any more out of you and you'll regret ever drawing your first breath."

I couldn't resist. "Alice, such language! What would dear Aunt Darla say?" That earned me another right palm to left cheek, and this one caught my nose hard enough to start it bleeding.

"Gag this son of a bitch!" she said to Harrison. "There's a roll of duct tape in the bottom left drawer. And hurry it up."

Harrison searched through that drawer and then rifled through the others. "It's not here."

"Shit," Alice hissed between clenched teeth.

Just then there was a light tapping on the interior door. Alice stomped over and swung it open.

If I hadn't been tied to the chair I would've fallen out of it when I saw Dr. Lawrence Garrett walk in!

CHAPTER 29

"Well, if it isn't the righteous Reverend Dr. Lawrence Garrett," I said. "How's the diamond-smuggling business these days?"

Garrett stared at me with icy eyes topped by those thick, cottony brows. "Mr. McClellan, I heard you were honoring us with your presence this weekend. To be quite honest with you, the governments have clamped down on the diamond trade the past few years and have made things a bit more difficult. We've had to adjust our business model somewhat to accommodate the new circumstances. But thank you for asking."

"Hmm, no more diamonds, huh? What're you swindling the natives out of nowadays?"

Alice started to chime in, but Garrett raised a hand to stop her. "We've managed to make many sound investments with the means the Lord has blessed us with that continue to provide for the well-being of those we've been led to serve. I consider it a privilege and honor to be able to continue shepherding these worthy souls with what God has so richly provided, both spiritually and materially."

I laughed out loud. "You know, Garrett, you take the proverbial cake, no pun intended. You are by far the most pompous and disgusting hypocrite I've ever had the displeasure of meeting in my entire life."

Garrett reached inside his coat, and for a second I thought he was pulling a weapon. Instead, he produced a pocket-sized Bible. "Are you right with the Lord, Mr. McClellan? I would hate to know you entered eternity with your soul still in the clutches of Satan."

This guy was certifiably nuts and belonged in a loony bin, but I didn't have very many options except to buy more time by keeping him entertained while I hoped for a miracle of my own. "You've got a lot of nerve spouting your religious crap to me, Garrett. It's you who's exploited the poor people you claim to serve and lined your filthy pockets at their expense, not me."

Again Garrett stopped Alice from ramping up her game on me. He pulled a pair of eyeglasses from a front coat pocket and put them on. "Please, allow me to read a passage from God's sacred Word, Mr. McClellan," he said, flipping through the pages of the small Bible. "Perhaps it will help you understand God's will for the people we serve, and why, in the long run, we are helping these poor unfortunates rather than causing them harm." He stopped flipping and ran a finger down a page. "Hear the words of the Apostle Paul from his epistle to the Ephesians, chapter 6, verses 6 through 8:

> *Bondservants, be obedient to those who are your masters according to the flesh, with fear and trembling, in sincerity of heart, as to Christ; not with eyeservice, as men-pleasers, but as bondservants of Christ, doing the will of God from the heart, with goodwill doing service, as to the Lord, and not to men, knowing that whatever good anyone does, he will receive the same from the Lord, whether he is a slave or free."*

Garrett finished his rambling and then closed the book and bowed his head for a moment. "Does that not touch your heart, Mr. McClellan?" he said when he looked up. He returned the Bible and glasses to his coat pockets. "Do you now see that we are doing the Lord's will for these poor creatures, helping them to continue receiving God's plenty rather than causing them harm?"

I laughed. "How? By stealing their diamonds?"

"The diamonds were of no use to them, Mr. McClellan," Garrett said, "but by using the diamonds for the greater good, we've been able to provide for the people's needs and continue to shower them with the Lord's blessings. Can you not see the Lord's hand at work?"

"What I see is that you're a damn two-bit thief and a raving lunatic, Garrett. Whatever happened to the Golden Rule?"

I turned to Alice and Harrison. "Christ on a crutch, you two don't buy into this crap, do you?"

Before either one of them bothered to answer there was another knock on the door. Harrison did the honors this time opening the door, but not enough that I could see who stood at the other side. "They're ready, Mr. Weston." It was a female's voice and sounded a lot like Maryann, the masseuse maven. Harrison nodded and closed the door.

He glanced at Garrett and then turned to Alice. "It's time."

"Okay, untie him from the chair, but before you do, make sure his hands are still tight," she said to Harrison. She moved back to the desk and reclaimed her perch. "You'll be taking a little ride in a few minutes, Mac. Be cooperative and behave yourself, and you might just get lucky."

I believed that about as much as I believed I could put a quarter in one of the slot machines and win a million-dollar jackpot on my next try. Harrison stepped behind me and started struggling with the ropes while Garrett shuffled to one of the bookcases a few feet from where I sat and leaned against it. Harrison tugged on the ropes and let out a few expletives that I'm sure the good reverend didn't approve of.

"Hurry it up, Wes, we—"

Alice never finished the sentence. With a loud bang and a blinding flash of orange the outside door burst open and something black hurtled through the doorway onto the floor. Other figures dressed in black stormed into the room and along the walls. Alice screamed and bolted for the inside door but found her escape blocked by still more black-clad cops. Garrett slipped a hand inside his coat. My gut told me he wasn't reaching for his Bible this time. I flung myself headlong into his midsection and heard the air blow from his lungs as he collapsed to the floor with me and the chair falling hard on top of him.

I glanced across the room just in time to see a prone Dakota roll and come up on her elbows, Glock at the ready. From the corner of my eye I saw Wes Harrison draw a pistol from under his coat and point it at Dakota. His pistol barked, but the Glock beat him by a split second. Harrison missed. Dakota didn't.

Harrison dropped his weapon and stumbled back a few feet until the wall stopped him. His eyes were wide with surprise, and both hands clutched his chest. Blood poured through his fingers, dyeing the front of his shirt crimson. His knees buckled, and he sat down hard. His mouth opened, and out came a guttural "uuurrgghhh" along with pinkish, frothy blood. Then his eyes rolled back in their sockets, and he slumped face-first onto the floor.

~~⁓

In the confusion immediately following I saw that Dakota was still stretched out prone. What the hell was she doing here with busted ribs? The girl was tougher than I thought. I kneed Garrett in the jaw for good measure, then scrambled to my feet and rushed to her side, chair and all. A chill ran through me; maybe Harrison hadn't missed his target after all. Somebody wearing black stopped me and quickly cut me free of the chair. Alice Spence was already handcuffed and sitting in a chair next to the interior door. Sheriff Pickron sat on the edge of the desk with his arms folded, facing her. A paramedic was attending to Lawrence Garrett. I hoped I'd broken the hypocrite bastard's jaw and a couple of ribs to boot. Another officer was bent over Wes Harrison checking for a pulse, but I'd seen enough center-chest shots in Iraq to know he'd most likely already bought the farm.

To my immense relief Dakota moaned and said something, but with all the commotion my name was the only clear word I caught. I knelt down and gently placed a hand on her shoulder. "Where are you hurt?"

"Where the hell do you think, McClellan? *Every*-friggin'-where. Now, would you please help me up like I asked you to? And don't bleed on me."

I looked down and saw that a few drops of blood had dripped from my nose and splattered near Dakota's face. I grinned. Good old Dakota, back to her sharp-tongued, witty ways. I eased my hands under her shoulders as carefully as I could so she wouldn't accuse me of sexual assault. "Try to roll and sit up when I lift," I said.

She groaned and directed a few choice words at me, but we got the job done. "Now, put your arm around my shoulder and lean into me." She winced as she slid an arm around my neck. I supported her back with one arm and slipped the other underneath her knees. "Ready? Here we go." I braced my foot against the polished tile and stood, trying to be as smooth and easy as I could as I lifted her off the floor. She grabbed my shoulder and dug her nails hard into it against the pain. I carried her across the room to the desk and eased her down onto the plush swivel chair behind it.

Dakota's eyes were shut tight. A single tear leaked from one of them and traced down her cheek. I pretended not to notice and backed away as a female paramedic moved in and began examining her. After several minutes she handed Dakota a couple of pills and a bottle of water, and then turned to me and smiled. "She's a tough girl. She'll be fine."

I'd seen my share of suffering and death during combat with the Marines, and I considered myself to be pretty damn hard-core. I don't know what came over me then, but I was suddenly fighting back tears of my own. Just as I was brushing them away, Dakota glanced at me. "Jeez, McClellan, what're you crying about? We rescued your ass, didn't we?"

My throat was tight, and I couldn't speak right away. In less than a year I'd been saved from impending doom by young J.D. Owens and now his cousin, Dakota. I knelt beside her, swallowed hard, and managed to put on a smile as my throat finally unclenched some. "You Owens kids are something else, you know that? You've saved my bacon twice in a year."

Dakota gave her head a slight turn, flashed the Elvis snarl, and glared at me. "I am *not* a frigging' kid, McClellan!"

I took a deep breath, let it out slowly and shook my head. "No . . . no, you sure as hell aren't a kid, Dakota Blaire Owens. You're my friggin' hero."

CHAPTER 30

Over the next few days precious few bits of info leaked out about what had gone down at the Palmetto Royale Casino & Resort. I had Dakota to thank for what I learned that hadn't been released directly to the media.

Dillon, last name Drew, had glanced my way just in time to see me being escorted away from the tiki bar by what turned out to be one of the two Atlanta bruisers Alice hired to do her dirty work. Her suspicions aroused by my flirting, Dillon immediately slipped the bill from her pocket and read the note. She then threw caution to the wind and tailed us until she saw me get hammered and dragged through the doorway. She grabbed her cell phone and called 911, who in turn alerted the sheriff's department.

Pickron immediately notified Dakota (a promise she'd coerced him into making) to see if she wanted in on the action and then scrambled his forces outside the Palmetto Royale. A squad of investigators dressed in tourist attire targeted the building and the door from the info Dillon had given the 911 dispatcher. Pickron then moved his forces to a staging position while the plainclothes officers sealed and cleared the surrounding area as unobtrusively as possible. When the all-clear was given the cavalry mounted up. They used a shape charge to blow the door. The rest, as they say, is history.

Wes Harrison was dead, and Alice Spence and Dr. Lawrence Garrett and company weren't exactly being paragons of cooperation. Alice had quickly contacted her topnotch team of lawyers—longtime friends and business associates of the Ramey family—to do their talking for them. One of the goons had mentioned being hired by "some lady in Atlanta" but then recanted his story and was now claiming that he was tricked into saying it by sheriffs' investigators. The two men flatly denied any knowledge or involvement in the death of Caitlin Medlin or the disappearances of Whit Coleman and Summer Tyson. They also pleaded innocent to having anything to do with rigging Kate's car or trying to snuff me with the .45 at the campground.

As far as Rachel Todd and Eric Kohler were concerned, Alice and Garrett insisted that poor Rachel had perished in the plane crash somewhere in the dense jungles of South America, and Kohler had died with Robert Ramey when the explosion caused Ramey's vintage Chris Craft to founder and capsize in the heavy seas kicked up by the squall.

Miraculously, Wes Harrison was blown free of the vessel, and when he came to, found himself clinging to a large ice cooler that had been aboard. Adrift for two days, he was finally rescued by a passing Mexican fishing boat and arrived in the town of Progreso on the Yucatán coast when the vessel returned to port.

Having suffered a fortuitous loss of memory, and with no identification on his person, Harrison had escaped the questioning and clutches of the authorities. Local doctors did what they could for his mangled face. Harrison eventually made his way to the Cayman Islands where skilled plastic surgeons put the finishing touches on his face in a series of operations. And he assumed the name Russell Weston, a convenient leftover from his memory bank.

Of course I wasn't buying any of their BS, and I had one hot ace up my sleeve to prove they were lying. I talked Dakota into showing Sheriff Pickron the satellite photo of the Ramey estate I'd downloaded early in the case. In that photo, dated 2009, there was an outdoor Jacuzzi located a few yards from the swimming pool. When I'd snooped around the back of Alice's house on my second trip, the fancy statue of Neptune riding his three water-snorting steeds stood where the Jacuzzi had been located.

"Dig there," I insisted, "and you'll find the body of Robert Ramey."

To my surprise Pickron was impressed enough to contact the Fulton County authorities, and the statue was removed and the foundation excavated. After digging down several feet past the last traces of concrete, plumbing, and reinforcing steel, nothing was discovered but bucketfuls of red Georgia clay.

Oops.

Turns out Alice had been on a business trip to Kansas City, Missouri, and saw the original statue there at some big plaza. She did her research, found where she could buy a smaller replica, and had it shipped and installed. That fiasco did little to enhance my relationship with Sheriff Bocephus Pickron. I started to suggest they contact the proper authorities on Grand Cayman and start digging around Alice and Harrison's compound. On second thought I decided it would be wiser to keep my trap shut on the matter.

The diamonds and paperwork Kate had discovered were turned over to the FBI, and it was likely that a decision as to whether or not she had a legal claim to some of them was probably several months if not years away. Oh well, honesty is its own reward, or so they say.

Because the diamonds were in Kate's possession via her relationship with Wes Harrison, and because the two had been friends with Eric Kohler at the time of the boating incident, Kate would likely be called as a witness in the case *if* it went to trial. Money talks, an assistant DA reminded me off the record, and Alice Spence had plenty of it to ply her pack of slick-talking attorneys.

On a brighter note, I presented Dillon Drew with a check that would more than cover the expenses for her and Tyler's move back to her parents' home in California. I didn't think she was in any real danger around these parts since the raid, but one can never be too sure. At first she balked about taking the money, but I told her it was a reward from the management of Hightower Investigations for helping solve the case and saving the life of its most valued employee.

I don't think Dillon bought it, but it did earn me some kind words about there still being decent and trustworthy men in this world, plus another nice kiss on the cheek. All in all, not a bad deal.

Finally, the Bible-thumping "I told you so!" crowd scored a major victory—at least temporarily—when authorities shut down all operations at the Palmetto Royale Casino & Resort. And with all the brouhaha that followed about the evil sin of gambling for filthy lucre begetting the even more vile sins of drug trafficking and rumored prostitution, it seemed highly unlikely the county fathers would allow the doors to reopen in the foreseeable future. Never mind the loss of thousands of bucks in annual revenue along with a few hundred jobs. Vengeance is mine, saith the Lord. Hallelujah, and pass the bingo cards.

*   *   *

A few weeks later Kate and I were sitting on a secluded area of beach watching the sun slowly sink toward the horizon. Gulls laughed and wheeled on the late afternoon thermals, and a cool onshore breeze cut the day's lingering heat.

It was a celebration of sorts. I'd finally completed all the coursework and passed the required tests with semi-flying colors, and was now the proud holder of an official Class "CC" private investigator's license from the state of Florida. Which meant that I would have to intern under Frank's tutelage for two years before being eligible to apply for my own Class "C" license and branch out on my own, if I so chose. To commemorate the auspicious occasion, Frank presented me with a set of my very own business cards. A nice enough gesture, but I was hoping for a case of Dewar's or at least a gold watch.

Kate had made small fancy sandwiches and an assortment of raw vegetables, fruits, and dips. Since returning from Destin she'd been on a health kick and was encouraging me to go along with the program. I'd brought a cooler of Michelob, light and regular, and a flask filled with The Dalmore. This was a celebration, after all. When it came down to specifics, liquid bread wasn't all that lacking in nutrition. That was the reasoning I presented to Kate, and I was sticking to it.

Kate washed down a bite of cucumber and bean sprouts sandwich with a sip of Michelob Light. "Do you think Eric and Rachel could still be alive?" It was a question she'd brought up more than once as the wheels of justice in the case continued to speed along like a snail through wet concrete.

"Travis Hurt and Rachel, you mean." I searched through the sandwiches, looking for one that had anything resembling meat inside. "The real Eric Kohler is buried in Arlington National Cemetery." The salty breeze caught and lifted Kate's hair as she stared out toward the west end of Five-Mile Island where the gulf blended into the bay. She bit her lower lip and nodded.

"Anything's possible, Kate, but my guess is they're both dead."

I had explained till I was blue in the face how I believed things boiled down. Sometime after Robert Ramey grew suspicious that some type of hanky-panky was going on with his diamonds, he, his lover Eric Kohler (for the sake of keeping things simple), and Wes Harrison set out together for a supposed fishing trip. While at anchor, a strong squall developed, making the premeditated job that much more plausible. Kohler and Harrison killed Ramey, weighted down his body, and sent him to Davy Jones' Locker. They allowed gasoline fumes to build up in the engine compartment and cut the anchor line. One of them hit the starter and followed the other overboard wearing lifejackets. The fumes ignited with a bang, and the old Chris Craft caught fire, took on water, and eventually capsized in the rough seas.

Shortly after the explosion, Kohler and Harrison were picked up by a second vessel waiting in the area, most likely operated by Rachel Todd, and sped the hell away from there to some nearby predetermined safe location. Rachel had a rented airplane waiting, and they took to the skies aboard that freedom bird and flew to their newly adopted home in the Caymans.

Realizing the golden opportunity of eventually gaining control of the Ramey fortune, Alice Spence had been in on the ruse from the get-go. With her education and business savvy, she soon became the brains of the group. Using the hefty profits from the illegal and switched diamonds, and the Ramey money Alice managed to get her sharp-clawed paws on, the gang made some very profitable investments and built quite a life for themselves in their Caribbean paradise. Of course, Alice had to spend the majority of her time with dear Aunt

Darla, but she managed to get away often enough to keep the flames burning hot with Wes Harrison.

Eventually something turned sour among the group. Maybe Eric and Rachel tried a power grab or felt they were being shorted in some way. Whatever the cause of the rift, the two longtime lovers and fellow scammers were rubbed out of the picture for good.

At some point, Harrison grew bored with the easy but mundane life in the Caymans. Maybe he missed the thrill of living life on the edge. Whatever the reason, he convinced Alice that investing in the Palmetto Royale would be a sound move. There was excitement and good money to be had in legalized gambling, and with silent partner Lawrence Garrett's accumulated diamond fortune for extra revenue, the venture had all the markings of a surefire moneymaker for everyone involved.

More than a decade had passed since the boating disaster, and chances were that the incident had long been forgotten. Harrison had a rap sheet, but with the plastic surgery he'd voluntarily undergone to change his appearance, what were the odds anyone would recognize him? That is, until the night at O'Malley's Theater when he'd gotten careless and forgot to wear the brown contacts to camouflage his striking eyes.

Kate wrapped her arms around her knees and sighed. "It doesn't really make a difference if they're dead or alive, because they're dead to me, anyway." It was the first time she'd said that, and I couldn't help but feel pleased, although I didn't let it show. I hoped the Destin gang and her ties to it were over for good.

Patches of aqua sky peeked through clouds painted red and gold by the retreating sun. I opened the flask and offered it to Kate. She took a ladylike sip, and I slugged down a healthy swallow. We sat in silence for a few more minutes listening to gulls and terns as they hunted their evening meal, and the surf rushing ashore. Just as the orange ball of the sun touched the horizon I held the flask up and turned to Kate. "Here's to us."

She tapped the flask with her bottle and smiled. "To us."

ACKNOWLEDGMENTS

Special thanks to my agent and friend, Fred Tribuzzo, for his tireless efforts not only to sell but also promote my work. To my editor at Seventh Street Books, Dan Mayer, who knows his business inside and out and always coaxes the best out of writers. My copyeditor, Julia DeGraf, for her sharp eyes and knowledge. And my wife, Karen, my "Kate." The best first reader, critic, lover, and friend a man could ask for. I am blessed.

ABOUT THE AUTHOR

E. Michael Helms is the author of *Deadly Catch*, the first Mac McClellan mystery. His memoir of his Vietnam combat service, *The Proud Bastards*, has remained in print for more than two decades. Originally published by Kensington/Zebra in 1990, it was republished in 2004 by Simon & Schuster/Pocket Star, and has sold over fifty thousand copies (Pocket Star edition). The memoir is a past hardcover selection of the Military Book Club. Helms is also the author of *Of Blood and Brothers*, a two-part novel about the Civil War, and the novel *The Private War of Corporal Henson*. He currently resides with his wife, Karen, in the foothills of the Blue Ridge Mountains in South Carolina.

Photo by Karen M. Helms